Their gazes met

A welcome moment of harmony. It felt like an oasis in the desert of this difficult journey. Neither of them spoke right away, as if they were both afraid another word would make the feeling break like a mirage.

"Kitty—"

She held up her hand. "No, it's all right, David. I know it's hard to accept. Hard to believe. And you've got a lot of things to consider. I'm sure you'll want to talk to your lawyer before you—"

"No."

She stopped cold. "No?"

"No. I don't need to talk to Colby. I don't want Colby's advice. I know what I want to do."

She held her breath.

"I want to marry you."

Dear Reader,

The last time you saw David Gerard, he wasn't a happy man. He'd just been dumped by the woman he'd hoped to marry. But Belle Carson found her happily-ever-after with Matt Malone in *For the Love of Family,* the book I wrote for Harlequin Superromance's wonderful Diamond Legacy series. And that locked gorgeous David out in the cold.

Thanks to your emails and letters, I couldn't leave him there. Apparently we're all die-hard romantics. We don't buy into the myth that nice guys finish last!

David doesn't take the easy road to true love. When he decides to tap into his inner bad boy, he makes some terrible mistakes—the worst being a one-night stand with a green-haired bartender he meets in the Bahamas. Then Kitty Hemmings shows up pregnant, and David realizes it's time to pay the price for being such a fool.

First thing to go? That level-headed life he's worked so hard to build. Because Kitty is one lady who won't be tamed—not unless this sensible guy is willing to go all out to win her heart.

I hope you enjoy their spark-filled journey toward becoming a family. I love to hear from my readers, so be sure to mail me at P.O. Box 947633, Maitland, FL 32794, or email me at KOBrien@aol.com. Or let's be friends on Facebook! See you online!

Warmly,

Kathleen O'Brien

For Their Baby
Kathleen O'Brien

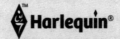

TORONTO NEW YORK LONDON
AMSTERDAM PARIS SYDNEY HAMBURG
STOCKHOLM ATHENS TOKYO MILAN MADRID
PRAGUE WARSAW BUDAPEST AUCKLAND

Recycling programs
for this product may
not exist in your area.

ISBN-13: 978-0-373-71737-8

FOR THEIR BABY

Printed in U.S.A.

ABOUT THE AUTHOR

Kathleen O'Brien was a feature writer and TV critic before marrying a fellow journalist. Motherhood, which followed soon after, was so marvelous she turned to writing novels, which could be done at home. She works hard to pack her backyard with birds, butterflies and squirrels. Indoors, her two cockatiels, Honey and Lizzie, announce repeatedly, if not humbly, that they are "pretty birds." Her colorful Gouldian finch, who lives in her office, fills every day with music.

Books by Kathleen O'Brien

To Nancy, Kris, Leslie, Deirdre and Dawn,
the SHU buddies who have,
over the past couple of years,
added so much fun and focus to my writing!

CHAPTER ONE

SHE WAS GOING to marry *him?*

Kitty Hemmings stared at the cell phone and tried to process the words she'd just heard on her voice mail. Surely her mother hadn't said *marry.* No matter how low the woman's self-esteem had plummeted, no matter how desperately she needed a Y chromosome by her side, she wouldn't—she couldn't—actually *marry* Jim Oliphant.

The beachside bar speakers launched into a steel drum version of "Red, Red Wine," and the breeze, always warm here in the Bahamas even in November, gusted gently across her hot cheeks. Suddenly Kitty's hands began to shake. She gripped the handle of the beer spigot for balance.

Lucinda Hemmings had pulled some pathetic stunts in her time. But marrying that bastard would top them all. Jim was a dozen years younger than her mother. He was slick and charming, but stone-broke, of course, just another barnacle trying to attach his empty wallet to Lucinda's bank account.

He'd hung around more than eight years, a record for any of her mother's boyfriends. Kitty had been hoping, any day, to hear that he'd given up and gone away. She'd even dreamed about Lochaven last night, about the Virginia oaks covered in Spanish moss, and the red tile roof, and her own bedroom, where her poster of Johnny Depp still hung on the door. For the first time in eight years, she'd let herself imagine what it might be like to live in a real house again, and not a crummy efficiency apartment or service-industry dorm.

But now…with Oliphant permanently installed…

Her mother had sounded so happy. Kitty bit down on her lower lip, remembering the lilt in the voice, and the subtle slur that said Lucinda hadn't declined an extra flute of champagne with dinner. Of course not. Jim Oliphant didn't drink alone. "I know you don't like him, sweetheart, but…"

Like him? Kitty's lunch rose briefly into her throat, an acidic reminder of the mandarin oranges she'd wolfed down between shifts. Like him? Who could like Jim Oliphant? He might be square-jawed and handsome on the outside, but on the inside he was what her father called *âme de boue.* Soul of mud.

Kitty swallowed hard, forcing herself to release her death grip on the spigot. She couldn't dwell on this now. She was on the clock another ten minutes, that was all. Just until midnight. Then she'd go back to the dorm and, since her roommate, Jill, was working till two, she'd have a little alone time.

Maybe she'd bake something sweet, something from her childhood. Comfort food.

And then, when she let herself think again, maybe her mother's news wouldn't hurt so much.

"Hello? Earth to barmaid? Two Slim Spiffies? Heavy on the cherries?"

She looked up, trying to compose herself. She'd seen

this guy before. The bartenders had a nickname for every customer. They called this one Mr. Sleazy. She suddenly realized he could have been Oliphant's older brother. The too-bronze tan, the overly highlighted hair and the sucked-gut vanity that begged you to believe he was twenty-five instead of forty.

"Sure." She slid the cell phone under the bar and smiled. "What's in a Slim Spiffy besides cherries?"

Mr. Sleazy leaned in, and she got a whiff of his breath. Oh. So that was a Slim Spiffy. Gin, cranberry juice, orange slices and the guarantee that, before the night was over, he'd puke his guts out into the sand.

Her smile stiffened. His eyes probably weren't nice on his best day, and this was definitely not his best day. Tiny red spiders crawled across the whites, and the pupils didn't quite track. She felt her hand begin to tremble again. She hated mean drunks. Jim Oliphant had been a very, very mean drunk.

"Just cherries," he said, then flicked his tongue over his lower lip. "That's all I'm interested in. The boys and I made a little bet over there. About whether you've still got one."

Kitty considered pretending she didn't understand. That was usually her first resort. But she could already feel her blood in her ears. It sounded like the incoming tide. He couldn't imagine what a really bad time he'd picked to get nasty. She needed this job, but she was inches from either bursting into tears or breaking his ugly nose.

They'd both get her disciplined, but the nose option would at least feel good. She hadn't cried in eight years, and, by God, she didn't intend to start tonight.

She scanned the tables, the dance floor, even the artificially lit beach, looking for Jill. Jill actually thought this guy was cute. And Jill owed her—Kitty had covered for her about half a dozen times lately, when Jill wanted to slip out with some hunky customer she'd just met.

But Jill was nowhere to be seen. As usual. That meant the bouncer, one of Jill's lovers this week, was also MIA.

"Look, the bar always has plenty of cherries," Kitty said, though her teeth would hardly open to let the words through. "Let that be enough, okay? Just play nice, and tell me what's—"

"No, no, not the *bar*." He winked. "See, honey, we're thinking you can't be more than, what…maybe nineteen? We think that green hair, that eyebrow ring… they're just for show, to cover up that baby face. Come on, baby face. We think maybe you've still got a cherry."

Bastard.

She was twenty-six years old, and felt every year of it, so the "nineteen" comment was pure hogwash. And "baby face" was what Jim Oliphant had loved to call her.

She leaned closer, lowering her voice. "Well, let's see, *honey*. What I've got…I've got a low tolerance for butt-ugly morons and a big, fat can of pepper spray." She glanced at his crotch. "Any of that make you feel spiffy, Slim?"

His bloodshot eyes hardened as he processed the insult. "What the—" He reached out, as if to grab her arm. "I'll have your job, you little—"

Technically, this wasn't a problem. She'd been a bartender less than a year, working her way up from waitress. The first thing you learned, though, was how to handle a drunk. But as she saw his meaty hand move toward her, something snapped and she found it hard to breathe. She inhaled, but choked on the tears she'd been trying to hold back. Suddenly all she could see were sparkling crystals, fracturing the colored lights strung between the poles that held up the bar tent.

Oh, God. She was losing it. Where was the bouncer? Fumbling with her apron, she turned, made an inarticulate sound and started to head for the beach.

"Hey!"

She glanced over her shoulder—he was coming around the bar, head lowered like a bull. An icy feeling spread between her shoulder blades.

And then, out of nowhere, another man was standing in his path.

"Steady, now," she heard the other man say as he put a palm against the charging bull's chest. "I think the lady needs—"

She didn't hear the end of the sentence. She saw her chance, and she took it. She walked fast, and then faster, until she was running. She ran beyond the party lights, through the bright landscape spots that turned the incoming tide to a frothy milkshake, and finally into the darkness of the natural night.

Even when she'd left the noisy bar far behind, she didn't stop. The Sugarwater Resort was built on a crescent-shaped spit of beach, and she blindly traced its eastern curve. When the soft piles of sand got too thick, she kicked off her sandals and continued to run.

Though her lungs burned, she kept going until she found herself where no lowly bartender should be, out at the very tip, beside the luxury cottages that were rented only by the month, only to people who never asked "How much?"

She finally ran out of steam, and beach, at the last stand of palm trees. She looked around, as if she thought there might be another way out, but of course there wasn't. The ocean was just a yard or two from her toes. Its dull, scraping sweep was louder than the blood that roared in her ears. She tried to focus on the sound. She tried to find something steady, something to hang on to.

But it was hopeless. She'd run as far as she could, as far as there was, and she hadn't outrun the memories or the fury. Without her permission, hot liquid began to stream down her cheeks. She pushed her fingers against her eyes, as if she could force the tears back.

No, no. She wasn't this weak. She was tough, and in control of her life, her body, even her tears. She wasn't afraid of Mr. Sleazy. She wasn't afraid of any man. She wasn't afraid of anything.

But damn Jim Oliphant. Damn him for exiling her from the home she loved, the home that held the memories of her father, who would never have let anyone treat her like…

With a strangled sound, she dropped to her knees. The sand gave under her weight, and then, at the last minute, something sharp bit into her skin. Heat flashed up her leg like lightning. She rocked back on one heel, shocked by the pain, and lifted the other shin.

She must have landed on a sharp shell. Or a broken

bottle. Blood—it had to be blood, though it looked black in the moonlight—seeped from a curved gash along the fleshy edge of her shin. And it hurt. It hurt like hell.

"Are you okay?"

She looked up, glaring, furious with herself that she hadn't heard the man approaching her along the beach. What if it had been that sleazy jerk, arriving for another round? Men like that were gluttons for punishment.

But it wasn't. Instead, it was the man who had stood in his way, giving her a chance to get free. Now that she was thinking clearly, she realized she knew him— all the female bartenders did. Their nickname for this guy was Gorgeous.

Blond. Blue-eyed. Six-one, with the body of a god, and an endearing way of seeming unaware of any of that.

His real name was David Gerard, and for the past few weeks he'd been renting one of the premium cottages, the best of the best, right here on the tip of the crescent. She'd processed his room card a dozen times or more at the bar, but he'd never hit on her. Oddly, he never hit on anybody. She'd seen about a dozen different big-breasted blondes try their darnedest to snag him, if only for one night, but he always brushed them off gracefully and left the bar alone.

It was kind of fascinating, actually. He ate dinner at the beachside bar every night, as if he were looking for someone, but he never hooked up. He nursed a couple of beers for hours, and spent the rest of the night throwing darts with the oldest, loneliest regular in the place.

They all wondered what his story was. Kitty said he acted like a guy with a broken heart. Jill disagreed. Any woman lucky enough to get her hands on that heart, she said, putting a wry stress on the word *heart,* would be careful not to let it slip away.

Kitty wondered why he'd followed her out here.

"I'm fine," she said now, and pulled herself to her feet. Grimacing, she brushed the bloody sand from her leg, then wished she'd dealt with her face first. She lifted her chin, daring him to mention the tears. "It's just my shin. I think I fell on something."

He bent down and took her calf between his hands. He didn't seem alarmed, but his grip was firm. "Let's get into the light. My cottage is right behind us. Can you walk?"

"Of course," she said, but the first weight she put on the leg made it sting. "It's no big deal. I should just go back to—"

"No. My place is right here. So is my car. If you need stitches, I can drive you to the E.R."

She glanced back toward the hotel, registering how far away the service dorms really were. "Fine. I mean… yeah, okay. Thanks."

She saw him smile as he lifted her arm and put it over his shoulder. She knew she sounded edgy and ungrateful, but, damn it, she felt like such a fool. There she'd been, ranting about how tough and independent she was…

Sugarwater's luxury cottages were impressive, but luckily she'd seen the interiors before, so she didn't embarrass herself by gasping or gawking. He flicked on the living room light switch—she noticed it was set to the recessed mood lighting, which didn't compete with the view of the ocean through the big picture window.

He deposited her on the wide leather sofa, then fiddled a few minutes in the wet bar behind her. When he returned, he had a plain brown bottle of hydrogen peroxide, some gauze and a bandage.

She stared. "You keep a first aid kit in the bar?"

He laughed, but he was already down on one knee in front of her, gently cleaning off the cut. "Yeah, well, I put a gash in my own leg the first week I was here. Apparently I still can't surf worth a darn." He smiled up at her. "Ten stitches. Just came out a week or so ago."

She smiled in spite of herself. He didn't seem clumsy. His hands felt sure. And kind.

He went through several pieces of gauze, all of which came away bloody and crumpled. He used the peroxide liberally, and thin, pink blood inched down her calf in dotted lines. He wiped it clean, with light strokes that made her feel strangely warm and tingly.

God. Just how weak was she tonight? Was she actually letting this Boy Scout routine turn her on?

It took a while, as he was clearly conscientious. But it wasn't all vaguely erotic TLC. Some of it was pure, sensible first aid business. She flinched as he scrubbed away a few last grains of sand.

"Sorry," he said. He bent closer and probed with careful fingers. Then he dabbed one last time and started peeling the plastic backing from a large square bandage.

"It's not as bad as it looked. No need for stitches,

probably. But you're going to want to get a tetanus shot."

"I had one a few months ago," she said. Her voice sounded husky, and she cleared her throat. "When you work around here, you don't take risks."

He nodded. "Good." He wadded up the used gauze and got up to put it in the trash can behind the bar. Then he ran water to wash his hands.

"How about you?"

She swiveled.

He was pointing to the military lineup of booze along the glass wall. The standard new-guest stock that came with the cottage. It didn't seem to have been touched, though David had been here several weeks. "Want something to take the edge off?"

For a minute, she didn't answer. Surrounded by sparkling crystal, he looked like the suave, unattainable hero of every movie she'd ever seen. So easy, so comfortable in his own skin, dressed casually in khakis and blue polo shirt, which probably hadn't been chosen to set off his taut chest and sexy hips, but did anyhow.

Something inside her stirred. It shifted restlessly. Something that had been asleep for a long, long time.

She tried to ignore it. He was too good-looking. She didn't trust such handsome men. His blond hair seemed to gleam, and his perfect profile was both manly and beautiful. And, yet, in some indescribable way, he didn't seem like…like the rest of them.

But that was ridiculous. Green-haired bartenders with edgy pasts were undoubtedly not his type, and Boy Scout gods weren't hers. And yet…that restless spot inside her felt odd, as if it were being tugged toward him. She wondered if he felt it, too. Something in his eyes made her think he might.

"No, thanks," she said. "I don't drink."

"Water, then." He brought over two glasses straight from the subzero fridge and sat beside her on the sofa. "Here's to a little peace and quiet for the rest of tonight. You've certainly earned it."

They both unscrewed their caps and drank a toast. She found herself watching the column of his throat as he swallowed. His neck was bronze and manly, but without that thick, muscled look she hated. The Jim Oliphant look. In fact, he had the kind of body she was usually attracted to. Lean, simple, graceful. As if he would be good at tennis.

Or sex.

He was watching her, too. She felt a blush creep over her cheeks, and she was suddenly aware that their bodies were only inches apart, and that this sofa had obviously been designed for nights of impulsive passion. She wondered whether he'd brought her here with casual sex in mind.

If only he knew how long it had been since sex had been casual for her. She could tell him—almost to the day. Eight years. Of all the things Jim Oliphant had stolen from her, the easy acceptance of her sexuality was the thing she missed the most.

Since the day Jim had pulled his disgusting stunt, she'd had one lover. Just one, a quiet law student she'd met at her first waitressing job. In Atlanta, where she'd settled after she'd come to the end of nearly two years of running. She'd stayed there a whole year, letting Allen erase the memory of Jim's grabbing hands.

Then Allen graduated, she had moved on…and she'd passed into a long, lonely five years, avoiding intimacy of any kind.

She turned away awkwardly and focused on the picture window. It framed a magical view. Just yards away, the ocean waves angled in, rolling toward the shore. Just before they broke, moonlight created a flashing vein of silver along the glassy curls.

She felt something silver winking deep inside her, as if a shaft of moonlight had penetrated her own murky layers of numbness and fear. It was almost as if somewhere, way down deep, below the scars, below the memory of Jim Oliphant, the real Kitty Hemmings still survived.

"You know, I didn't thank you. For tonight. It was nice of you to…to step in." She looked down at her water bottle, then risked a glance up at David. "Usually I handle jerks like that much more smoothly. It's just that—I was rattled. You see, I got some bad news tonight."

If he'd asked her what the news was, she probably would have clammed up. But he didn't. He just waited. Serious. Attentive.

"I found out my mother is going to marry a guy I can't stand. A very bad guy. I've told her about him, but she doesn't believe me. She doesn't want to believe me."

David frowned slightly, but he still had the sense not to speak.

"The hard part is…just tonight I'd been thinking maybe I could go home soon. I've been here—or somewhere—for eight years now. I've started to get homesick. But now…now that he's going to be there permanently, I can't go home. Not ever."

He was silent for a minute longer.

"I'm sorry," he said finally. "That must be hard."

She nodded, wondering why she was unburdening herself like this. He couldn't care. He didn't even know her last name, which they never printed on the name tags, for "security" purposes.

But maybe that was why it was possible to speak the truth. He didn't know her. He couldn't judge her. And he didn't seem the judgmental type, anyhow. He actually seemed surprisingly kind.

"It's even more painful than I thought it would be," she went on. "I don't know why. I knew my mother didn't believe me about Jim. I knew he was still in her life. Logically, this engagement thing shouldn't be such a big deal."

He shrugged. "I don't think pain responds very well to logic. I—" He smiled over at her, a strangely sad smile. "It hasn't been the best day in my world, either."

Now it was her turn to wait. She wondered whether this was it…the answer to the question the staff had all been asking. Why did such a hunky, gorgeous guy always look so haunted and alone?

He turned his glass, watching the light glimmer on the water. "A woman I used to be in love with married another man today. We broke up a long time ago, and it's far from a shock. He's a great guy, actually. We're all friends now, and I'm actually even happy for her. I thought I could go, but at the last minute I couldn't. I just…couldn't."

He let the explanation taper off. Their gazes held, though, and something invisible arced between them.

Then she knew he felt it, too. In spite of her green hair and her tough-girl attitude, in spite of the fact that someone this gorgeous clearly should spend all his time with beauty queens, he wanted her.

Correction. He wanted *someone.* For the first time since he'd arrived at the resort, the loneliness had overpowered him. His voice was calm, his body at ease, and yet she heard the undercurrent of confusion, of betrayal, of loss. It spoke to her, even more than his gentle hands or his bedroom eyes.

She considered the situation, well aware it was foolish to risk a one-night stand with a guest. And yet…it would be such a comfort, not to be alone for a while. Not to think about home, of Jim Oliphant, or where she would go next in this nomadic exile she'd chosen as a life.

This David Gerard was a good man. She could feel it. He was sensual, but gentle. And he was as haunted as she was.

Her father had a French phrase for someone like this, too. *Âme perdue.* A lost soul.

She hadn't ever been able to master French, though she'd tried ever since her father's death, hoping it would bring his memory closer. She wished her accent weren't so awful. She might say that to David Gerard now.

Deux âmes perdues. Two lost souls.

Did it have to be more complicated than that? Just this once, couldn't something be simple and sweet? He wanted her, and she wanted him, too. She wanted to make love to him. Right now. Tonight.

He was leaving tomorrow, she remembered suddenly.

A man who was leaving tomorrow was perfect. A night in his bed wouldn't complicate anything, really. She would break this cycle of loneliness by sleeping with this lovely man, and maybe she'd wake up tomorrow lighter, easier in her own skin.

She felt the anger and bewilderment lift from her, like the sky lifting as the sun came up. Maybe her subconscious mind had guided her feet tonight, as she ran away from the bar. Maybe destiny had directed her here. Maybe it was fate.

The word startled her. Ordinarily, she didn't believe in fate. Her mother did, and used that convenient imaginary entity to rationalize all kinds of self-destructive behavior. But, even though Kitty was a committed cynic, she couldn't ignore this powerful feeling.

Look at the two of them, sitting on the sofa with sparks of lust going off like invisible fireworks. Two lonely people, two sets of painful memories that had reached an unbearable climax today. Each facing a long, miserable night of trying to forget.

She touched his upturned palm with her fingertips. His eyes darkened slightly, and a flash of electricity shimmered under her fingers, but otherwise he didn't react.

"I'm sorry," he said politely. "I didn't mean to whine on about my problems. I must sound like an idiot."

"No, you don't." She held his gaze and kept her fingers against his palm. "You sound like someone who doesn't want to be alone tonight."

He started to say something, then stopped. He closed

his fingers around hers and shook his head. "No, don't. This isn't right. I didn't… I promise you, I wasn't looking for this. I didn't follow you onto the beach hoping that—"

"I know you didn't." With her other hand, she reached out and touched his cheek. She had to lean over to do it. "Does that mean you don't want it? Because I do. A lot."

"I—" He frowned. "Wanting is…I don't want to take advantage… It would be—"

"It would be lovely," she said.

"Yes." He closed his eyes, still frowning. "But—"

"Isn't that enough? It doesn't have to be complicated. You're just a man, and I'm just a woman, and we're hurting. But we can help each other tonight."

"Listen." His eyes fell to her name tag. "Kitty. You're right. It's a bad time for me, and I came to the Bahamas thinking maybe I could just—" He broke off and ran his free hand through his hair. "But now, with the way you're feeling tonight, if I take—"

"You're not *taking* from me any more than I would be taking from you. I want you, and I think you want me. There's…something. You feel it, don't you?" She took his hand and guided it to her breast, where her heart thudded with hunger. "Don't you?"

She felt the heat of his palm through the cheap polyester of her uniform. He scanned her face with somber eyes. He took a long breath that seemed to catch on something as it entered his lungs.

"Of course I do," he said. He grazed her cheek with one knuckle, and then, slowly, he bent his head down and whispered against her neck, "Yes. Of course I do."

His breath was warm and sweet, and went through her like a honeyed summer breeze. She began to shiver as he dragged his mouth up her throat, and goose bumps cascaded down her body, all the way to her toes.

She had wondered whether, in the end, she would change her mind and back away, as she had done so often, but his sudden human warmth was blissful. Easy and, at the same time, thrilling. She groaned in hungry relief, and pressed her body closer, as close as she could get.

Take that, Jim Oliphant. She wasn't ruined. She was still a woman, and she could still catch fire from a man's touch. It just had to be the right man. The right touch.

David seemed to understand that she didn't want him to waste time with a gentle seduction. She didn't want to change her mind. He lowered his mouth over hers and took her parted lips. His kiss was fierce, and the inside of his mouth was hot and sweet.

She heard herself moan, and for just a flash she wondered…what was he going to think of her? They'd just met, and—

But she didn't care. Tomorrow he'd disappear back into his real life, and she'd never see him again. He wasn't David Gerard, and she wasn't Kitty Hemmings. They were simply bodies, doing what healthy, hungry men and women did.

His hands slid across her back, down to her hips and up again, into her hair, and everything he touched tingled—her scalp, her ears, her spine, her arms.

She felt a sudden wetness under her eyes, but it wasn't tears this time. She'd been frozen, and now she was melting. The ice water was seeping out, over-flowing. She felt it around her heart, too, and between her legs.

She reached between their bodies and touched him, hoping she could urge him to hurry. She was ready. She'd been ready for years.

He was ready, too—she could feel how ready. But though she stroked that exciting, swollen warmth and traced the strong contours with her fingertips until she could hardly breathe, he never lost his focus.

His lips were still doing fiery things to her collar-bone, even while his fingers found the metal pull to the zipper that ran down the front of her dress. Her stupid, too-tight, too-short bartender's costume.

As the fabric peeled open, David bent his head fur-ther, kissing each new inch of exposed skin. The moon-light glistened on his dark blond hair, as if he'd been dusted with glitter.

She threaded her fingers through his hair and arched toward him. Oh, she wanted this so much. It might be midnight outside, but as he slipped the dress from her shoulders she felt suddenly full of sunshine. Her nerve endings sizzled, just like the ocean on a bright sum-mer afternoon.

She reached out, tugging at his button, and he smiled. He shed his clothes quickly, without a trace of self-consciousness.

And why should he be self-conscious? He was amaz-ing. She shut her eyes against the overwhelming beauty of him, and the power. He made every other man on the island look like a child.

Gently, he eased her back against the cool leather.

They both knew that his bed was too far away, but it didn't matter. Only the moon watched through the picture window, and the palms shifted in the breeze, throwing shadows across their bodies.

He got up long enough to find a condom, and soon, so soon, the moment had arrived. She tried not to think about it. She tried just to feel, and to let it flow through her.

His body was hard, intimidating in its primitive strength, but he was sensitive and gentle, and besides, in spite of the fear, her body ached for him. Those silver flashes exploded everywhere now, and her core was tugging toward him.

She felt him, so wondrously rigid and velvety at the same time, pressing against that tingling spot between her legs. Her lungs tightened. Her fingers dug into his shoulders. She tried to find enough air to breathe.

He kissed her again, his tongue driving that spiced sweetness into her mouth, and she inhaled sharply. And then she let her knees fall apart to welcome him.

After that, for a very long time, nothing seemed quite linear or logical. She was all body, all sensation, with no brain to interfere. She was all aching and pushing, panting and exploring.

Finally, even the body was unnecessary. He had, with his amazing hands and his clever lips, unwound the spiraled fortress of that outer shell and found the vulnerable truth inside. She was sunshine and starlight and invisible currents that were ready to carry her to places she'd never been.

But at the very end, in that point-of-no-return

moment before the currents took her away, like a fool she opened her eyes.

And David Gerard's strong face was above her, gleaming with the sweat of their lovemaking. And so, as she twisted away into the most shattering climax she'd ever experienced, she was looking into his eyes. And God help her, he wasn't just a man.

He was *this* man. *Âme perdue.*

She wasn't going to be able to forget him now.

DAVID WOKE in the purple hour before dawn, and he sensed immediately that he was alone.

He lifted up just enough to squint toward where her clothes had fallen. Nothing. The carpet was bare. His sweet, mysterious lover—he knew only that the name on her badge had been Kitty—was gone.

He fell back onto the couch, irrationally disappointed. Had he really expected her to stay all night? What, in fact, had he expected from any of this?

He sleepily relived the strange events that had led to...

To this.

If anyone had told him that he'd mark Belle Carson's wedding day by picking up a tough-talking, green-haired bartender whose badass attitude barely covered up the fact that she was really a little girl lost, he'd have laughed in their faces.

If anyone had told him that the bartender would make crazy love with him until he collapsed and passed out stark naked on his own couch, he would have said they were crazy.

And if anyone had dared to suggest that, when he

woke up, he'd still be hard as a rock and hungry for more, he'd…

But he was. He was exhausted, and yet he was fully aroused, still on fire, as if she'd cast a spell on him. Why the hell had she left? He wondered if the hotel would give him her room number. If he could stand the pain of putting on pants, maybe he could go and…

He laughed at himself. He couldn't even walk right now, much less go out in public.

Could he find her before he'd have to leave for the airport? His plane was at two, which gave him…

Not long enough.

Not nearly long enough.

How much would it cost him to change his flight? He rolled on to his side and groaned as the cool leather pressed against the sensitive places.

He didn't care if it was a thousand dollars. There was something about his little green-haired Kitty with no last name. Something clever and sexy…and something else, too. A haunting quality he couldn't put a name to.

He remembered the look in her eyes as she made love to him. She'd been frightened, and at the same time so alive, so in love with the feeling. He could almost hear her whimper, and feel her pulsing helplessly around him. He groaned again. Oh, yeah. Once with that woman was definitely not enough.

And then, suddenly, as if his hunger had summoned her up, he felt the cushions bend, and he felt her warmth slide onto the sofa behind him. He felt her breasts press into his back as she spooned up against him. He sighed with pleasure, and more than a little relief.

She reached around and pressed her hands against his chest.

"Ahhh," she said. She nipped his shoulder, purring in a delighted murmur.

Slowly, she began to slide her palms up and down, from collarbone to hips. For a moment, he shut his eyes and let the bliss wash over him.

"Kitty," he said softly. He stilled her hands just below his rib cage, but he felt his control slipping.

"No," a strange voice said, breaking the moment as brutally as a hammer shattering a mirror. "But obviously Kitty wasn't exaggerating about you."

He turned sharply, and faced a voluptuous brunette, dressed in the same bartender's uniform that Kitty had worn. But different, so different…such dark, almond-shaped eyes over full, hungry lips.

"Kitty said you were a carnival ride like no other." The woman licked the skin on his shoulder. "And now I see it's true."

It was the other bartender. Jill. He'd seen her a dozen times, pulling drafts and raking in big tips. She'd flirted with him, night after night, as she did with every male customer she encountered.

But what the hell was she doing here, on this sofa? And what did she mean, "Kitty said…"?

He sat up, grabbing her shoulders and moving her out of the way as he might have moved a child who had become a pest.

She chuckled softly, clearly undaunted, and reached out to smooth his tousled hair.

"Don't you remember me, sweetheart? I'm Jill. Kitty

said to say she's sorry. She had to go, but she sent me to see if you needed anything…" Her eyes slid down. "Anything else."

CHAPTER TWO

Eight weeks later

BY THE TIME the Brantley deposition was over, David Gerard couldn't see anything but January's darkness outside his law office window, and he was tired. Not just go-to-bed-early tired. The kind of disgusted bone-weariness that made people burn their houses, move to Costa Rica and spend the rest of their lives drinking piña coladas out of conch shells.

Unfortunately, he'd promised to take Marta Digiorno, a friend who also happened to be an attorney, out to dinner. They'd been circling the idea of dating for the past few weeks, though he wasn't crazy about mixing the courthouse with pleasure. Tonight would be a trial balloon. Not quite a date, but not completely business, either.

"Do you think Barker and King will settle?" Marta stuffed file folders into the pocket of her briefcase, then sat on the edge of his desk and smiled. Amazingly, she didn't look an iota less crisp and professional than she had at eight this morning, when they'd passed in the hall, each heading into the courthouse to take separate depositions.

She had a good legal mind, and David answered the

question honestly. The chauvinistic weasels at Barker and King, Inc., had clearly discriminated against his client, a former employee who had been let go because she got pregnant.

"They should settle," he said. "But they might not. They know the case is pro bono. They might think they can stonewall until we get tired of paying out of our own pockets."

"Watch your pronouns," she said, cocking one graceful eyebrow. "I'm not representing anyone for free. You're the bleeding heart around here. So, any chance your heart feels sorry enough for a fellow lawyer to rub her tired feet?"

She kicked off her high heels and rested her left foot on his thigh.

Okay, that certainly shifted the evening squarely into the personal column. He hesitated, then decided he was being a fool. It had been two months since he'd had a date. Longer, really, because that Bahamas madness didn't really qualify as a date.

Still…eight weeks since his vacation, when for the first time in his boring, Mr. Nice Guy life, he'd been propositioned by two women in one night. Not his usual style, not by a long shot. And sadly, not as exciting as people might think. Kind of foolish, actually, and, in the end, oddly depressing. Another prepubescent dream busted.

Anyhow, the green-haired bartender and her trashy friend, whom he'd tossed out of the cottage in about ten seconds without wasting much time on tact, were history. Belle Carson, who had been happily married eight weeks now, too, was also history.

Marta was smart, classy, witty and obviously interested. And she was here. So what was he waiting for?

Nothing. He nestled her heel in one hand and began flexing her long, slim toes with the other.

She leaned back, palms down on his desk, and let her eyes drift shut. "Mmm," she said in a low purr. "Nice."

A sudden commotion in the outer office stilled his hands. He glanced toward the closed door, not alarmed but curious. It was at least eight o'clock. He didn't have any appointments tonight.

That is what his paralegal, Amanda, was clearly trying to tell someone. A woman, from the sound of it. A woman who was refusing to take no for an answer.

Within two seconds, his door flung open. A young female with crazy green curls stormed in, her eyes fiery and her head pushed forward, like a determined goose. Behind her, Amanda stood helplessly, hands up in defeat. "Miss—Miss, I told you Mr. Gerard is unavailable and—"

The young woman scowled over her shoulder at the paralegal. "And I told you I don't care. What is it with you people? He's not the president, for God's sake!" Then she turned toward David, and he saw her face harden as she took in Marta lounging on the desk, her jacket on the chair, her foot cradled in David's hands.

"Oh," the newcomer said. "*That* kind of unavailable."

David's mind wasn't working fast enough. He knew what he saw, or what he thought he saw, but it was so impossible his brain wouldn't accept it. The hair was green, just like before. And the eyes…

He knew those eyes. And yet, how could it be? It couldn't. It couldn't be—

He'd called her "the green-haired bartender" in his mind so long he couldn't, for a minute, remember her name.

Marta had already moved her foot and let her legs slide down, so he stood.

"Miss…" He took a breath. "Katie?"

But the instant he said it, he knew it was wrong. Not Katie. *Kitty.* Of course it was Kitty. In his mind, he could still see the white rectangle of her name tag, moving up and down as she panted…

What on earth was she doing here?

Her eyes narrowed. "Close," she said icily. "Partial credit. It's Kitty. Kitty Hemmings. You look surprised to see me. I guess this means none of your bodyguards called to give you a heads-up."

"My what?"

"Your bodyguards. I've been trying to get in touch with you all afternoon. But your receptionist, she's not that friendly, is she? Neither is your housekeeper, for the record."

She'd been to his house? Of course Bettina, who was a terrible snob, would have been rude to a visitor with green hair and…whatever that geometrically patterned green and pink sarong-like thing was supposed to be. Bettina was rude to *him* if he wore sweats or brought home fast food.

How had Kitty found his house? He hadn't known her last name, and he wouldn't have thought she knew his. In the end, though, *how* she'd found him was relatively unimportant. Relative, that is, to the real sixty-four-thousand-dollar question.

Why had she found him?

Out of the corner of his eye, he noticed that Marta had slipped on her shoes, and she'd put on her game face, too. As he'd just been observing, Marta was smart as hell. She clearly knew something wasn't right about this scene.

Half a dozen explanations raced through his head. Could Kitty need a job, a recommendation, a lawyer? Surely not. People didn't expect their one-night stands to give them career references. His shoulder muscles tightened. Crap—had he picked up a stalker?

Or was she bringing bad news? An STD? He always, always used condoms. Blackmail? God help him, she wasn't underage, was she? She looked mid-twenties, but you never knew these days. He'd assumed the bar wouldn't employ anyone...

But assumptions could be lethal. Any good lawyer knew that.

"Of course. Kitty." Years of poker-faced negotiations saved him from revealing the chill that ran through his veins. "How can I help you?"

It sounded stilted, almost rude. He saw her recoil slightly. But what the hell had she expected? Whatever he'd briefly, brainlessly, believed might be going on between them that night—he'd been wrong. He'd just been her flavor du jour, a tourist novelty to be shared with her horny girlfriends. *Fine.* He was a grown man. No one had held a gun to his head. *No big deal.*

But with that kind of cheap treat, no one came back for seconds.

"How can I help you?" he repeated. He didn't change his tone.

"We need to talk," she said flatly. Her gaze slid to Marta. "Alone."

The other lawyer didn't budge.

He touched Marta's shoulder. "The reservations are for eight-thirty. If you go ahead now, we won't lose the table. I'm sure this won't take long. I can meet you at the restaurant."

A frown line bisected Marta's perfect, pale forehead. "David, it might be better if—"

"It's fine." He smiled. He hoped he was right. "I'll meet you there."

Marta nodded, though she didn't look convinced. The room rang with silence as she gathered up her briefcase and her coat. She moved to the door, then turned.

She looked at David. "I'll mention to security that you're still in the office."

"Oh, *brother*." Kitty dropped her purse on the desk and crossed her arms. "He's twice my size, and I'm not packing heat." She glared at David. "But if you're afraid to be alone with me, I'd be happy to have a group discussion. Invite security. Hey, invite everybody. The *alone* part was for your benefit, not mine."

"It's fine," he said again, giving Marta a straight look. "Really."

Marta knew he meant it. She slipped through the door, shutting it behind her.

And then he and Kitty were alone. With Marta gone, he was much more aware of her, of her deep, island tan and a scent with a hint of strawberry. For a minute, he could smell that little beachside bar again. Salt in the air, lemons and limes and kiwi fruit, an undercurrent of barbeque smoke.

She glanced around, and her frown deepened. "Nice office," she said cryptically.

Did that mean she was surprised? By what? How dull it was? By the decorator-chosen beiges, the bland paintings that even Belle, who was ten times as conservative as Kitty, had hated? Had he seemed more interesting in the Bahamas?

Or was she surprised by how luxurious it was? Half his clients were pro bono, but the other half required impressing. So the decorator had hauled in solid mahogany paneling, carpet like velvet air, a marble bust of Thomas Jefferson for the corner. If Kitty had come for blackmail, this probably looked like the jackpot.

But something in him couldn't believe that. What blackmail could possibly stick? He wasn't married, and the sex had been consensual. Even if she'd caught the whole thing on tape, up to and including the second offer from her friend, he'd be nothing worse than embarrassed. Lunches at the University Club would be awkward for a while, with everyone asking why he'd turned down Lady Number Two, but he'd survive.

He watched Kitty as she roamed the room, proving it didn't intimidate her. She even gave Jefferson an affectionate tap on the nose. But the gesture didn't ring true. Her body looked tight, as if she were nervous, but hell-bent on hiding it. He wondered how rude Bettina had actually been. Or Amanda. Both women had maternal streaks where he was concerned.

He felt like a blind man playing a game of chess,

aware of all the possible strategies, but unable to see the full board. He had no idea what her ultimate gambit was. Surely a polite neutrality was the best first move. No need to assume the worst.

"Would you like to sit down?"

Kitty turned. Her green eyes were bright, sparkling under the overhead fixture. Anger? Or tears?

"No. Thank you." A hint of a smile played at her full mouth, and it wasn't a reassuring look. "You might want to, though."

Ah. Not good news, then. Of course not.

"Thanks for the warning." He tilted his lips in an equally mirthless smile. "I think perhaps you'd better get to the point."

"So you can make your reservations? So you can meet your date?" She glanced toward the door. "Is she your girlfriend?"

"I don't see that my relationship with Marta is relevant."

"How serious is this relationship? Was she your girlfriend when you…eight weeks ago?"

"Again," he said, though he had to work to keep a patient tone, "I think you'll need to establish the relevance before—"

"You want relevance?" She hadn't ever unfolded her arms, and he saw her fingers tighten until the knuckles were white. "Okay, I'll give you relevance."

He waited. The room was so quiet he realized neither one of them was breathing.

"I'm pregnant."

THE NEXT AFTERNOON, Kitty nursed a glass of ice water in the restaurant of her hotel, trying to occupy herself by mentally critiquing the bartender. Unfortunately, because the hotel was half empty and down on its luck, nothing much was happening except the occasional request for an after-work beer.

She'd considered booking a room somewhere glitzy—a fancy hotel that would show David Gerard she wasn't someone who could be pushed around. But that idea had evaporated after a nanosecond. She didn't have much left in her savings, and she had no idea whether David was the type who might tell her to go to hell, and take the baby with her. She had to hang on to every penny.

Still, she had to do something to take her mind off the fact that he and his lawyer would be here in about five minutes. She was determined not to spend the time second-guessing what they might say.

She needed, more than anything else, to stay calm.

But…how could she have been such an idiot? How could she have let herself end up in such a wretched mess? Everyone knew sex with strangers was dumb. Everyone knew condoms weren't foolproof.

Everyone except Kitty Hemmings and David Gerard, apparently. She'd seen the shock in his eyes when she announced that she was pregnant. And then she'd seen the cynicism, the disdain, the quick up-and-down glance that said he thought she was lying.

If only she were.

The last thing in the world she wanted was to have a baby right now. With her life so up in the air, no roots under her feet. With a man she barely knew. A man who thought she was, at best, a little island tramp and, at worst, a sociopathic gold digger.

But she was going to have a baby, and it was his, and he'd have to come to terms with the idea, just as she'd had to.

The restaurant door opened, letting in a long rectangle of light briefly, then shutting it out again as it closed. David was here.

Her heart lurched a little, partly fear, partly just the same reaction any female would have to someone that good-looking. And of course he'd brought the tallest, best-dressed lawyer in San Francisco, doubling the intimidation factor.

She held up a hand to help them find her, although she knew her green hair was as good as a neon sign. David glanced at the other man, who slowly nodded, his gaze piercing even from ten yards away.

She felt a blush creep over her cheeks.

Temper, temper. Getting mad at David wasn't just counterproductive—it was unfair. He hadn't forced her to have sex that night. Far from it. She was honest enough to admit it had been entirely her idea.

And he certainly hadn't poked holes into the condom. He was just as shocked and confused as she'd been when she found out a couple of weeks ago. By bringing a lawyer, he clearly just intended to protect himself. What was wrong with that?

In the end, wasn't that what she was doing, too? The only difference was, she was also protecting her child.

"Kitty." He had reached the table, and managed to summon up a smile. That was nice, anyhow.

"David." She didn't rise or hold out her hand because it felt wrong. Everything about this meeting felt wrong.

"Kitty, this is my attorney and friend, Colby Malone. He's advising me today."

Malone didn't seem to have any scruples about the standard courtesies. He probably dealt with awkward situations every day. He held out his hand with such authority it didn't occur to her not to take it. "Hello, Ms. Hemmings. I hope you don't mind if I sit in on the meeting."

She shook her head. "No, of course not. Whatever."

Both men sat, and Kitty shifted her glass over, just for something to do with her hands. What a pair. Their pictures were probably in the dictionary, illustrating the phrase "looks like a million bucks."

Malone smiled at her, his eyes cool but kind. "Ms. Hemmings, David is—"

"No." David lifted his palm. "Colby, thanks, but… let me."

Malone hesitated briefly, then leaned back in his chair, putting his elbows on the padded arms to signal his easy agreement. "Of course. Sorry."

David cleared his throat, then began.

"Kitty, I—"

The waitress, of course, took that moment to come by. The men ignored the woman's flirtatious blinks and calmly ordered coffee. Kitty decided to get an order of unbuttered toast. For the past few weeks, her stomach had been unsteady, not just in the mornings and not just when she was arranging the future of her unborn child. She'd always heard what a tough time her mother had with pregnancy, and apparently she'd inherited the problem.

In fact, it was when she puked on Sugarwater's best beach bar customer that she'd lost her job.

"Kitty." David turned to her one more time. "I want you to know, right from the beginning, that if this baby is mine I don't intend to shirk responsibility."

She pressed her hands together in her lap. *"If?"*

David was careful not to glance at Malone, though Kitty could see that the other lawyer was listening very carefully to this part. He looked as serene as ever, but Kitty could sense the spiked awareness. He was ready to intervene should David utter a syllable that wasn't in the script.

"I have to assume you've come to me because you're looking for some kind of financial commitment. And if the baby is mine, you'll get one. I don't walk away from my mistakes. But first I'm going to need indisputable proof that this *is* my mistake."

Malone's eyes flickered. He might as well have groaned out loud. He obviously knew, even if David didn't, how damned rude that sounded.

She felt her throat tightening. "No, David. First you need to wrap your mind around the idea that this is a child, not a *mistake.* And then, you need to take your legalese baloney and—"

"Ms. Hemmings." Malone smiled again. "I think what David is trying to say—"

"I know what he's trying to say. He's trying to say I'm such a tramp the baby could be anyone's. But I'm not, and it isn't." She looked at David. "Unless…you don't have me mixed up with Jill, do you? I was the *first* one."

Neither man looked surprised. That hurt, because it

killed her last real hope that Jill had been lying when she said she'd gone to see David after Kitty left. It destroyed the illusion that David hadn't really slept with Jill, too, as if he'd booked a room at an amusement park of sex.

But he wasn't even trying to deny that there had been a second whirl on the roller coaster that night. Her heart hardened a little, processing its disappointment.

The unruffled demeanor of both men also answered another question: whether David had shared all the dirty details with Malone. She wondered when David had told him. Just today, to prepare for the meeting with her? Or eight weeks ago, when David had arrived home from the Bahamas with a good tan and a great locker-room story?

"I'm perfectly clear about the two of you," David answered coldly. "But I have no idea what you might have done before that night, or in the eight weeks since."

She scowled, then leaned forward, her mouth open, her cheeks as hot as if he'd held a match to them. "I don't—"

"Kitty, listen," David said, forestalling her. "I can understand why you might think I'm a fool, because I certainly acted like one in the Bahamas. But I'm not. Before I accept…" He stopped, and for the first time he looked uncertain. "I need to establish beyond a doubt that the child is mine."

Suddenly she was precariously close to tears. Damn these hormones. She blinked hard and narrowed her eyes.

"Well, we'd better find a way to establish that in

a hurry. I lost my job because of this pregnancy, although of course they cooked up some other excuse. And I don't have insurance. This pregnancy isn't going to be easy. I'm Rh negative, but you're probably not, which is a problem. My mother had two miscarriages, and my family has seen three sets of twins in the past three generations. I'm not a high-risk pregnancy, but it's not exactly a cakewalk, either. So if you think I'm going to see some quack at some third-rate charity clinic, where God only knows—"

"Hey." He put his hand over hers. It was the first physical contact since that night, and even through her anger she sensed the warm sizzle of skin against skin. She moved her hand up onto the table. She didn't want his pity pats.

"Kitty, please," he said. "Relax. It's absurd for us to—"

She lifted her chin. "Too late," she said. "This whole thing is absurd, and believe me, I know it. But, still, here it is."

David shook his head, as if he didn't quite know what to do with such an emotional female. Well, let him try being pregnant. Let him try being jobless and homeless, and counting pennies, and waking up in the night doubting yourself, wondering if your own child would be better off adopted...

"There's a test we can have done right away," he said.

She frowned. "It's too early for an amniocentesis."

"I know, but—"

Everyone fell silent as the waitress set down coffee and toast. Great. The kitchen had buttered the toast, though Kitty had made a point of asking for it dry. Little greasy yellow puddles glistened on the brown surface. Nausea twisted Kitty's stomach. She swallowed hard and pushed the toast to the side, out of sight behind the silver coffee carafe.

When they were alone again, Malone took over, as if handling Kitty were a relay race, and the baton had been passed to give David a rest.

"The test David's referring to is called CVS, which stands for Chorionic Villus Sampling. It's quick—a week, maybe ten days at most for the results. If it's done properly, through an obstetrician we mutually agree upon, David will accept the results as definitive."

She looked from one man to the other, wondering if she could trust any of this. Was she being set up for some kind of fall?

She hadn't researched Colby Malone, of course, since she hadn't known whom David would consult. But she had used Google to research the heck out of David, and she hadn't found anything squalid or dishonest. In fact, at worst, he appeared to have an overactive social conscience. All kinds of charity functions and do-gooder lawsuits, lots of sober interviews in boring, peer-reviewed journals.

So apparently the indiscriminate sex had been an aberration. What happens in the Bahamas, and all that.

She had pretty strong feelings about the importance of a father in a child's life, but still. If David had turned out to be a true sleazeball, she would never have breathed a word to him about the baby. She'd work five jobs if she had to, rather than saddle her child with an untrustworthy, deadbeat dad.

But David clearly was, with the occasional lapse, a good guy. He had a right to know he was about to be a father, and he had an obligation to assume his half of the responsibility.

The two men waited, apparently patiently, for her answer. Malone never seemed to look anything but pleasantly confident, but David's face was tight and wary. Suspicious. She wondered if he hoped she'd refuse to submit to the test—which he could take as proof that her accusation had been a con from the start.

She breathed through her mouth, so that she didn't smell the coffee, which suddenly seemed too bitter.

She'd heard of this CVS thing, read about it somewhere, maybe, but she hadn't paid enough attention. Why should she have? She'd never imagined it could matter to her. "Are there risks?"

Malone started to shrug, but David nodded.

"Yes," he said. "The risks are very small, but I want you to understand completely. Colby brought some materials."

Malone retrieved a colorful brochure from his briefcase. She took it from his outstretched hand, wondering where he'd picked it up on such short notice. Did his practice specialize in paternity suits or something?

She leafed through the brochure blindly, the words indecipherable through the haze in her brain.

"You don't have to read it now," David said. "Take your time. Obviously you can consult any physician you like while you make your decision, though, as Colby said, the test must be performed by someone we agree on. Colby has a few names to suggest."

"Of course," she said, and accepted Colby's doctor

list, printed on creamy, classy letterhead that said Diamante, Inc. Whatever that was.

The brochure was glossy and obviously expensive, as well. That meant the test wasn't cheap. "Who will pay for this CVS test? I know you said you wouldn't be drawn in before—"

"Since it's in my interests to settle the problem definitively, one way or another, I'm willing to pay for it." David waved the issue away, as if payment were sublimely unimportant.

And she knew, from her Google searches, that, to him, it was. A few hundred, a few grand, he'd never miss it.

Suddenly her anger surged back, full force. Well, bully for the big guy, to whom her pregnancy was the "problem." The "mistake." When he realized the baby really was his, he'd probably have Colby sue the condom company, and her child support checks would all come marked Trojan, Inc.

Jerk.

She slid the brochures into a neat stack, like folding a bad poker hand. She stood, pushing her chair back with a scrape that echoed through the nearly empty restaurant.

"Make the appointment," she said. "I'll be there."

CHAPTER THREE

DAVID SAT in the waiting room of the obstetrician's office, surrounded by pregnant women, hyperkinetic toddlers and hovering husbands. He hadn't ever been so uncomfortable in his life.

It might as well have been tattooed across his forehead: *I don't belong here.*

He flipped through the newspapers he'd found on the magazine table and tried to remember who was running in the upcoming special elections. But real life, or what he used to call real life a week ago, seemed remote. Kitty's announcement had blasted him into an alternate dimension. He still met clients, took depositions, researched case law, but it all had the muted, out-of-focus quality of something seen through dirty glass.

And yet, this "baby" and "fatherhood" world didn't seem real, either. That left him…nowhere. Suspended in some murky, slow-motion half-life.

He wondered if things would snap back into clarity when the results of the paternity test came through.

Or would life just get weirder still?

He glanced at the closed door through which the nurse had escorted Kitty at least forty-five minutes ago. Their cheek swabs had been done earlier, when they first got to the office. Now the CVS test was supposed to take no more than half an hour. Had something gone wrong?

He stood. He paced to the check-in window to see if he could glimpse anything going on down the halls. He couldn't.

When he turned back, he saw that a little kid with a runny nose had stolen his chair. In the far corner, a woman who had to be about eleven months pregnant inexplicably burst into tears, and her husband knelt in front of her, apologizing and chafing her hands.

God. This was the waiting room of one of the most respected and most expensive obstetricians in San Francisco. David could only imagine what it must be like at a free clinic. No wonder Kitty had been so adamant that she wouldn't go to a cut-rate place.

He checked his watch. Fifty minutes.

And then, suddenly, Kitty came through the door. For a second, her small, oval face was pale and oddly woebegone under the chaos of green curls—and then she spotted him. Instantly she rearranged her features into the feisty, chin-up expression he knew best.

But all the pride in the world couldn't put the color back into her cheeks.

"Everything go okay?" He had already paid, days ago, so they had nothing to do but leave. He fought the urge to put his arm around her shoulders. She might be pale, but he knew she'd rather collapse on the carpet than admit any weakness.

"It was fine."

They walked a few feet, and she stumbled over a

board book some brat had left by the door. She reached out and used the wall to steady herself.

"How about if you wait here," he said, "and I'll bring my car around?"

"No, thanks." The door to the obstetrician's suite opened just a little way from the elevator, and she punched the down button quickly. "I'm all right. They said to take it easy, but no one said I needed a wheelchair and a keeper."

He wanted to ask her again how the test had gone, but the stiffness in her shoulders told him she wasn't in the mood to discuss it. At least not with him. Once again that surreal detachment swamped him. How was it possible that he might be having a baby with this woman who wouldn't even talk to him?

She spent the ride down adjusting the folds of her cloth purse to avoid making eye contact, as if he were some disreputable stranger who had crowded her and might ask for a handout.

He tightened his jaw and backed away to lean against the farthest wall of the glass elevator. Fine. If she didn't want to talk, he knew how to be silent. He put his hands in his pockets and pretended to watch the luxuriant fern and ivy of the atrium slide by.

When they reached the ground floor, though, and the doors slid soundlessly open to release them, he saw her hesitate, her fingers tightening on the shoulder strap of her purse. And then it hit him. How had she gotten here this morning? And how was she going to get back? Her hotel was halfway across San Francisco, and he had no idea whether she could afford a cab.

Damn it. He should have picked her up. Or at least

sent a cab to get her. He'd promised he'd handle the cost of this test—all the costs. But he hadn't even thought about transportation. Obviously, he'd been spending way too much time in ivory-tower lawyerland. And she probably despised him for that, probably assumed he had been born to the cushy life and had always been smugly oblivious of details like this.

Ha. If she only knew.

"I hope you'll let me give you a lift back to the hotel." He smiled, working at sounding politely professional. Nothing judgmental, patronizing or overly familiar.

He seemed, thank God, to have hit the correct tone. She didn't smile, exactly, but her face wasn't as gray and hard as it had been upstairs. A little color had come back into her cheeks.

"Thank you," she said. "But I'm fine."

"I'd like to." He thought fast. "And it wouldn't be out of my way. I have to meet a client over in that part of town, and—"

"No, really. Thanks, but I'm fine." She pushed a curl out of her forehead with a tense hand.

Had a hint of chill returned to her voice? Had she taken "that part of town" as an insult? He hadn't meant it as one. Her hotel had obviously been chosen to get maximum clean-and-respectable points for minimum price, which seemed like common sense to him.

He wasn't a silver-spoon snob; but of course she didn't know that. All she knew of him was the luxury cottage at the Bahamas, the overdecorated office in Union Square and maybe a glimpse of the Victorian house he'd just bought in the Marina district, which looked okay from the outside but was crumbling to bits on the inside, like a facade for a film set. That moldering interior was partly why his housekeeper stonewalled anyone who came knocking at the door.

Someday, he'd have to tell Kitty about the two-job, Ramen noodle years of law school. And the loans that had crippled him financially for a decade. And how, now that he'd been fool enough to buy that fading lady of a house, he would have to restore it, plank by plank, with his own time and sweat.

Someday. Yeah. If the test came back with his name on it, and they actually had a someday.

Right now, though, he had to get her into the car and back to her hotel so that she could rest. She had dark circles under her eyes that hadn't been there ten minutes ago.

"Kitty, I—"

She shook her head firmly. "I'm not going straight back to the hotel, anyhow. I have an errand to run first. I'm fine with the bus."

The bus? A half-hour standing in the cold, waiting for it to rumble by, followed by two hours of bumping and jostling, hanging onto a ceiling strap and nosing the next guy's armpit?

"Can't the errand wait? You really should take it easy and—" But she was already shaking her head again, so he tried another tack. "Tell you what. I'll take you to do the errand, whatever it is, then drop you back at the hotel. I guarantee we'll get it all done before the right bus even shows up."

He almost had her. Though she probably didn't know it, a tiny worry line had formed between her eyebrows.

He could practically see her willpower fading as she glanced uncertainly toward the front doors. He knew very little about her, but he knew, from the quick bar-side chitchat, customer to bartender, that she was from Virginia.

He would have known, even if she hadn't told him. Her accent, with its soft I's and almost inaudible G's, spoke of a childhood spent playing under the magnolia trees of the Deep South, not on the foggy hillsides of northern California.

Besides, even natives occasionally found the public transit system daunting.

"Kitty." He put his hand on her shoulder—and almost pulled it away again, shocked to find that his palm instantly recognized the exact shape of the curve, the exact feel of the warm, satiny, sun-bronzed skin. "Let me help. You look done in, and that can't be good for you—or the baby."

He wondered whether she'd say something snarky, something about how charming it was that he suddenly gave a damn about the baby, but she didn't. Maybe she was too tired.

She nodded slowly. "All right," she said. She took a deep breath. "Thank you."

She stood somberly by his side, without chitchat, as he gave his ticket to the medical complex valet. When the car came, she settled herself gingerly, and leaned her forehead against the window for a few seconds, with her eyes closed.

As he pulled out onto the street, she finally spoke. "The errand is…well, I have to go buy and pick up the uniform for my new job. It's near my hotel, though, so it's not far out of the way."

She had taken a job? Here, in San Francisco? Thank God he was accustomed to controlling his face in court, so he didn't let his shock show. But...surely she wasn't planning to stay here long enough to need a job!

And that's when he realized that, despite everything, he had continued to believe that this whole mess might go away soon.

That *she* might go away soon.

He tried to relax his hands on the wheel. "Where's the job?"

"At the Bull's Eye," she said. Her chin tilted up maybe an eighth of an inch. "Weekend bartender."

The silence that followed the statement was loaded, like a gun. A hundred incredulous phrases leapt to the tip of his tongue, and though he somehow bit them back, she obviously guessed at every one. She didn't look at him, but the muscles in her body seemed coiled, ready to strike if he dared to criticize.

But a bartender? Damn it, a *bartender?* On her feet, in the middle of the night, in that neighborhood? As fragile as she looked? She'd lost ten pounds since the Bahamas—ten pounds she didn't have to spare. Did she really think the Bull's Eye was any place for a pregnant woman? Hadn't she had enough of groping drunks to last her a lifetime?

Something hot and tight moved through his chest, and he found his fingers clenching the wheel in spite of his best efforts.

He knew how any of those questions would sound.

Controlling. Patronizing. Snobbish. The mother of *my* child, a bartender?

He could hear her comeback now. *Guess you should have thought of that, jackass, before you slept with a bartender.*

He turned right onto Market, his tires complaining as he took the corner a little sharply. He eased back on the gas and forced himself to take a breath. Regroup, he ordered himself. This wasn't about snobbery, but he'd be damned if he knew what it *was* about.

He had no say over where she worked. And whose fault was that? His own. He was the one who had dictated the rules here. He had rejected any official investment in Kitty, her life or her unborn child, until and unless the tests proved the baby was his.

So what was this sudden overprotective reaction all about? Why did he care what she did to earn a few bucks while she waited for the test results?

Because—

Because the whole thing was impossible, that was why. Insane. She was nothing to him today, but tomorrow they might be as intimately connected as two people could be. Nothing in between. Either she was a lying nutjob who would vanish like a bad smell, or she was the mother of his child, who would change his world forever.

And he couldn't do anything but wait to see which way the coin fell.

This shouldn't have happened. They'd had one sexy, rather sweet night together, the way millions of people the world over did all the time. They'd both been trying to drown some sorrows, forget some ghosts. Neither of them had dreamed they might be stepping into this kind of trap.

So what the hell was he supposed to say? What the hell was he supposed to *feel?*

The silence stretched on, but eventually grew less tense as she seemed to realize he wasn't going to lecture her. She gave him directions as needed, and by the time they reached the Bull's Eye, David felt back in at least some semblance of control.

He parked near the door—it was far too early for a crowd, even in this neighborhood. He turned off the engine and swiveled toward her. She looked pale, as if the wordless emotional standoff that had just passed between them had taken its own kind of toll.

He offered a smile as a truce. "Would you like me to come in with you?"

She shook her head. "I won't be a minute."

She was as good as her word. Less than sixty seconds later, she emerged from the small, dark, brown-planked building, hugging a white plastic sack to her chest. Her face was bent over the sack, and she walked so quickly he wondered if she was running from someone.

Had her new boss given her a hard time?

She pulled open the door and lurched in.

"Is everything okay?" He couldn't see her expression. Ducked down like this, her face was hidden by a cascade of springy green curls. "Did you get your uniform?"

"Yes." Her voice sounded odd. Was she crying?

"Kitty—"

"Please," she said in that same muffled strangeness. "Could you take me home now?"

"Of course." He started the car and pulled back onto the main drag. She still hugged that bag, wrapping her arms around it as if it were a life raft.

He tried to think of something to say, but failed. He had an insane urge to tell her that if she hated the idea of taking that bartending job, she didn't have to do it. He'd help out, financially. Hell, even if the baby wasn't his, he would help. He didn't want her to have to serve drinks in that greasy, half-rotted dump.

But he couldn't say any of that. He had no idea what he *could* say. He'd never felt so wrong-footed in his entire life. Thank God her hotel was only three blocks from here. All he had to do was get there without saying or doing anything to upset her more.

From the moment they'd met at the doctor's office, he'd seen that she was angry with him, desperately angry at being forced to submit to the test. What he saw as common sense, she saw as a monstrous personal insult.

Or perhaps a cowardly attempt to dodge responsibility.

That, he realized, wasn't entirely untrue. He'd never pretended to be a saint. He didn't want to be a father, not now, not like this. He didn't want to bring his first child into the world…like this. So, yes, damn it, he did want a way out of this impossible situation. If by some miracle the baby wasn't his, what a get-out-of-jail-free card that would be.

For him.

But… He glanced at Kitty's huddled body and her

trembling fingers. What about for her? The baby wasn't going to go away just because David found out it wasn't his. What would she do then? If he wasn't the father, and she knew it, why would she have come to him in the first place?

Because she had nowhere else to go. No other safety net below her, ready to catch her fall.

"The lab has promised to expedite the results," he began awkwardly. She made a strange sound he couldn't identify, and he wondered if she thought *expedite* was pompous and absurd. Hell, this was like trying to have a conversation with someone from another planet. You didn't know what the simplest words meant to them.

"They've promised an answer by Wednesday," he soldiered on. "So I'll call you as soon as—"

She waved her hand toward him, making another peculiar noise. She fumbled with the bag.

"Kitty, look," he said, frustrated, but starting to get worried. Why wouldn't she tell him what was wrong? "I know this is rough on you, but I want you to know that, no matter—"

And then, with one final, strangled moan, she opened the bag and promptly vomited all over her brand-new bartender's uniform.

THE FOLLOWING MONDAY AFTERNOON was crisp and windy, the blue sky filled with long scalloped rows of clouds that looked like fish scales. It would have been a great day to feel healthy, rested and free.

Instead, Kitty felt sick, exhausted and trapped.

It was only the second day of her job selling puppets

at Punch and Judy—the retail job she'd taken at the wharf because the bartending gig didn't offer enough hours. And already her patience meter was sagging toward Empty.

She had hoped this store, which sold gorgeous, quirky hand puppets, might be less boring than other retail jobs she'd had in the past. But the novelty had worn off quickly—about the time she realized the customers expected her to perform full puppet plays, complete with voices and dancing about, for their spoiled, impossible-to-please children.

This particular family, who had asked her to bring down every dragon puppet in the store, was really getting on her nerves. The parents kept backing into the corner to continue what looked like The Neverending Fight, counting on her to keep their seven-year-old son entertained enough that he didn't overhear.

A losing battle. She'd seen too many little kids like this as she toiled at her various service jobs. She'd even *been* a little kid like this. And they always heard. They always knew.

What was worse, the family's stop at the puppet store was probably just a ruse. At the last minute, the parents would undoubtedly refuse to buy, with some lame excuse like their luggage being overstuffed already.

The kid would go home empty-handed. That was rough, because, for once, this little boy wasn't a brat. And he really, really liked the green dragon with crystal-teardrop scales and the red felt fire trailing from its nostrils. It cost about fifty dollars, and she wanted to warn him before he got his hopes up.

She glanced over at the dad. Good-looking guy, until you got to the smug face. And doing well for himself. Haircut, two hundred dollars. Sweater tied around the hips, five hundred dollars. Hips? Well, clearly, in his estimation, priceless. He'd just informed Mommy that he had janitors in his office who took better care of themselves than she did.

He caught Kitty looking at him, and lowered his voice. Right. God forbid anyone should think there was trouble in Yuppie Paradise.

Hypocrite.

She pulled off the puppet and wiped her hair back from her face, which felt suddenly sweaty. *Aw, please,* she thought, tightening her stomach. No vomiting now, not on this fifty-dollar dragon.

And all at once she'd had enough. She plucked one of the crystals from the dragon's tail and turned to the dad again. "Oh, look. There's a little damage to the scales here. I don't know if that bothers you, but it does mean I could offer a pretty good discount."

A discount she'd have to cover out of her own pocket, unfortunately. But the kid's face was so hopeful, and she couldn't stand it. She could make up the difference in her own budget by bringing a bag lunch the next week or two.

And maybe a few peanut-butter sandwich dinners.

She thrust the puppet out a bit farther to show the dad. "It's only a tiny flaw. I'm sure your son would still love it."

She turned to the boy. "I bet your dad does a great dragon voice, doesn't he?"

The boy nodded. "Daddy, do your dragon voice! I'll be Sir Galahad, and we can fight."

The cheapskate was still considering saying no. His wife put her hand on his arm and said hesitantly, "Honey, surely we—"

He brushed her hand away. "How big a discount?"

Kitty smiled placidly. "I think it's fifty percent. When there's damage."

The little boy squeezed his hands together so tightly the blood flow stopped, and his fingers were as white as marble. Kitty glanced down at him, then up at the dad with a smile that said she knew he was a great father who wouldn't dream of breaking his kid's heart.

With a low murmur of irritation, the man finally dug out his wallet. Kitty took a deep breath of relief.

She kept up a running chatter, to keep Dragon Dad in a good mood so that he wouldn't take his frustration out on the family later. When they left, she pulled out her phone and calculated what her half of the dragon would be, including the tax, then took her wallet out with a sigh.

She was so focused that it wasn't until she'd slipped her cash into the register that she noticed David Gerard standing on the other side of the store.

Her heart stumbled slightly. Now that was a sight that qualified as priceless. Muscled grace from head to toe. His thick, golden hair wind-tousled, a suit made for winning cases and breaking hearts, not necessarily in that order.

He was watching her with a dark, unreadable gaze. She flushed, wondering how much he'd seen. Did he think she'd really been flirting with that jerk? Had he seen her rip off the crystal? She'd have to explain. She didn't need any more black marks against her in his mind.

And then her breath caught. She forgot about the little boy, the dad and the dragon, all in one swoop. Because she knew why David was here.

Though it was two days early, only one thing could have brought him all the way out here.

The test results were in.

She didn't move from behind the register. She couldn't. Her legs didn't seem connected to her brain. She held on to the counter, just in case the legs gave out entirely.

She'd pictured this moment a hundred times. She'd known what the test results would be, of course, so she'd never felt any anxiety—only an eagerness to be vindicated.

She'd imagined how satisfying it would be to see his face once he understood what a bastard he'd been. How ego-soothing to listen to him try to find the words to apologize.

What she hadn't realized was how intimate this moment would be.

The moment they looked at each other, not as adversaries in some paternity chess game, but as parents. As two people who, whatever else they might become, would be "Mommy and Daddy" to the child she carried inside her now. She didn't want to be enemies. For her baby's sake she wanted peace in whatever kind of family they formed. But, if not enemies...what were they?

The current sizzled across the store, connecting

them like a glowing thread of awareness. He moved, then, but slowly, as if walking through a dream. By the time he reached the cash register, she felt her nerve endings spark painfully. Her mouth was dry, and it hurt to swallow.

He stopped only when the counter got in the way. "Can we talk? Outside?"

She shook her head. "My replacement will be here in a few minutes, but I can't leave till she arrives."

He frowned. "Kitty, we have to talk."

She wondered what he expected her to do. Quit? For a minute he reminded her of the dragon dad, who expected everything in the world to run on his schedule.

"So talk. There's no one in here but us. The puppets aren't going to repeat anything they hear."

Her voice sounded rougher than she intended it to. But she didn't know what to do, what to say, and her voice wasn't fully under her control. No part of her was. She still clutched the counter as if her knees might fail her at any minute.

She wasn't exactly a pro at situations like this. If her voice sounded tough, so be it. One thing was certain—she'd rather sound like an unforgiving bitch than a breathless beggar.

"Okay," he said. "We'll talk here. If that's the way you want it."

Want it? *Want* really didn't come into this, but she let that go. "I take it you've received the test results."

He nodded. "It's conclusive. The baby is mine."

She waited. Strangely, now that the moment had come, she no longer felt the slightest urge to say "I told you so."

She was still angry, of course. Still hurt, still frightened. But she recognized his expression. That unique mixture of shock and dismay, and under it all, that blind, gutsy determination to find a way to face the unfaceable. It was exactly what she'd seen in the mirror the day she found out.

For the moment, anyhow, that expression bound them together, made them teammates in this dangerous game. So she didn't say she'd told him from the start that of course the baby was his.

"I'm sorry," he said simply.

She lifted her chin. "Sorry it's yours?"

"Sorry I didn't believe you." He ran his hand through his hair. "And sorry that we've found ourselves in this situation. I know it's just as hard for you as it is for me."

That made her smile, and he understood the wry reaction instantly. He shook his head at his own stupidity. "No, I didn't mean it like that. Of course it's harder, much harder, for you. It's your body that's changing. Your life that's completely disrupted—"

"My uniforms that need to be dry-cleaned."

"Yes."

Their gazes met. A welcome moment of harmony. It felt like an oasis in the desert of this difficult journey. Neither of them spoke right away, as if they were both afraid another word would make the feeling break like a mirage.

"Kitty—"

She held up her hand. "No, it's all right, David. I know it's hard to accept. Hard to believe. And you've got a lot of things to consider. I'm sure you'll want to talk to your lawyer before you—"

"No."

She stopped cold. "No?"

"No. I don't need to talk to Colby. I don't want Colby's advice. I know what I want to do."

She held her breath.

"I want to marry you."

CHAPTER FOUR

KITTY FLUSHED, turning her face away slightly. "Don't make a joke of this, David. We—"

"It's not a joke. I want to marry you, if you'll have me. We can work out the details with Colby and with your lawyer. We can consult every lawyer in San Francisco, if that'll make you feel safer. I want to do this."

She could tell he was serious. "But…why?"

The question seemed to surprise him. "For the baby, of course. It may be old-fashioned, but I don't want my child to be illegitimate."

"It's the twenty-first century, David. Terms like *illegitimate* aren't just old-fashioned. They're dead. Why would you marry a complete stranger just because—"

"Because I think our child deserves a shot at having a family. I think he deserves a chance to have a mother and a father, both at the same time, not on alternate weekends. We created this child. Don't we owe him something?"

She nodded, struck by the intensity in his voice. She knew how he felt. Once she wrapped her mind around the idea that she was going to be a parent, she saw all the terrifying power of that relationship.

She suddenly realized that, sometimes, all the clichés were true. As a mother, a woman would drag the evening star out of the sky for the baby's first birthday candle if she thought it would make him happy. She'd work till she bled, and negotiate with God, and lie down on the proverbial railroad tracks.

Well, not *her* mother, maybe. But normal mothers. And thank God, she already knew that she would be a better mother than her own. Her pregnancy had already triggered a ferocious, protective passion for her unborn child.

"We owe him everything," she said. "But marriage won't necessarily—"

"No, I know. It won't necessarily fix anything. I have no idea if we can make it work. It's a dark-horse long shot at best. But we should at least try. For a while—a reasonable try. We can put together a contract, so that you can be sure you'll be protected."

He drew a long breath and put his hands, palms down, on the counter. "What do you say, Kitty? Will you do it? Will you give this crazy thing a chance and marry me?"

She hardly knew what to say. What was the "right" answer?

She looked into his gorgeous blue eyes and remembered the feel of his hands on her naked skin. She thought of the baby, no more than a delicate pea inside her, waiting with an absolute, unthinking trust. Growing silently, preparing to be born and loved.

But she also thought of her restless mother and her wounded father. And all the barnacle men who came after, right up to the unspeakable Jim Oliphant. She thought of the dragon dad she'd just waited on, who wanted everyone to believe he possessed the model family, though his son had anxious eyes and his wife was afraid to talk back to him.

She thought of all the brutal dramas that were playing out right this very moment, invisible behind neat doors and elegant lace curtains.

What, in the end, did marriage guarantee? Especially a marriage without love?

Not a damn thing.

"No," she said. "I'm sorry, but I don't think that's a good idea."

His blank face told her how shocked he was. She almost laughed. He hadn't even considered the possibility that she'd turn him down, had he? He'd come here so confident, like Prince Charming holding out the glass slipper. Every princess in town itched to wear it, so just imagine how ecstatic and grateful the little cinder maid would be!

And, in some ways, it was the fairy-tale ending. From unemployed bartender to lawyer's wife. From sooty rags to society pages. Wasn't that every struggling unwed mother's brass ring?

But she wasn't every unwed mother. How little he knew her!

That was, of course, the point. He didn't know her, and she didn't know him. They'd gone at this thing all backward.

At that moment, Cheyenne, her replacement for the evening, came in.

"Just let me clock out," Kitty said. "We can talk outside."

He nodded grimly and backed away from the counter. She went through the motions of turning the store over to Cheyenne, then met David at the door. They strolled out onto the boardwalk without speaking.

She tried to read his expression. When the shock of being turned down wore off, what kind of emotion would take its place? How he behaved right now might tell her a lot about who David Gerard really was. Would he be angry, insulted to have his generous offer rejected? Would he use it as an excuse to wash his hands of her? Would he be polite, but secretly relieved?

Of all the men she'd ever met, he was the most difficult to figure out. For a couple of minutes, he didn't speak at all. He moved to the railing and leaned his elbows on it, as if this were any lazy afternoon and he wanted to watch the water.

She joined him there, pulling her sweater close around her chest. The winter sun sparkled on the waves, but didn't provide much warmth. The wind was loud in their ears.

She started to say again that she was sorry, but she stopped herself. If he had a petty temper or a fragile ego, she wasn't going to play beta dog, rolling over and showing her belly. She wasn't asking for David's charity, but for his partnership. The child she carried was his.

A gust of wind caught her curls and began to play rough. She grabbed the longest ones and tucked them behind her ears. She clenched her jaw, so that she wouldn't shiver, and so that she wouldn't say anything before he did.

Finally, he took a deep breath and turned to face her. "I'm not sure what to say. I might have expressed myself badly. You don't have to answer right away, of course. Maybe it would help if you took some time to think it over."

"I don't need to think it over," she said. "I can't marry you. The truth is, I hardly know you."

He didn't quite let his gaze drop to her stomach, but one corner of his mouth turned up, acknowledging the irony. "Fair enough. But I promise you I'm healthy, law-abiding and relatively sane. If you'd like, I can provide references."

"This isn't a job application." She smiled, in spite of herself. "Although I'll be darned if I know quite *what* it is."

For a second, he smiled, too. Then his face sobered, and he reached out to touch her wrist with cold-tipped fingers. It was a gentle contact, and she felt no urge to pull back.

"It's the biggest decision we'll ever have to make," he said. "One that will change our child's life forever."

She didn't have an answer for that. Of course, as a lawyer, he would be good at framing arguments.

She stared at him, hoping for inspiration, but she got distracted by how elegant, handsome and intelligent he looked. How reasonable and calm. His hair lifted, sparking gold as invisible fingers of wind moved through it. The sun spotlighted his face, and his piercing eyes seemed an impossible blue. Just surface stuff, of course, but as baby-daddies went…

She had a feeling she could safely cross looks and brains off the list of DNA worries, at least.

"I know it's important," she said. "But illegitimacy, as I said before, doesn't exactly make a kid a pariah anymore. I won't enter into a sham marriage just to keep people from talking."

He shook his head. "Legitimacy isn't about what people think, or how the birth announcement looks on the society pages. It's about how our child feels about himself. About whether he grows up feeling wanted and safe, and the equal of anyone he meets."

She gave a small cynical snort. "It takes more than a mommy and daddy in the house to pull off that miracle of confidence. I can tell you that firsthand."

"Perhaps. But having a mommy and a daddy is a pretty good place to start."

"Not always. Having a pair of parents who argue for years, then divorce and battle over the pieces can be a lot worse than having just one."

He was silent a moment.

"Our child already has two parents, Kitty." Maybe it was a trick of the sunlight, but his eyes seemed to harden, the blue turning icy. "And he always will. There is no scenario, short of death, in which he could have just one. I am his father. If you wanted to keep me out of this baby's life, you should have stayed in the Bahamas."

She felt her cheeks burn under the surface cold. "That isn't what I meant. Of course he, or she, will have two parents. Just not necessarily always in the same place, at the same time."

David shook his head. "Can't you hear how wrong that is?"

"Of course I can. But you're suggesting that two total strangers—" She paused. "Nearly total strangers…should exchange vows promising to love and honor, in sickness and health, till death do us part. It's ridiculous. Neither one of us would mean it. It would be a fraud, and it wouldn't fool anyone, not even our child, once he gets old enough to think straight."

He gazed at her thoughtfully, as if Kitty herself were a problem that needed solving, like a complicated algebra equation or a crooked bookshelf. Again, she tried to read his emotions, but couldn't.

"Have you talked to your attorney about this?" She tried to imagine the elegant, arrogant Colby Malone approving of such a reckless move.

David shook his head. "He's out of the country right now. I could have called him, or emailed, but I didn't. I don't need to. I know what I want. I know what I think is right."

She almost laughed. "Well, unfortunately it's not just about what you think is right. I'm afraid I don't see marriage as a solution here. I see it as yet another impulsive mistake."

He looked at her thoughtfully for several long, uncomfortable seconds. Then, to her surprise, he simply nodded.

"All right," he said, apparently without rancor. "I can see that I'm not going to be able to change your mind, at least not right now. But if marriage is too extreme for you, what would you suggest instead?"

"I—I guess I thought—" She heard herself stumble. "I don't know, exactly."

"You must have had something in mind when you came to San Francisco. You could have sent me a certified letter from your attorney, but you didn't. Why?

I don't believe you came all this way just to ask me to sign a check and disappear."

She raised her chin. "No, but I wouldn't have been surprised if that was all you offered. I had no idea whether you were the kind of man who—"

"Well, I'm not. So now what?"

She turned back to the water, buying a minute. The wooden rail felt rough and splintered under her palms. She felt, quite abruptly, like an idiot. With those two little words, "Now what," he had exposed something she hadn't quite acknowledged to herself. She really wasn't sure *why* she had come all this way instead of sending a letter.

A letter hadn't even occurred to her.

But why not? What exactly had she expected to accomplish in person that she couldn't accomplish through a lawyer?

She thought she'd been so sensible. And yet…

On the plane, she'd alternated between panic and defiance. To work up her courage, she'd fed her indignation. She'd imagined a dozen different ways the confrontation could end in a fight, or an insult, or a brush-off. She'd half welcomed the idea of getting in his face and forcing him to take her seriously. She'd stand up for herself, by God. And for the baby.

She'd been so disappointed, back in the Bahamas, when he hadn't called or stopped by to see her the next day. She knew that, officially, he'd been scheduled to check out.

But maybe, just maybe, their night together had changed his mind. Maybe he'd extended his reservation.

Like a fool, she'd actually thought he might, and every time a new man walked into the bar her stomach had fluttered. Midafternoon, she'd discovered that he'd checked out. Left the island entirely. And then Jill had clocked in, with her delighted laughter about how they were both members of the Double Dipper club now.

Thankfully, Jill had quit within the week to take a job at a bigger resort, because Kitty couldn't have stood much more of the winking and teasing and fake sympathy.

"Oh, poor little pussycat," Jill had said, right in front of Josh, the bartender she slept with whenever she couldn't find a cute customer. "Guys like David Gerard think gals like us come with the price of the room. Did you actually imagine you were embarking on a *romance?*"

Then, just when Kitty thought she'd put the embarrassment and disappointment behind her, *wham*. She'd missed her period. She started feeling sick. The pink plus sign showed up on the stick.

From that moment on, she'd had one single mantra, repeated over and over in her mind: David Gerard was going to be a father. He had a right to know, and he had a responsibility to help.

"Kitty?"

David's voice called her back to the present, to the wharf, which was teeming with tourists she had completely tuned out for—how many minutes? He didn't sound impatient, exactly. More puzzled by her continued silence.

"I don't really know *what now.*" She glanced at him, wondering how he could look so calm when she felt so close to tears. Hormones, no doubt. Men didn't know how lucky they were. "It was hard to make specific plans when I had no idea what your reaction would be."

Before he could answer, he was tackled by a little kid who wasn't watching his step, clearly too fascinated by the huge gold balloon that floated above him, bobbing and shining in the sunlight. He ran straight into David's leg, so hard it must have hurt.

"Careful, buddy," David said pleasantly, steering the boy back toward the open walkway with a smile at the child's worried mom. Kitty couldn't help noticing that the woman thanked David with more warmth than was strictly necessary. And more words, and more minutes. The woman did everything, in fact, but write her phone number on his cheek.

Great-looking men who were patient with silly little boys—pure catnip for a certain kind of woman, Kitty supposed. She didn't like the sensation the woman brought out in her, though. It felt a lot like jealousy, which was, of course, ridiculous. David wasn't hers, and even if he were, he'd still have the right to exchange pleasantries with women on the boardwalk.

Annoyed with herself, she looked back at the water, but its gray sequins activated her nausea. She became intensely aware of the fishy, oily smell.

Eventually she shut her eyes and waited for the one-sided flirtation to be over. She wanted to go home. If that shabby hotel, which still cost more than she could afford for long, could be considered "home."

When the woman finally clacked away on her high heels, Kitty opened her eyes. "I'm not sure I can think very clearly right now," she said, taking up where they'd left off without preamble. "My emotions have been a little tangled, ever since..."

She swallowed, wondering where this quavering quality in her voice came from. "Ever since..."

"I understand," David said, the calm of his voice such a contrast to hers it almost sounded like a criticism. "But maybe we need to step back from the emotions for a minute, and just look at the facts."

She swallowed again. Step back from the emotions? How was she supposed to do that?

She scanned his composed features. She wondered if his emotions were always on such a tight rein. Or was it easier because he didn't, in the end, care very much about any of this? Perhaps, to him, her pregnancy was a surprise and a nuisance, but neither a miracle or a tragedy.

To her, it was all those things. It was a potent cocktail of contradictory emotions, deadly to rational thought.

"Really," she said dryly. "And what do the facts tell us?"

"That what we need is time. Time together. To get to know each other. And, unless I have completely misunderstood, you need a place to stay that doesn't rent by the night. Luckily, I have a solution for both those problems. It doesn't involve signing anything, or making any long-term promises, so it's perfect for people with commitment and trust issues."

Commitment issues? Trust issues? Did he mean himself? Or her? Or both?

"And this perfect solution is...?"

"Move in with me. I have four spare bedrooms in

that white elephant of a house I just bought. Bettina, my housekeeper, sometimes uses one of them when she needs to stay in town, but you can have your pick of the others."

Kitty almost laughed, it was so surreal. This outwardly conservative, buttoned-up lawyer was full of surprises.

"Move in with you?" She realized she'd begun to sound like an echo. "Seriously? Instead of a wife, you'd settle for a pregnant, live-in girlfriend? Think of the gossip! What would your neighbors say?"

"To hell with the neighbors." He smiled. "I came here hoping for a wife, Kitty. But I'll take what I can get."

CHAPTER FIVE

WHEN ANGELINA MALONE and her grandsons put on a party, they went all out, turning the sloping lawn of their waterfront Belvedere Cove home into a glittering fairy tale of Japanese lanterns, candlelight and music.

Once, it would have seemed impossible that David would get invited to any of these parties.

On the surface, David and the Malone brothers didn't seem to have much in common. Colby, Matt and Red Malone were playboys, surfers and heartbreakers. Heirs to a small pizza company fortune. Adored by their elegant grandmother, Angelina.

David, on the other hand, had fought and scraped just to survive his childhood, and he'd been working too hard all his life to have any idea which end of a surfboard to grab.

More importantly, though, Matt Malone was the reason David had been in the Bahamas that fateful night in November. While David had been drowning his sorrows in sun and sand and sexy bartenders, Matt had been marrying Belle Carson, the woman David had once hoped to make his wife.

Matt hadn't "stolen" Belle, of course. David and Belle had broken up months before she ever met Matt, and, hell, to be honest, things had gone sour long before that.

He'd known they were in trouble even when he bought the four-karat diamond ring, because he felt kind of like a guy on a kamikaze mission. He knew something was wrong, but she wouldn't ever talk about it. Probably because she didn't want to hurt him, she seemed willing to let their relationship drift in limbo forever.

He wasn't. So he bought the ring.

She tried to stall. She said she needed time to think it over. But one look at her pained, anxious face had told him everything he needed to know. She didn't love him. As a friend maybe, but he wasn't willing to settle for that.

God, what a line. "I need time…"

Compare that to Matt's whirlwind conquest of Belle's heart. She'd gone to work for him in June, and he'd been in her bed by July. And then, that November day, Matt had put his wedding ring on her finger.

By then, the Malones had also applied their considerable charisma toward making David their friend, too. They'd started by using him to consult on a few legal issues and had moved smoothly from the professional to the personal. Dinners at Belvedere Cove; his "own" table at Diamante Pizza, their family business; windy outings on their MacGregor sailboat; quick lunches after handball at the downtown Y.

He had to smile, thinking of the ease with which they'd absorbed him into their circle of favorites. The whole Malone clan was pretty irresistible when they put their mind to it.

"David!" Colby must have been watching for him. He appeared almost instantly, putting his hand on David's shoulder. "Glad you could make it! Just a heads-up. Don't go within ten feet of Matt tonight. He's pushing wedded bliss on every poor fool he meets, like a street preacher. I thought Red was going to deck him."

David laughed, glancing over to where Matt and Belle were dancing under a maple tree. The lantern light slid over her blond curls, and he imagined he could hear her laughter. He braced himself for the usual sting, but when it came it was duller than usual, more like a pressure than a stab. Maybe his other problems blocked the signal.

His other problems. His thoughts shifted to his half-empty Victorian house, where an hour ago he'd left Kitty unpacking in the tower bedroom she'd picked as her own. He had invited her to come to the party with him, but she'd said no. He'd offered to stay home with her, but she'd rejected that idea even faster. She would rather have the evening alone in her new quarters, she said, so that she could begin to settle in.

So here he was, feeling a bit disjointed. He wondered whether she'd even be there when he returned. Her movements had been jerky, skittish. She'd reminded him of a bird perching nervously on a feeder, ready to be startled into flight.

He looked back at Colby. "I need a drink," he said. "And we should probably talk, if you can spare a couple of minutes."

"Yeah, sure. I got your message, so I haven't drawn up any paperwork, but I ought to get going on it soon."

David nodded, aware that Colby was in for a shock. Colby had just arrived back in the country this morning, so he had no idea what David had done in his absence. Rather than go into the details long distance, David had simply emailed a request that Colby hold off on the child-support agreement they'd discussed.

They each got a beer from the bartender, dodged a couple of women who seemed to think it was Colby's duty to dance, and made their way to the water's edge.

No crowd down here, probably because few partygoers relished the idea of the return trudge back up to the house. But it was the best view on the property and well worth the walk. The purpling sky seemed to melt onto the lapping waves, and in the distance the mound of Angel Island rose darkly.

They didn't launch into conversation immediately. Both of them sipped the cold beer, enjoying the peace of the place. A cormorant flew overhead, black against purple, croaking softly.

"So," Colby said, when the beer was about half gone. "Before we get to the other thing, there's something I wanted to mention. Diamante is looking for a squeaky-clean, upstanding citizen type to take over the Drivers' Fund." He grinned. "That eliminates all Malones, past, present and future. Then I remembered we do know someone who fits the bill. You."

David had to laugh. "I'm your token boring friend?"

"You're our token sensible friend." Colby raised his beer bottle in a mock salute. "Seriously, we've revamped the fund, made it bigger and better. But as you know, we've got to keep a close eye on it. We want the money to go where it'll do some good, not into the administrator's pocket. It's just part-time, so it wouldn't interfere with your practice. It was Nana Lina's idea, but we are all on board. We all hope you'll agree to take it over."

David understood what a compliment this was. Diamante Pizza had been started as a single restaurant by Colby's grandparents and had grown into one of the most-beloved chain of pizza delivery franchises in California. Its reputation was extremely important to all the Malones, especially the matriarch, Angelina.

The Drivers' Fund was the company's charitable program, financed partly by Diamante itself and partly through employee contributions. Through the fund, money was channeled to employees in need.

A great idea, but, unfortunately, the last fund administrator, a troubled family friend they had been trying to help, had channeled most of the money to himself. He'd rejected the applications from needy employees, while cooking the books to make it look as if everyone got the help they needed.

A real black eye for a company that prided itself on being an honorable, caring employer. Obviously, the Malone family wanted to be extra careful about what kind of person they put in charge of the program now.

"I appreciate the vote of confidence." David took a sip of his beer, which was warming and losing its appeal. "But are you sure my image is still as squeaky-clean as you need?"

One of the things David valued most about his new Malone friends was how utterly straightforward they could be, when it mattered. Colby didn't play dense.

"You mean because of the situation in the Bahamas?"

Colby shrugged. "Unless you're planning to embezzle from the Drivers' Fund to pay your green-haired friend to go away, she isn't an issue."

David felt his bottle turning even warmer under his grip. Now it was his turn to be straightforward, but it was hard to find the right words.

"I don't plan to try to make her go away," he said. "If anything, I'll probably have to pay her to stay."

An edgy silence followed. The cormorant, or one just like it, had circled back, calling hoarsely. The sound was more mournful now, in full night, than it had been ten minutes ago.

Colby's eyes glimmered in the rising moonlight, but he didn't speak right away, obviously aware that David had more to say.

After news of the test results, Colby had asked David to refrain from contacting Kitty until Colby got back to San Francisco and they could draw up some kind of legal acknowledgement and offer of support. Initially, David had agreed to do exactly that.

But then, on impulse, David had driven out to the puppet store and pretty much lost his mind.

He knew Colby wouldn't like it, but so what? Sometimes you just had to follow your gut. The deed was done, and even though he felt as if he were walking on razor blades, he didn't wish it undone.

"I know I said I'd wait," he said now. "But I couldn't do it. I went to see Kitty at work after I got the results. I told her the test had been conclusive. That I was definitely the baby's father."

"What did she say?"

"She was fairly restrained, all things considered. I

don't think she ever once used the phrase 'I told you so.'"

"Really." Colby moved his lips, and David caught a hint of a smile. "*Restrained* isn't a word I would ordinarily have associated with that one."

Suddenly Colby's tone rubbed David the wrong way. *That one?* Colby didn't know Kitty. Neither of them knew her, really. Neither of them had any right to measure her and find her lacking.

"I asked her to marry me," he said bluntly.

Colby's only response was a slow release of breath.

"Don't worry." David's jaw was tight. "She turned me down."

Colby shifted his stance and ran his hand through his hair, as if he'd just dodged a bullet. "Well, thank God for that. David, I don't know if this is some misplaced sense of chivalry, but you know you have to protect yourself from—"

"She's agreed to live with me instead." David broke into whatever the other lawyer had been going to say, before he could say something he'd regret later. "For a while, anyhow. We're going to see if we can start over. Get to know each other the normal way."

"Ah, hell." Colby shook his head. "David."

"I know what the playbook says I should do. But this isn't a game anymore. It's not a simple lawsuit, where we can see who has the best strategy for beating the other guy."

"But if you'll just be patient, we might be able to work something out. You might be able to get—"

"Get what? Joint custody? You think I want to be one of those weekend fathers? Sunday at the park, pizza every other Wednesday night? Or were you thinking I might be able to get it all, and cut her out of the baby's life instead?"

Colby hesitated. "No."

"Damn it, Colby. Whether I like it or not, Kitty is going to be the mother of my child. My *child.* If it were reversed, if it were you, wouldn't you do the same? Wouldn't you try damn near anything to somehow get it right?"

It had been rhetorical, but Colby flinched slightly, as if David had thrown a punch instead of a question. Colby took a couple of deep breaths, and the silence stretched on just a minute too long for comfort.

When he finally spoke, his voice was hard and strange.

"No, I probably wouldn't find a way to get it right. In fact, I'm pretty sure I'd make a total mess of everything. But that doesn't prove anything, except that I'm a fool. So don't listen to a word I say. If you want to try to make this work, go for it. I'll be here, David, to help you any way I can."

David wasn't sure how to read the vehemence in his friend's tone. Obviously he'd struck a nerve, but he couldn't even apologize without making things worse. Every inch of Colby's body language said he didn't want to talk about it.

"Thanks," he said neutrally. "That's good to know."

They stood a minute, letting the truce sink in. Then David gestured toward the house, where the flickering lanterns dotted the grounds. "Should we go back, do you think?"

"Yeah." Colby squared his shoulders, and they began

to walk. "So what about the Drivers' Fund job? You'll consider it?"

"Do you still want me to? With Kitty living at my house, people are bound to talk, and—"

"Welcome to the club." Colby's chuckle had no mirth in it. "They've talked about me since I was maybe ten."

"Yeah. But…" That was a dead end, so David let it go. "What you said earlier. About being a fool? I want you to know I'm aware I'm probably being a fool here, too. Going to see her—asking her to marry me—it was impulse. Pure gut instinct."

"Hey." Colby shrugged. "No explanations needed. I'm just the lawyer."

David laughed. "*Just* the lawyer?"

"Yeah. I'm just the guy who picks up the pieces if your gut decides to steer you off a cliff."

AFTER DAVID WENT TO THE PARTY, Kitty had tried to make herself unpack, but stress had left her exhausted. She fell asleep and didn't wake up until it was pitch-dark. The house was silent, except for the occasional creak of old wood settling, and she felt shivery and unnerved.

That would never do, not if she really intended to live here. So she got up, turned on every light in her room, wiggled her feet into sneakers and set out to explore the house.

Half an hour later, she still hadn't seen it all.

David hadn't exaggerated when he called the place a white elephant. It was absolutely huge, way too big for one person to live in alone. Plus, it was a holy mess. Only about half the rooms were habitable, and the rest were either completely empty or crammed with remodeling debris. Some of them looked almost eerie. The moonlight poured in through large windows, turning dust covers to gleaming ghosts, and ladders to milky gray skeletons.

But the underlying structure of the house, she had to admit, was fantastic. Three stories, fanciful with gingerbread-encrusted gables above wide, gracious porches. Stained glass and mahogany paneling from the turn of the last century. And, of course, the octagonal tower that rose up the east side.

She'd arrived this afternoon, determined to choose the bedroom farthest from David's…just to keep a little breathing room between them. But then she saw the tower. It was the first part he'd finished restoring, so it was in the best condition, and his own room was the second-floor suite.

But that wasn't why she picked the third story as her quarters. She picked it because it was like something out of a storybook, and it appealed to some childhood memory she couldn't resist.

Six tall windows circled the room, each topped with a large violet stained-glass flower set in a Celtic knot of gold. The sunset poured in, buttering the hardwood floor with yellow stripes. David had furnished it with a big four-poster bed, a dresser and a rocker, but the room could have held three times that much.

Kitty's tour had finally led her to the kitchen, which was fully restored and every bit as well designed as the one back at Lochaven. She could create amazing things here, she felt instinctively. It would be so comforting to peel apples, stir cream…

She wondered if David would mind if she investigated the cupboards, turned on the oven, made herself at home.

At home. There was the rub, of course. She sternly told herself to stifle the urge. Baking was so...domestic. So soft. Such a wife-and-mommy thing to do. She wasn't ready to show him that side of her.

She opened the fridge and pulled out a carton of fat-free milk. She set it on the counter and was looking for a glass when she heard a whimper just outside the door.

Apparently her nerves hadn't completely settled, because the sound made the hair on her arms stand up. She froze in place and listened.

Almost instantly, the whimper repeated. If she hadn't known better, she would have said it was an infant's cry. She carefully walked closer to the Dutch door at the back and put her ear to the glass. Again, the soft, unhappy sound could just barely be heard.

In the movies, this was where she always irritably instructed the heroine not to be an idiot, not to open the door, to call the cops, for heaven's sake. But that seemed silly now. Whatever was crying out there wasn't big enough to hurt her.

She turned the handle, inching the door open slowly. As her gaze instinctively dropped toward the ground, a little voice in her head noted how ironic it would be if someone really had left a baby on David's doorstep.

But it wasn't, thank heaven, either a psycho or a newborn. It was a puppy. Tiny, shivering, adorable. A glossy reddish-brown coat, a fat, beige muzzle, and the saddest black-button eyes she'd ever seen.

He was soaking wet. She glanced out, surprised. She hadn't even realized it was raining.

"Oh, honey!" She scooped him into her arms and brought him into the warmth of the kitchen. He blinked at the bright light, shivered another second or two, then relaxed against her and stared trustingly up into her face.

Her heart melted on the spot. "You poor little thing."

"Mr. David isn't going to approve of that." A deep voice behind Kitty seemed to come out of nowhere. "You've brought a dog into this house? He's not going to like it one bit."

Pressing the puppy to her chest protectively, Kitty whirled around, startled and half-guilty, though she wasn't sure what for.

Bettina, David's middle-aged, skin-and-bones housekeeper, stood on the stoop, scowling. "Mr. David won't allow a dog in his house."

Kitty tried to reclaim her poise, though this stern-faced woman, with her heavy jaw and her chocolate-brown, piercing eyes, was ridiculously intimidating. When Kitty had first arrived in San Francisco looking for David, Bettina had made her feel about as welcome as the plague.

She wondered exactly how David had explained the new, pregnant houseguest.

"I'm not bringing a dog," Kitty said. "I mean, not my dog. Not to stay. I just found him, just now. He's obviously lost, and I'm making sure he doesn't freeze to death."

Bettina shook her head as she entered the kitchen, removing her plastic rain scarf and setting it into the sink to dry. She didn't seem to feel the need to explain her presence, though she didn't live here, and, besides, she was supposed to be visiting her sister in Marin County all weekend.

"The dog's here, though." Bettina raised her brows and stared at the puppy, proving her point. "And Mr. David won't like it. He'll be very angry."

Kitty frowned. "He'll be very angry because I helped a lost puppy? I doubt that."

Bettina folded her wiry arms over her flat chest. "Yes, he will. He says no dogs. Miss Belle tried to give him a puppy, two years ago. He would do anything for Miss Belle. Anything. But he wouldn't keep that dog."

Kitty hesitated. Who was Belle? David's little sister, maybe? His mother? Kitty's internet searches hadn't turned up any mention of family, but maybe he kept a firewall around his private life. Lots of high-profile business people did.

Kitty felt impaled by Bettina's watchful stare. It was almost as if the older woman were daring her to admit she didn't know.

Well, she *didn't*. She wasn't going to pretend she did. Mind games like that annoyed her. "Who is Belle?"

Bettina looked surprised that she should be so straightforward. Good. Kitty wanted the housekeeper to understand that she wasn't going to be lured into this "Mrs. Danvers vs. the timid new bride" routine. Her bravado might be half charade, but she wasn't going to let Bettina put the mind whammy on her already.

"He didn't tell you?" Pursing her lips, Bettina brushed an imaginary speck off the countertop. "Belle is his fiancée."

Okay, that sucked the air out of Kitty's lungs. Round One to Bettina. But it didn't take long to piece it together. David had been so dejected that night in the Bahamas. Now she remembered why. The lost love who had married someone else.

Kitty raised her chin and met Bettina's gaze steadily. "You mean *was* his fiancée."

Bettina shrugged. "She married Mr. Malone, but it was a terrible mistake. Miss Belle is the love of Mr. David's life."

Was the love of his life, Kitty wanted to say, but she didn't. She didn't know whether it was true, and she had a feeling Bettina would enjoy setting her straight.

David had warned her that Bettina was protective—she'd been his housekeeper for years—but this was ridiculous. Why had she come back so late at night, anyhow? Why wasn't she safely in Marin Country? Maybe her sister didn't want her sour puss around, either.

Oblivious to the tension around him, the puppy sighed once, then put his head against Kitty's collarbone, shut his eyes and fell into sleep like a potato falling off the table. A few drops of rain still dusted his coat, so Kitty pulled a dishcloth from the drying rack and wrapped it around his little body.

"Well," she said. "If David's mad, he'll just have to deal with it. I can't leave the poor guy out there in the cold."

Suddenly Bettina's dark eyes grew wide, and the sight made Kitty feel more irritable than ever. It was just a puppy, for heaven's sake! It wasn't as if she'd picked up a T-Rex egg and decided to hatch it in the bathtub.

The sound of the rain increased, and she realized they hadn't quite latched the kitchen door. The wind must have blown it open again.

She went over to it, and put her free hand on the knob to shut out the weather. "Don't worry," she said, exasperated and tired of the whole thing. "If David throws a fit, I'll accept responsibility."

Even as the words were leaving her mouth, she saw him. David stood on the stoop, his hand on the other side of the doorknob. That, of course, was why the door had "blown" open.

He smiled. "Say that again? Why would David throw a fit?"

Kitty couldn't decide whether to laugh or let out one of her father's favorite French curses. She decided against the curse, because her French accent was embarrassingly bad. But really. Tonight just wasn't her night.

"She's brought home a dog." Bettina pointed accusingly at the bundle Kitty cradled against her chest. "Probably has fleas. Ticks. Who knows what else?"

Kitty watched David's face carefully. She had a pretty low opinion of people who didn't like dogs, and she couldn't believe he might be one of them. He didn't look angry, but his expression did kind of flatten out into an emptiness she'd seen before. She was learning to read him just a little, and she suspected this was the look that meant he was trying to conceal what he really thought.

"I didn't know you had a dog," he said neutrally.

"I don't."

He raised one brow, and she realized how idiotic that sounded.

"Well, I mean, obviously I have a dog right now. But I don't usually have one. This one isn't mine. I don't know whose it is. But it was on your doorstep, and the poor thing is just a tiny baby, and he was freezing." She tried not to sound defensive. "So I brought him in. And just for the record, Bettina told me not to. As usual, she did an admirable job of trying to guard your castle gate."

He chuckled. He knew exactly what she meant, of course.

"Thanks, Betty," he said, smiling at his housekeeper. "But I'm sure we can survive the invasion, at least until someone shows up to claim it. We can put a 'found puppy' notice up on the internet right away, and I'll make some calls to the neighbors. If we can't find anyone tonight, I'll put an ad in the *Chronicle* in the morning."

Wow. A five-star general couldn't have mobilized any faster than that. He really wanted to unload this puppy, didn't he? Kitty couldn't help noticing that he hadn't even taken a peek under the towel to see what the dog looked like.

It made her feel, perversely, as if she ought to push the point. In the weirdest way, it scared her to think her baby's father would be a man who couldn't stand dogs.

"Want to see him? He's really cute."

David held up a hand. "I'll take your word for it. I've got a lot to do tonight, and if I'm going to canvas the neighbors to see who's lost a dog, I'd better get started." He turned to his housekeeper. "Betty, you decided against going to see Fran?"

Bettina nodded, and her sour face grew even more so. "Her boyfriend is staying over. She knows I don't come when he's there. She should know better than to—"

The woman caught herself just in time. Poor lady, Kitty thought wryly. Caught between one unacceptable domestic situation and another.

"Okay, then," David said, polite as ever. "Would you mind making up a pallet for our four-legged visitor tonight? A couple of old blankets. Maybe in the mud room, where it can't—"

Bettina looked shocked. "You're really going to let him—"

"Actually—" Kitty interrupted, pressing the puppy a little closer against her breast as if to guard against having him ripped away. "I thought he'd sleep with me."

That startled both the others into silence. Seizing the moment, she squared her shoulders and set her jaw. She grabbed the milk from the countertop and, without waiting for permission, turned and headed toward the tower staircase.

Behind her, Bettina sputtered, but David was strangely silent. Certainly he didn't try to stop her.

Good, she thought as she began to climb the stairs to the third floor. She couldn't explain why, but she wasn't letting go of this puppy until she had to. At the moment, he felt like her only friend in the house.

CHAPTER SIX

"I DON'T KNOW." Colby eyeballed the salvage wood laid out along David's damaged library floor. "It's a pretty good match, but it's hard to tell until you've seen it in every light. Might be safer to redo the whole floor. Do you have enough wood for that?"

David groaned. "No. Not enough wood, and definitely not enough time. I'm going to have to settle for patching the bad spot. Maybe it'll look awful, but that's why rugs were invented, right?"

He didn't mean it, of course. He wouldn't settle for a bad patch. He was spending insane amounts of both money and time restoring this house authentically. He'd just knelt here for almost ninety minutes, for instance, laying out an arrangement for this original-vintage salvage wood, so that all the grain patterns lined up nicely and the lengths were staggered just right.

Colby, who had stopped by to drop off some account books for the Drivers' Fund, probably thought David was nuts for spending his Saturday working indoors. Like his brothers, Matt and Red, Colby preferred outdoor sports, and his sunburned cheeks proved that this winter morning had been no exception.

But though Colby never wasted a dollar, he had never needed to stretch one, either. And he'd never had to live in a crap apartment, or bunk on one of his mother's friends' sofas till the family could save enough money to get the electricity turned back on.

This ramshackle old Victorian was the first house David had ever owned. Sweating the restoration details was a hell of a lot more gratifying to him than surfing, or tennis, or whatever Colby had been doing this morning.

He frowned at the wood, then knelt back down and switched out a couple of pieces that didn't look right.

"God, Gerard. Could you be any more OCD?" Colby was clearly bored. He wandered to the windows that overlooked the backyard. "It's such a great day. We're going to take out the MacGregor this afternoon. Want to come?"

"Can't." David squinted at the wood. "Thanks, though. Hey, open that curtain all the way, would you? Let's see what happens in direct sun."

Colby shook his head, but obeyed. A shaft of winter light as pale and hard as frozen lemonade angled in through the window, laying a rectangle on the floor.

"Still looks okay. That's good." David got to his feet, and beat the sawdust from his jeans. He knew Colby wasn't really listening, but—

And then he saw why. Kitty had just entered the backyard, with that ridiculous dog in tow. She wore a pair of loose jeans, a pink sweater and a navy blue sweatshirt that half fell off one shoulder as she ran along, encouraging the puppy. The sweatshirt had a hood, but her head was bare, and her green curls bounced and shone in the sunshine.

The dog clearly hadn't ever spent much time on a

leash. It kept getting tangled, which seemed to delight Kitty, who would kiss its nose every time she bent down to unwind it.

David joined Colby at the window, and the two men watched for a minute in silence. David had already told Colby about the dog, secretly hoping that maybe Colby's girlfriend, who adored animals, might be in the mood to adopt one more. Or even Belle, maybe. But while Colby had commiserated, he hadn't taken the bait.

"She looks happy," Colby observed, his voice studiously casual. "She's settling in all right?"

David shrugged. "I guess so. I'm not sure I'd know. She works two jobs, and she mostly keeps to her room the rest of the time. Some nights she even brings her dinner home from a take-out place and eats up there."

Colby gave David a glance. "It's going to be pretty hard to get to know each other that way."

"Tell me about it. I'm trying not to rush her, but at this rate the kid will be in college before Kitty and I have our first real conversation."

Colby nodded. "What's spooking her, do you think?" Then he smiled. "Wait. I know. It's Bettina, right? She may be a good housekeeper, but she's got a glare that will burn the skin off your body."

David knew exactly what look Colby was referring to. "Yeah, Betty isn't Kitty's biggest fan so far. You know how she is."

"Yeah, I do. She's scary as hell. Why don't you suggest she take a little paid vacation?"

David had considered that. Bettina had a soft side, but few people ever glimpsed it. Three years ago, she had worked for the maintenance company that serviced his office building. One night when he'd come back unexpectedly to finish up a brief, he'd found her slumped in the lobby, crying. She'd been fired. She was too slow, too methodical, too much of a perfectionist for the company's taste.

David had hired her on the spot. Though he didn't technically require a full-time housekeeper for his apartment, he'd always known he'd buy a real home as soon as he could afford it, and she'd be just what he needed then.

He didn't mind her dour personality—he knew it masked a tender heart. Plus, she was unflinchingly honest. If she found so much as a nickel on the floor, she put it carefully on the edge of his desk. She was thorough, and she took pride in her work. And she was terrified of being unemployed. That was enough for him.

Unfortunately, she'd made too much of his white knight moment, and she'd developed a passionately protective streak. She'd given Belle the cold shoulder for the first full year after Belle moved in. But eventually her fierce guard-dog mentality had extended to Belle, and the housekeeper had been brokenhearted when Belle moved out.

"A vacation is a good idea," David said. "At least then Kitty and I could have a little more privacy."

Colby fiddled with the cord to the blinds. "I'm sure you set some sensible ground rules before Kitty moved in," he said. "You talked about sex, right? About whether there is going to be any?"

David could hear the concern in his friend's voice,

though Colby cloaked it well. Colby always thought like a lawyer, wanting every *t* carefully crossed and notarized. It had driven Colby insane when David insisted on waiting a while before asking Kitty to sign any agreements.

But this topic, the subject of sex, had definitely been covered.

"Yeah," David said, laughing wryly. "We talked about it. She brought it up, in fact. She was adamant that we couldn't include sex in our arrangement."

"She said it's off-limits?"

"Not exactly. She said if we included sex as part of the deal, she'd feel like a prostitute. And if we decided it was forbidden, she'd feel like a fool. Nothing, she said, was guaranteed to make two people obsess about having sex like telling them they couldn't."

Colby laughed out loud. "Man. She's one of a kind."

"She's—yeah. She's unique. She's not a fan of hypocrisy or beating around the bush."

"So?" Colby raised his eyebrows. "Is that why you're OCD'ing about planks of salvage wood? Are you using the restoration as a distraction so you don't obsess about sex? I have to say, when I first met her, I didn't quite see it." He glanced out the window. "But now…"

David looked, too. He knew what Colby meant. Even David could hardly reconcile this laughing girl-woman with any of the Kittys he knew—not the sad-eyed bartender longing for a savior, and definitely not the tight-lipped, tense stranger who had showed up to make him pay for his sins.

But, unlike Colby, David had found all her incarnations fascinating—and dangerously seductive.

"It's not easy," David admitted. "Sometimes, just knowing she's upstairs, I'm not sure I can…"

Colby waited, but David didn't really know how to finish the sentence. He didn't talk about these things. No guy talked about these things. The sex, maybe. But the strange, romancy longings and chivalrous constraints that kept him awake at night, listening to her footfalls overhead… *Hell, no.*

David watched as she picked up the puppy, which had to be at least ninety-percent Irish setter, practically a purebred, and began spinning around with it in her arms, laughing. Her sweatshirt slipped down around her elbows, and her cheeks grew as pink as a china doll's.

"The thing is, Colby, sometimes she's so… I'm not sure I can—"

Abruptly, Kitty stopped spinning. She set the puppy down quickly, and put her palm to her mouth. David could see her eyes, wide and panicked, casting about the backyard in sudden desperation.

She clearly considered the mulched flower beds at the back of the property, but didn't have time to get there. With clumsy hands, she yanked one of the little blue plastic bags out of the dispenser attached to the leash. She tugged it open roughly, just in time to bend over it and lose her lunch.

The men watched in silent horror.

And then Kitty sat on the grass, wiping her hair from her face and looking more angry than ill. In innocent oblivion, the puppy chewed on her shoelaces.

Colby chuckled. "Yeah. Well, there's your salvation, my friend. Morning sickness. Works better, I'm thinking, than a cold shower any day."

WHEN COLBY LEFT, David went out back. Kitty had recovered, for the most part. She was on her feet again, and she must have dumped her bag into the trash bin, because her hands were empty. A wet stain spread across her pink sweater, and the garden hose was dribbling, so he assumed she had rinsed out her mouth as best she could.

But she still looked pale, and her curls stuck to her damp forehead. He wished, suddenly, that he could take this away from her. It didn't seem fair that she had to go through so much, while he just sat back and watched.

"Hi," he said, moving toward her slowly. The puppy had claimed the sunniest square of lawn and fallen asleep. David didn't want to wake it. "Everything okay?"

"Yeah. I felt a little sick there for a minute, but I'm fine now. Just another lovely day in hormone-ville." She smiled half-heartedly. "I think I brought this one on myself, though. I was feeling pretty good, almost like normal, and I dropped my guard."

"I thought it was called morning sickness. It's almost four in the afternoon."

She lifted a shoulder. "Guess if it was called twenty-four/seven sickness, the whole let's-have-a-baby idea would be a little tougher to sell."

He agreed completely. And that was before you ever got to the labor and delivery room shockers. And they called women the weaker sex. Right. "How long is the nausea part supposed to last?"

"It's *supposed* to last three months. But my mother said that, with me, she was sick the whole time." She made a face. "Just one of the many things I hope I didn't inherit from her."

He wondered whether they might actually be about to have a substantive conversation. This was the first time since the Bahamas she'd mentioned her mother—obviously one of the most important, and probably most destructive, relationships in her life. He was eager to know more. It had undoubtedly shaped her ideas about marriage, family, motherhood—and love.

But she seemed to realize she'd opened a door she'd intended to keep locked. She concentrated on rubbing the water stain on her sweater and walked away a couple of feet.

Once she reached a safe distance, she looked back. "Has anyone phoned about Murphy?"

"Murphy?"

"The puppy. That's what I decided to call him. He's an Irish setter, so something Irish seemed appropriate."

He glanced at the dog, who twitched in some kind of doggie dream delight. Hell, she'd named it?

"Not yet," he said. "But it might be a good idea not to get too attached. It's a purebred, which means it undoubtedly belongs to someone. It's just a matter of time till they claim it."

Clearly that was the wrong answer. She turned an appraising look his way, and it was obvious his value hadn't risen.

"Do you always calculate the odds before you let yourself care about anyone? Is that a lawyer thing?"

She had a point. He did have a habit of guarding himself. People with trust issues usually did. And she should know. "Has trust issues" was a tame way to describe a woman so prickly she fled from his offers of both marriage and friendship, then hungrily turned to a stray puppy for affection.

Suddenly, he saw a completely new way to look at the Bahamas mess. Trust issues. Commitment issues. That was probably why she'd crept away while he slept. And it was probably why she'd sent Jill, too. Not to insult him so much as to protect herself. To prove to herself how little the encounter had meant.

Or maybe he was reading too much into the whole thing. He told himself, not for the first time, just to forget about the Bahamas. They needed to start over, clean slate, if they had any chance of building something decent here.

"No, it's not really a lawyer thing," he said, deciding to be honest. "Just a personal quirk. I suppose I protect my emotions the same way I would protect any of my assets."

She shrugged, obviously no more comfortable with this topic than she had been with talking about her mother.

"Whatever works, I guess." She glanced at her watch. "I probably ought to go take a shower. I have to work at eight."

"How about if I give you a ride? You could save an hour or two. Maybe you could grab a nap."

"That's okay," she said. "Thanks, anyhow, but I'm fine."

Her polite stonewall frustrated him. Why wouldn't she let him help, even in the smallest way? She had to be tired. She'd been out on the Muni already today, apparently going to the pet supermarket. She'd brought back food, the leash, a crate for the dog to sleep in and God only knew what else.

"How late do you work tonight?"

"Just till ten." She frowned. "But tomorrow night, I have the whole shift. Eight to two. Surprisingly, the bar's pretty busy on Sunday nights. Thank goodness. I could use the hours."

That frustrated him, too. She knew he didn't expect her to pay for anything while she was here. Why did she continue to work and worry as if she couldn't be sure there would be food on the table next week?

"Then let me give you a ride tomorrow. Coming home alone in the middle of the night isn't a great idea. Working in that neighborhood isn't anything like bartending at Sugarwater. The drunks are different there."

Her unblinking gaze was cool on David. "Thanks. But I have tended bar in quite a few places, not all as nice as Sugarwater."

Somehow, he kept a lid on his frustration. The only change in his voice was a slight drop in timbre. "I have no idea where you've worked," he said. "How could I? You don't exactly volunteer a lot of personal information. Frankly, Operation Get Acquainted seems to be dead in the water."

"I'm sorry." She flushed. It was one of the things that intrigued him most about her. She presented such a tough-kid attitude, but she blushed whenever she realized she'd been rude or unkind. He wondered what her childhood had been like. Someone had taught her manners, though she pretended to think such things were phony affectation.

Suddenly, on the street in front of the house, a driver honked, leaning hard on the horn. The puppy, who had been sound asleep, jerked to its feet, bewildered and terrified. It stumbled once, then raced straight for David and tried to launch itself into his arms.

Of course, it couldn't make it—it crashed somewhere around David's thigh and fell to the ground. Mindless in its desperation, the puppy jumped up again, clawing David's jeans as if he were the only safe place in an insane world.

There was no way to avoid it. David leaned down and picked up the puppy.

"Hey, buddy," he said softly, trying to hold it at a distance. "It's okay. Welcome to big city life."

The puppy scrabbled across his forearm, trying to get to his chest. When David finally relented, the puppy buried its nose deep in the crook of his elbow, shuddered once, and promptly went limp with sleep again.

With a helpless shake of the head, David smiled at Kitty. "At least Murphy seems to think it's okay to accept a ride from me."

She almost smiled back, but didn't quite make it. "I'm sorry," she said. "I probably sound ungrateful. But…it's just that I don't want to be a problem."

"You're not. I offered."

"Well, I—I also don't want to grow dependent. I don't want to get used to being chauffeured around in that cushy car of yours. The bus will just seem worse when I have to go back to it."

Did she really think that, after the baby was born, he would make her return to riding the Muni at all hours, trying to juggle a couple of part-time jobs *and* a baby? Did she really see herself as Cinderella, let out for a brief visit to the castle but doomed to slink back to the ashes on the stroke of midnight?

For God's sake, even if they decided not to marry, he would still make sure she had a house, a car and whatever it took to give his child a comfortable life.

"I don't think you'll get addicted to luxury in one night, Kitty," he said. "Look, I'd like to give you a ride. We don't even have to talk, if you'd rather not. If you want to stop for food or something, you can just point."

Finally, she let the lid off her smile. She had an amazing smile.

"Okay," she said. "You're right. I'm being silly. That would be nice. Thanks."

Awkwardly, she reached out for Murphy, and he handed the puppy over. The dog didn't even open its eyes, just traded David's chest for Kitty's arms without complaint and slept on.

David watched her walk away, her head bent over Murphy's little satiny body, her green curls glimmering in the sunlight. The natural honey-brown that had just begun peeking through at the roots gave him a tantalizing glimpse of what the real Kitty might look like. He wondered if she had decided to let it grow out.

Her shoulders were stiff as she walked, as she was uncomfortable knowing David was watching.

Still, he'd offered her a ride and she'd said yes.

It wasn't much of a concession, he warned himself. Not nearly enough for him to be so pleased. Still. Enough baby steps, and eventually they'd make progress.

But then he shook his head at his own foolishness as she disappeared into shadows of the back porch. Baby steps?

At this rate, he'd be lucky to learn her middle name by Christmas.

CHAPTER SEVEN

ORDINARILY, Kitty didn't mind bartending. Whenever she discussed it with her mother, during their rare phone calls, Lucinda started weeping, woefully asking herself where she'd gone wrong.

But Kitty knew that, if her father had been alive, he would have understood. He'd always said people should never feel above honest labor. Work hard, and work with pride. That was all that mattered, he'd insisted.

Of course, she'd been only ten when he died, so he probably hadn't considered the possibility of Kitty bartending. He had been a university professor of French literature, a far cry from pulling drafts. Still, she liked to believe he would have given her his blessing.

This job paid well. And as long as the customers weren't pigs, bartending was just challenging enough to keep her mind occupied. In spite of David's snobbish uptown disdain for the neighborhood, the customers at the Bull's Eye were pretty nice people. The bar abutted a huge call center, and whenever a shift let out, the place swarmed with telemarketers eager to forget the depressing reality of their jobs.

She'd only worked here a short time, but she'd learned that all she had to do was be nice to the customers, treat them with normal human kindness. The contrast between her understanding smile and the rejection they faced on the phones all day created an outpouring of gratitude and tips.

Plus, the Bull's Eye had both a busboy and a bouncer. She couldn't remember ever being that lucky.

Unfortunately, it also had an ape for an owner. In his late fifties, he had a face as grooved as old oak bark. Addicted to working out, cigarettes and his own liquor, Harry was the kind of guy who always hired female bartenders and then talked to their chests instead of their faces.

His only saving grace was that he didn't like to bother watching his shop. He was off property as often as he was here. He hadn't even been the one to hire her.

But tonight, for some reason, he decided to hang around all night. With every passing hour, he got on her nerves worse. It didn't help that she felt tired and a little nauseated. She prayed that she could get through the shift without vomiting.

She made it until about one-thirty, just half an hour before her shift ended.

When Kitty had arrived at eight, Harry had told her he needed her to try out the new uniforms he was considering for the staff. He'd narrowed it down to three possibilities, and he wanted to see which one handled the best on a real work night.

Though she wasn't in the mood, she really didn't have a choice. The first uniform wasn't too bad. She could actually bend down without flashing her underwear at everyone. Harry got bored with it within the first hour, and told her to switch to possibility number two.

Not great, but she could probably stand it. A little short and tight, but basically respectable. She'd worn that one for hours, while he asked her to retrieve one silly thing after another from the lowest shelves, and watched her from the back every time she bent down.

Eventually, when her thighs were burning from trying to squat without leaning forward, he'd decided he didn't like it. Time to try possibility number three.

And that's when everything went wrong.

She lifted the scrap of material out of the box, held it up just long enough to see the low neckline, short hem and bull's-eye pattern over the left breast. She let it drop immediately.

She stared at Harry. "You can't be serious. If we wore that, we'd be in violation of about a hundred decency laws."

The busboy, a nice guy named Chip, laughed nervously.

"So?" Harry pulled back his lips, exposing his nicotine-stained teeth. "If the decency police drop by and fine us, we'll pay it. Cost of doing business. Let's see it on."

She glanced again at the uniform, the red-and-white bull's-eye dramatic against the pale blue dress. She waged a small war with her common sense. She could try it on, at least. Maybe it wasn't as short as it looked. Maybe the bull's-eye didn't fit directly over her breast.

Heck, she could at least pretend to consider it. Maybe he just wanted to pull rank, to prove he could make her put it on. She could give him a minute to think it through, and maybe he'd realize how impossible it was.

Or she could make up some other reason. Her religion. Her polyester allergy. Her scary, possessive boyfriend...

"No, Harry. I'm not wearing this. No way."

Harry pulled his head back, feigning shock. "What did the lady say, Chip?"

Chip wouldn't make eye contact. He pretended to be scanning the customers, making sure none of the tables needed to be bused. He and Kitty had gotten along well, so far, and he clearly didn't want to gang up on her. But he also didn't want to lose his job.

Harry put his index finger in his ear and dug around dramatically, as if it must be full of wax. She watched and tried not to shudder.

He pulled his finger out and inspected the tip. "Okay. Come again, honey? I said *let's see it on,* and you said..."

"I said no." Kitty took a breath. She knew where this was headed, and she refused to grovel to this creep, only to have him fire her anyhow. "I'm not wearing that uniform. It's indecent. Everyone will think you're running a brothel, not a bar."

"You might want to reconsider." Harry's eyes narrowed. "You don't wear it, you don't work here."

She bent over and grabbed her purse, and the sack that held her own clothes, from behind the bar. "I already don't work here. I quit."

She stalked out, through the throng of customers, passing in and out of the light from neon brand-beer signs, making for the door with all the self-assurance she could muster.

She hoped Harry wouldn't follow her, but of course he did. Damn it. Where was she going to go? It would be at least twenty minutes before David showed up. She'd just have to start walking. She refused to huddle in some dark doorway, looking pathetic, while Harry laughed at her.

"You think you're going to quit? That's a joke, with your green hair and your flat chest. You haven't got boobs big enough to quit, honey."

She yanked open the door, terrified that she might turn around and smack him. *Don't follow me, don't follow me...*

But, again, of course he did. "You think anyone else will hire you? And don't think you can come back here when you get hungry, begging me—"

And then, miraculously, as if it had been orchestrated by a fairy godmother, she saw David. He leaned gracefully against the long nose of his elegant car, which was still running to keep the interior warm. The red bull's eye of the bar sign glowed in the flawless polish of the elegant curves. The car's headlights cut crystalline swathes through the darkness.

When he heard Harry's ugly voice, David unfolded himself like a tiger waking up to the scent of prey. He walked to Kitty's side and stared at Harry, apparently as surprised to see him as he might have been to see a cockroach wearing a top hat.

"Hey, there," he said, putting his arm around her shoulders. "Everything okay?"

She didn't look at Harry. She didn't want a scene.

She didn't want David to see what a horrible person she'd been working for. She bit her lip and willed the old creep to go back inside.

Let it go, Harry.

"Yes." She tried to smile at David. "Everything's fine."

"You ready to go home?"

She nodded.

"Hang on. I don't think so. That's my uniform you're wearing." Harry tried to sound belligerent, but it wavered oddly in the chilly night air. "You can't leave here without paying for it."

Kitty glanced at David. He frowned, and then he began walking toward Harry, with a slow menace that made her feel strange. She'd never seen him lose his temper. What was he going to do?

Harry didn't run. Kitty had to give him credit for that. David exuded disgust, and if he'd been coming toward her that way, she would have bolted as fast as her legs would carry her. Harry held his ground, though he seemed to shrink as he drew into himself. No question. The weasel was terrified.

David stopped about six inches from Harry's face. As if in slow motion, he reached into his pocket, withdrew his wallet and extracted a bill.

It must have been a large one, because Kitty saw Harry's eyes widen. David didn't say anything. He folded the bill, then nudged it down into the older man's greasy breast pocket.

Harry swallowed.

And then David returned to Kitty. He opened the

passenger-side door, and she gratefully slid in, her legs shaking.

When David got in and put the car into drive, she let her head fall against the headrest.

"Thank you," she said. "I'll pay you back when—"

"Forget that. It was cheap if it bought you freedom." He glanced at her, his eyes shining in the cool blue dashboard lights. "I take it you quit?"

She nodded.

He smiled. "Fantastic." He flicked his left-turn blinker and began to twirl the wheel. "This calls for a celebration."

HALF AN HOUR LATER, they were in another world.

Kitty knew so little about San Francisco—she had no idea exactly where David was driving. He'd climbed high into the hills, and she'd been too drained to question anything. For once, she just shut her eyes and trusted him.

When she heard him put the car into Park and kill the motor, she opened her eyes. Ahead of her, she saw something that looked kind of like…a playground.

"Come on," he said, opening his door. "I want to show you the San Francisco I love."

She got out and followed him toward the large mulched clearing tucked in among a cluster of lovely trees. In the dark, she couldn't really identify them, but they smelled fresh and clean, with a hint of pine.

The real view, though, was straight ahead, just beyond the swing sets, monkey bars and whirligigs that dotted this clearing. He walked to the very edge of the playground, and pointed.

"This is why I live in San Francisco," he said.

It was as if she'd entered an enchanted land. Everywhere she turned, the darkened hills sparkled, as if the trees had worn diamonds to bed. In the valley below them, glowing nuggets of yellow, white, amber and gold flickered. It was just the city at night, she knew, but it looked like Aladdin's cave.

She thought of a French expression her father had often used. It meant something like... *magic hides everywhere.* But, though she could hear him saying it, whenever she tried to form the words herself her tongue mangled them.

So she didn't try.

"It's amazing," she said. "It's hard to believe that this place and the Bull's Eye Bar exist in the same universe."

"They don't," he said. "The Bull's Eye Bar doesn't exist at all anymore. You've erased it from your world map. That's why we're celebrating."

She drank in the scene a few more minutes. Then, as the cool air and the beauty revived her, she turned to check out the playground.

"Did you live in this area as a child?" She walked toward the whirligig and put two fingers on the cold metal bar, spinning it a few inches.

"No," he said. "I grew up a million miles from here."

His voice wasn't sad, exactly, but it was somber. She glanced at him, and he smiled, as if to shake off the mood. He touched the whirligig, too, and brought it to a stop.

"I guess this would be tempting fate? Especially since you don't have your doggie bags with you?"

She laughed. "Definitely. Although I used to love these things." She gazed around the rest of the playground. She pointed toward the swing set, which rose in shadows over near the parking lot. "I might be able to handle the swing, though."

"Perfect. But not those." He took her hand and led her to another set of swings she hadn't even noticed. These overlooked the twinkling hillside. "Climb on. I'll push, and you can let me know if you get woozy."

Another night, another place, she might have felt foolish. But being out here, at nearly three in the morning, felt a little like a dream, and anything could happen in a dream. She eased onto the heavy plastic strap that made the swing's seat, clamped her hands over the cold metal chains, and tucked in her feet so that they didn't drag on the dirt.

He started off slowly, giving her time to cry uncle. But the smooth up and down motion didn't make her feel the least bit sick. The shadow trees glided past her peripheral vision like melted chocolate, and, as she went higher and higher, the valley glittered into view, disappeared and returned, a magic show performed just for her.

Magic hides everywhere.

The cool night air swept past her face, tickling her hair against her cheeks. Impulsively, she laughed. She swiveled her torso, so that she could see David. He was smiling, too.

She could gladly have stayed here forever. But, too soon, the winter night proved too much for the skimpy uniform. Goose bumps broke out along her bare limbs.

She shivered, and let go of one chain to rub warmth back into her upper arm.

Immediately, David brought the swing to a standstill.

"You're cold," he said. "I should have thought of that." He shrugged off his jacket, a luscious brown suede windbreaker, and held it out. "Here. Put this on."

She wasn't too proud to accept it. She extended one arm, and he slipped it over her. She slid in the other arm, closed it around her chest, and murmured delightedly. It felt and smelled heavenly.

"You want to go home?"

She shook her head. She definitely did not want to go home. Here, in the dark, with a treasure trove of diamonds at her feet, she wasn't the tired, nauseated bartender of an hour ago. She was the Kitty she used to be, years and years ago. Protected and safe—and happy.

"No." She looked at him, standing in a shaft of moonlight, which turned his hair the same color as his pale gold sweater. "Unless, now that you've loaned me your jacket, you're too cold."

"I'm fine." He led the way to some wooden picnic tables tucked into a sheltered nook of trees. They sat on the same side of one bench, facing away from the table so that they could still watch the glimmering hills. A bird cooed softly, as if to remind them that some creatures were actually trying to sleep.

Kitty shivered one last time, as her skin thawed out. She pulled the jacket tighter. It was still warm from his body, and smelled faintly of his aftershave.

"I wish I'd brought a real coat," he said, reaching out

to lift the collar around her neck. "You must be frozen in that outfit."

"No," she said with a wry smile. She tugged at the hem, trying to stretch it even a fraction of an inch. Too bad she couldn't take that extra inch she didn't need in the bodice, and tack it onto the bottom. "Just a little chilly. And a lot embarrassed."

"You have nothing to be embarrassed about," he said. "You look terrific in it."

She grimaced. "Harry didn't think so. He's not really happy unless you're spilling right out of your uniform. He probably would have been a lot happier with a bartender like Jill—"

She clamped her mouth shut in horror. She had said Jill. God, she had really said Jill.

She tried to laugh it off, to fill the gap, to erase the echo. "Wait a minute. That's right." She pulled the sleeves of his jacket down over her fingers. "Harry doesn't exist anymore, does he?"

David seemed to hesitate. Then he put his hand over hers. The suede came between them, but she still could feel his warmth.

"Kitty," he began. But he didn't continue right away.

She waited, her stomach tightening. Somehow, she knew what he was going to say.

"You know we're going to have to talk about it sooner or later."

"It?"

He shrugged. "Okay. *Her.* We're going to have to talk about Jill. At first, I thought maybe it was better just to let it go. But I don't see how we're really going to move forward until we put that situation to rest."

The night suddenly seemed about ten degrees colder.

"I'm not sure what we need to talk about," she said. "It happened. It's over. As long as she doesn't show up on your doorstep, too, I don't see that it's a very big deal."

The wind kicked up, sending a few dry leaves skittering across the mulch. She kept her focus in the mid-distance, on the starry hillside, but she could feel David looking at her.

"Kitty." He applied a hint of pressure to her hand. "Look at me. What do you mean, if she shows up on my doorstep, too?"

She looked at him—she had to. Otherwise, he'd think she was upset about Jill. Which she wasn't. Not anymore.

"It seems pretty simple," she said. "We've learned the hard way that there's no such thing as one hundred percent reliable birth control. It would complicate matters a bit if she ended up pregnant, too, don't you think?"

A line formed between his brows. "Wait. Are you saying what I think you're saying? You're upset because you think I slept with your friend that night, too?"

"She's not my friend," Kitty said, more hotly than she'd intended. "And I'm not upset. You are a grown man, and you can do whatever you like."

"Okay, but…" He tilted his head. "I'm confused. Didn't you send her to me?"

"Send her?" Kitty almost lifted to her feet. "Of course not."

"Well, she told me you did."

"She told you—" Kitty subsided onto the bench. "That's crazy. Why would she have told you a ridiculous lie like that?"

But even as she asked, Kitty knew the answer. The other woman had always been competitive toward Kitty—compulsively so. If Kitty got bigger tips or a better schedule, Jill would sulk for hours. If a male customer wanted to flirt with Kitty, Jill always horned in and swept the poor guy off his feet.

Kitty remembered well the smug, sleepy-cat look in Jill's brown eyes as she talked about her night with David. She hadn't merely been enjoying the chance to share a little naughty girl talk. She'd been triumphant. She simply couldn't let Kitty have anything she didn't get a piece of, too.

Something electric and angry sizzled through Kitty's veins at the memory.

"Never mind," she said gruffly. "I know why she did it. She'd had her eye on you for days. She would have hated to hear that I—" She bit her lower lip, considering how it must have been. "I suppose she's just trashy enough to think it would turn you on, to believe I'd sent her. Like some girlie magazine's Swedish twins fantasy. She probably thought you were the kind of guy who…"

She let the thought peter out, realizing belatedly that there was no way to end the sentence that wasn't rude.

To her surprise, though, David didn't look offended. He was still studying her curiously. "Apparently, you think I'm that kind of guy, too."

She shrugged. "I didn't mean to sound so harsh.

I guess every man approached by a woman like that would—"

"No." His voice was flat. "Not every man."

She blinked against the wind that gusted across her face. "Are you—" She frowned. "Are you trying to tell me you *didn't* sleep with Jill that night?"

"Right. Not that night, and not ever."

He didn't? He'd sent Jill away without...? That would mean the whole story, all the X-rated details, had been one of her lies.

But....if that were true...

Kitty wasn't sure she could absorb all the implications of this. She wasn't even sure she believed it. The whole time she'd worked at Sugarwater, she hadn't ever seen a heterosexual male between the ages of twenty-five and fifty say no to Jill. Something about being on vacation, something about the moonlight on the water. Something about Jill's hourglass body and lick-you-all-over smile...

She narrowed her eyes. "Why not?"

He laughed, a deep baritone rumble that echoed across the empty playground. "You don't have a very high opinion of men, do you?"

"No."

"Well." He leaned his elbow on the picnic table and rested his temple against his knuckles. "First, she wasn't my type."

That part was probably true. After Bettina's cryptic comments about Belle Carson Malone, Kitty had taken her first opportunity to look the woman up on the internet. The love of David's life was a petite blonde princess, with a sweet, heart-shaped face, a curvy body and big, dewy blue eyes.

That meant that Kitty wasn't his type, either. And that hadn't stopped him from sleeping with her.

"And second?"

"Second, I was disappointed that she wasn't you."

With a small, irritable huff, Kitty turned her face away. She didn't want to be spun a fairy tale.

"It's getting late." She stood. "We should probably go."

He didn't move. "I take it you don't believe me?"

"I don't know what to believe." She wasn't angry. She was simply matter-of-fact. It didn't really make sense. If he'd been so disappointed to find her gone, why had he flown back to San Francisco on the first plane off the island? If he'd wanted to talk to her, he knew where she was. Standing there in the beach bar every day, she wasn't exactly a moving target.

"But I'm too tired to sort it out right now. And, in the end, it doesn't really matter." She pulled off his jacket and handed it back to him. "As I said, it's not that big a deal."

CHAPTER EIGHT

DAVID HAD ALMOST DECIDED to throw away the library chandelier, which was froufrou and grimy, and was also missing about a dozen hard-to-replace prisms. The ceiling medallion above it had cracked in at least six places. One of the pieces had almost hit the electrician on the head this morning while they'd been conferring about the new wiring.

But now that David was up here, on the highest rung of the ladder, he could see that the fixture was quite a work of art. Okay, the kind of art only some absinthe-crazed Victorian could love, but still. Serpents, rams' heads and cherubs all twisted together in the five bronze rococo arms, and the prisms were elaborately cut.

Someone had put a lot of work into this thing. And it was obviously original to the house. He grunted, resigned to taking it down, getting it restored and then lugging it back up here. More money, more time he didn't have.

He released the chandelier from the junction box and then, belatedly, wondered how the hell he was going to get it safely back down the ladder. It was like trying to carry a crystal snake.

"Bettina?" He twisted his elbow and got a look at his

watch, releasing a cascade of tinkling sounds from the prisms. *Hell.* She did the weekly shopping on Monday afternoons, and it was only six. She wouldn't be back yet.

"Need something?" Kitty's voice floated up to him around the clinking glass.

He was surprised she was downstairs. Last he'd heard, she'd gone to her room to compose an email to her mother, informing her of the pregnancy and the change of address. She'd warned him it would take a while, and not to expect her for dinner.

"Oh, wow." Her footsteps moved into the room, followed by the patter of puppy steps. "That thing's huge. Let me help you with it."

"Thanks," he said. She reached up with both hands, and he tilted it toward her carefully. "I've got it, but if you'll just balance that end a bit. I'll try not to drop it on you."

"I'd appreciate that," she said with a small smile in her voice. Her left hand took the closest arm of the chandelier, and she gripped it securely. The prisms dangled across her fingers, their sound muffled by her skin.

"Great." He descended the rungs of the ladder carefully. She held on to her end like a trooper, and though he didn't let her bear any real weight, the stability made a huge difference.

Together they carried it toward the window, where a large refectory table had been pushed to clear the way for the floor repairs. He'd draped a large mover's blanket over it, and they set the chandelier down on that.

"Thanks," he said again. "If you hadn't come along,

I'd probably just have a pile of broken glass by now." He scooped away a mass of gray cobwebs, exposing another scowling ram's head. "Although…I'm not sure that would have been such a bad thing."

"Oh, no. It's fantastic," she said with what sounded like genuine enthusiasm. She began whisking cobwebs away. The long beams of late-afternoon sunlight angled in through the window, caught fire in the bronze and lit rainbows in the prisms.

"See? With a little water, a little polish…" She traced one of the cupids with her forefinger. "A toothbrush along in these grooves, to clean away the green… It'll be a beauty."

He half grunted, half laughed, as he picked cobwebs out of his hair. "You've seen the rest of this house, right? Does it look as if I have time to clean cupids with a toothbrush?"

"No." She shook her head thoughtfully. "But I might."

She hadn't looked up, still mesmerized by the intricate designs. It was a rare chance to watch her. She wore a simple pair of jeans and a green sweater. She'd caught her hair in a plain gum rubber band, and she'd chewed off her lipstick everywhere except around the edges, probably while she tried to find the right words to send her mother.

Just another green-haired former bartender. He had to smile. She wasn't trying to turn him on, that was for sure. He shouldn't have felt any attraction. But he did.

Boy, did he.

"If you'd be willing to work on it, I'd really appreciate it," he said.

She glanced up at that. Her eyes were as green as tourmaline in the sun, fringed by dark lashes. Her cheeks bloomed pink, as if she'd been outside today, while he was at work.

He wanted her to stay. He wanted to talk to her. He wanted to know why she loved this goofy Victorian chandelier so much. Was it because she'd never had nice things? Or because she'd had them once and missed them?

"Want to start now?"

She tilted her head. "Can Murphy stay, too?"

Squatting, she lay her hand protectively across the puppy, who stared up at David with liquid black eyes. David realized he hadn't seen the dog much in the past day or two. Kitty had been so good at keeping it out of sight, he sometimes forgot that no one had claimed it.

Kitty pressed subtly on the dog's bottom, and it sat obediently, its little tail wagging with some nameless inner pleasure. Didn't take much, did it, to make an animal happy?

Yeah, it was definitely time to get more energetic about getting rid of the mutt.

But not right now. Right now, Murphy and Kitty were clearly a package deal.

"Sure," he said. He crossed to his toolbox, which he'd rolled in from the garage, since he was never sure what he might need next. He rooted around a bit, found some brass polish, a small brush and a rag. "Will these do?"

"They're a good start," she said, reaching out to accept the items. She was still crouched by the puppy, so she held the rag out for it to sniff. "You won't believe the difference in that chandelier when I get through."

He smiled. "Great. And maybe, if we're working together, we can actually talk a little."

She rose smoothly, and if he hadn't been watching he wouldn't have seen the slight tightening of her shoulders. "Sure. Talk about what?"

"Nothing in particular. Just talk." He tried to make light of it. "You know, I ask you questions, and you answer. Then you ask me questions, and I answer."

"Like a game show."

Her voice was dry, but he couldn't tell if she was making a pleasant joke or a complaint.

"Okay, sure." If that made it easier. "Like a game show. Let's say we each get to ask…say…three questions."

She looked suspicious, tapping the brush against the palm of her hand. "Just three?"

"Yeah. For now. But we have to tell the truth when we answer, okay? Otherwise, it's worthless. And not just yes, no, I don't know. A real answer."

She gazed at him for a long moment, as if trying to find the catch. "I guess so," she said finally. "Obviously, if I answer, I'll tell the truth. But if there's a question I don't want to answer, I'm just going to say so."

"Okay." He couldn't help wondering which question that might be. Did she have some special secret, some shameful skeleton, that she feared he might unearth? But he was glad he'd made it this far, so he didn't push. "Who goes first?"

"You do," she said. She turned toward the chandelier and began wiping it down carefully with the rag. Obviously she preferred not to make eye contact.

Again, he accepted her terms. He was busy trying to decide what his three questions would be.

How personal could he dare to get? He'd had plenty of experience framing his deposition questions, and he knew he could find a way to probe as deeply as he wanted. So…how deep was that?

In spite of his intense curiosity about her, he didn't want to assault her with anything too intrusive. But he'd be damned if he'd waste his precious questions finding out things like her favorite color. Who knew when he'd get his next three chances?

At the last minute, he decided to climb back up on the ladder and work on removing the ceiling medallion. He had a hunch Kitty would feel safer, freer to open up, if he didn't stand here staring at her like the Grand Inquisitor.

"Okay, then." He carried his small carbon-steel pry bar up with him. The symbolism didn't escape him. "First question. What do you like to do for fun?"

As interrogations went, it was fairly softball. But it would tell him a lot of useful things. Most importantly, it might tell him whether, someday, after all the weirdness had passed, they might be able to build a normal life together.

She kept wiping the chandelier.

"For fun," she repeated pensively. "Well, mostly I guess I like to cook."

She hesitated, then seemed to realize it wasn't much of an answer. "Cooking takes my mind off anything that's bothering me. It's a perfect mix of the creative and the practical. Deep inside, I'm a bit of a Puritan, I'm told, so I like that."

He glanced down, and saw that she was smiling wryly, probably assuming that he'd find the "Puritan" part surprising.

But he didn't. He'd already recognized that, under the green hair and the pierced eyebrow, in spite of the one-night stand and the unplanned pregnancy, she had a moral code as strict as any he'd ever seen.

When he turned back to his work on the medallion without comment, she seemed to relax a bit. "I'm not a great cook or anything, but I'm pretty good, I think. When I live in one place long enough, I like to have a few friends over for dinner."

She blew at a stubborn cobweb that clung to the edge of her hand. "I've always enjoyed it. When I was a kid, my dad was sick a lot, and I used to make things for him, things like soup and little cakes. I guess cooking still reminds me of him."

She paused again, as if waiting to see whether he was satisfied with the answer. He would have loved to ask about half a dozen follow-ups. What had been wrong with her father? When had he died? Who had taught her to make the "little cakes"? Her mother? Somehow he doubted that. But he would bet fifty bucks it was Mom who had tagged her with the Puritan label.

"Okay," he said, letting all that go for now. "Question two." He hesitated, then plunged ahead. "Why did you like your father so much more than your mother?"

He didn't look away from his work, but he felt the glance she shot at him. He dug gingerly around the medallion. The old plaster crumbled, raining on him like snow.

"That sounds like a cliché lawyer question," she observed wryly. "Like, when did you stop beating your wife?"

He chuckled, then wished he hadn't, because plaster landed on his lips. "I guess it does," he admitted, looking down at her. She'd picked up the dog and was holding it to her chest, like a shield. This question had apparently touched a nerve.

"I'm sorry," he said. "But I guess those questions are clichés because they work. I could just have asked, did you like your father better, but then you could have answered yes or no, and I wouldn't learn anything."

"Except I already promised I wouldn't do that." She bent her head and kissed the puppy, which was already sleeping, as it seemed to do every time she picked it up. "But you're right. I was closer to my father. He was… easier to be close to. He was a teacher. A reader. A thinker. He was a quiet man who knew how to listen."

David nodded. He didn't speak. He hoped she would go on, but he wanted it to be her decision.

The sun was going down, and they'd have to stop soon, since the electricity for this room was turned off at the main switch. He itched to prod her, but somehow he resisted the urge. He watched as she thoughtfully stroked the puppy's fur, which gleamed like copper in the dying light.

"He died when I was ten. He was very sick. His heart. He wasn't ever strong, not in my memory, anyhow. My mother is, though. She's one of those women who burn up all the oxygen in a room. She's big and pretty and eternally healthy. Outdoorsy, athletic. She loves parties and dancing, and all that stuff he couldn't do. He always said she was like a beautiful hot-air balloon, and he was the rope that held her down."

She bent her head again, and kissed the dog, which let out a small sleepy protest. David still waited, but his hand had tightened so hard around the crowbar that the metal stung his skin.

Suddenly Kitty looked up, and her eyes were glistening. "So it's not that I don't like her, exactly. It's just that I never could forgive her for proving him right. For being so obviously relieved when he died."

David backed one step down the ladder, instinctively. But before he could descend another rung, her cell phone rang. It was one of those pay-as-you-go cheapies, but she'd insisted it was good enough.

She shifted the puppy up onto her shoulder, pulled the phone out of her back jeans pocket with one hand, then frowned at the number displayed there.

"I guess I should take this," she said. As the phone rang again, she headed for the doorway. "I promise, I'll answer your third question later."

"That's okay," he said. And it was. The minute he'd seen that hint of tears in her eyes, he'd known what his third question would be.

What's your favorite color?

He climbed down, just in case she needed something. He didn't like the way the color drained from her cheeks when she saw the number.

She seemed to be gone forever, but probably it was only about five minutes. He could hear her muffled voice coming from the general area of the kitchen but couldn't make out any words. The volume rose briefly, then ended altogether.

She returned to the library, pausing in the doorway. Her cheeks were flushed, and her eyes were still bright. Her chin tilted unnaturally high.

"I'm afraid we'll have to break the rules," she said, remnants of something hard edging her voice. "I have to ask the next question."

He set down the tools. "That's fine. What is it?"

A pulse beat in her slim neck. She took a deep, ragged breath.

"How do you feel about houseguests?"

FOUR DAYS LATER, Lucinda arrived in all her hurt-mother glory to spend a long weekend. One piece of good news, for Kitty at least, Lucinda's plane had landed early in the afternoon, before David finished at the office. Kitty hoped that would leave enough time to get some of the inevitable drama out of the way.

When Lucinda emerged from the tram, they hugged stiffly. As usual, Kitty's mother was groomed as if she were heading to a beauty contest, with a blue suit that fit her like body armor, ostentatious blue-and-gold jewelry at her ears, throat and wrists, and a suede coat over her arm.

Kitty, who had worn her usual jeans and sweater, ignored her mother's disapproving up-and-down flick. She knew what her mother thought about her choices, and she didn't care. At fifteen, Kitty had bundled up her expensive "young socialite" wardrobe and donated it to the Richmond Battered Women's Shelter closest to their house. When she got home to her mother's incredulous fury, she'd announced that she would never, ever wear anything her mother picked out again.

Though she was still watching her pennies and ordinarily took the bus, Kitty had found a great deal on a week-long car rental. Her mother had expressed horror at the thought of trying to negotiate San Francisco public transportation.

As they drove from the airport to David's house, they kept the conversation neutral. Mostly Lucinda's memories of the last time she'd visited San Francisco. Kitty kept her answers brief and noninflammatory, and they made it without a single flare-up of the old tensions.

Finally, they got home, where at least they wouldn't be locked together alone in a small car. As they entered the hall, Kitty took her first real breath since she'd glimpsed her beautiful mother at the terminal.

"Interesting house," Lucinda said, glancing about as they stood in the foyer removing scarves and sweaters. "But it certainly needs a lot of work. I wonder if he used a Realtor. Someone like Jim could have warned him against these old houses that have been let go."

Out of the corner of her eye, Kitty saw Bettina scowl. Great, another strike against Kitty in the housekeeper's book. The two of them had just barely begun to negotiate a ceasefire.

"Too bad Jim couldn't get away," her mother went on, apparently oblivious. "Just too much work. He'll come Monday, though, to pick me up, so he'll meet David, I'm sure."

Kitty refrained from snorting at the idea of Jim "working." He might be a Realtor on paper, but in real life his "work" consisted of bad golfing, slick schmoozing and heavy drinking.

And, of course, pampering the meal ticket. Her mom.

However, as she led her mother up to the guest bedroom they'd picked out for her—on the east side of the house, as far from the tower as they could get—Kitty was proud of herself for saying nothing. Maybe some of David's remarkable restraint was rubbing off.

Good, because she was going to need it. In her first five minutes in the house, her mother had managed to step on Murphy, offend Bettina and, of course, irritate the hell out of Kitty.

Lucinda didn't like this beautiful house? *So go to a hotel,* Kitty wanted to say. She fantasized about tossing the heavy suitcases back down the staircase. She even imagined the satisfying thunks as they hit each step. Who needed three big suitcases for a three-day trip?

But that might have damaged the stairs, which David had refinished himself. So instead, Kitty chewed on the inside of her lower lip until she frayed the flesh, just to keep her mouth shut.

When she opened the door of the guest bedroom, in spite of herself, she paused expectantly. The room looked darn good, especially considering the shape it had been in just a few days ago. A handyman, quickly hired, had taken up and carted away the moldy old carpet. David had rehung three hinky windows. Bettina had teamed up to sweep, dust and polish, while Kitty had washed all the curtains, sheets and blankets.

But her mother just sighed, long-suffering as always.

"It could be worse," she said, running her finger across the windowsill and twitching the curtains, which, unfortunately, had shrunk in the dryer and were now about two inches too short. "I suppose the bare bones look has a peaceful quality. Like a nun's cell. But doesn't your…your friend…believe in *pictures?*"

Kitty's stomach began to burn. When would she learn? It simply wasn't in her mother's nature to offer a compliment. Even supposedly nice comments always hid a thorn inside.

"He's remodeling and restoring, Mom. It would be foolish to hang pictures before he's fixed walls, floors and ceilings."

Lucinda sighed. "The foolish part is buying such a damaged house in the first place."

Kitty was furious. Didn't her mother realize how generous it was of David to allow her to descend on them with next to no warning? Didn't she understand how tenuous this situation was? Did she really think Kitty and David needed a bitchy houseguest right now, while they were still trying to figure out how to interact with each other?

She should have told her mother no. She should have told her mother to go to hell. But David had insisted that they should try very hard to assuage her mother's fears. He'd been so rational, reminding her that Lucinda was probably shocked about the baby, worried that Kitty had hooked up with an axe murderer. If they could calm her fears, things would be much simpler for the next…oh, twenty years or so.

Compared to David's sensible, generous reaction, her mother's grousing seemed even more unpleasant.

"Look, Mom, I don't want you to say anything rude about this house to David. He loves it. He's pouring his heart into it. It's gorgeous, in case you hadn't noticed, and it means a lot to him."

Lucinda looked chastened. She was good at that—throwing the dart, then apologizing profusely for the sting. She put her purse on the mantel, untied her blue-and-gold Hermes scarf, and dropped herself onto the armchair next to the fireplace in a sugary poof of Chanel N°5.

"Of course I won't," she said. "I don't even care about the house. I care about you. We have to talk about..."

She waved her hand weakly toward Kitty. Her engagement ring caught the overhead light and tossed it onto the walls in tiny prisms of color. Quickly, she dropped her other palm over it, as if embarrassed by its magnificence. As well she should be. They both knew Jim couldn't afford a rock like that. Lucinda had surely paid for it herself.

"We have to talk about you, honey."

Kitty lowered herself onto the edge of the bed, resigned to the scene she knew would follow. There was no way to get through this quickly. The basic facts had been exchanged in emails and phone calls, but Lucinda wouldn't be satisfied until she'd had a good fight, a good cry, and a face-to-face chance to make Kitty feel like dirt.

Letting Lucinda have her melodrama was the only way to come out the other side, where maybe, just maybe, they could maintain their superficial, semi-civilized relationship. So many times Kitty had asked herself why she even bothered with that much. Surely her life would be safer if, as David had put it about the Bull's Eye Bar, she erased her mother from her world map.

Funny, really. If this woman had been a stranger, Kitty would have told her exactly where she could shove all her rude, condescending crap. But for some reason, in spite of everything, she couldn't quite bring herself to declare an open war with her mother.

Kitty and Lucinda were the only blood relations either of them had. Only children from only children didn't have a lot of relatives to spare.

And, somewhere deep inside, hiding like a fugitive from Kitty's efforts to kill it, hope lived on.

So now they needed to "talk."

She kicked off her shoes and put her feet on the ottoman beside the bed. "What about me?"

"About the baby, I mean. Oh, my goodness. Just imagine." Lucinda's eyes were already starting to redden around the edges. "My little girl's going to have a baby."

Her little girl? What a joke that was. Right from the start, Kitty had been more pawn than person. Pawn in the eternal battle between her parents. Currency in her mother's desperate bid for attention. Even Kitty's looks had been a tool her mother used to fish for compliments about the excellent gene pool. "Your daughter's beautiful, Luce, but of course she would be. What else would you expect?"

Kitty had been "invited" to help distribute drinks at Lucinda's parties since she was eleven. Her mother would lay out a blue dress and white pinafore that made her look like Alice in Wonderland. The guests couldn't get enough of the "Drink me" jokes. She'd been her mother's very own walking, talking conversation piece.

"I can't believe it, honey. Maybe if you were showing, I could..." Lucinda made a small choking sound. "Looking at you, I really could still think you're my little girl."

"The baby isn't due until August," Kitty responded flatly. "If I were showing in February, something would be seriously wrong."

Lucinda's misty eyes suddenly sharpened, and Kitty knew she was counting. The wedding was scheduled for June. By June, Kitty would be—

"Seven months," Kitty said. "I'll be seven months pregnant in June."

"But..." Lucinda looked stricken. "You'll definitely be showing by then."

"Yes."

"But..." Her mother shook her head, as if she could make the numbers change by sheer denial. "But the maid of honor dress I've picked out. You can't wear it if you're seven months pregnant. It would look absurd."

Kitty shrugged. "Ask someone else, then."

"Ask someone other than my own daughter?" Lucinda's glossy eyebrows shot up in horror. "Never. It would break my heart. And you know what people would say. They'd say you didn't approve of the marriage."

"Well, I don't. You know I don't."

Her mother folded her hands in her lap. She probably meant the pose to look calm, but her knuckles were white. "Kitty, I know it's hard for you, but you have to come to terms with this. You know how much I loved your father."

Kitty dug her fingernails into the mattress. She could see herself, gray and watery in the old glass of the windowpane. She looked like a ghost.

Her mother had loved her father? Kitty didn't know any such thing, though she couldn't say that out loud. This was the steaming center of the volcano that always threatened to blow their relationship sky-high.

"My feelings don't have anything to do with Dad."

"Well, what then?" Lucinda widened her eyes even further. She should have been an actress, Kitty thought. You'd think her mother had completely forgotten the whole thing. "No. Honey, no. That was a misunderstanding. If you only knew how terrible Jim feels that you'd ever believe he—"

"I don't want to talk about this, Mom. We've said all that can be said, years ago. If you're really going to marry him, let's just move on and get it done. Let's focus on something practical. What do you want to do about the dress?"

Her mother clung to her tragic heroine role another few seconds, but the lure of the wedding details was obviously too strong. She stood, emitting one last sigh for good measure, then walked over to one of the big suitcases and hoisted it onto the bed beside Kitty. The mattress bounced from the weight.

"I brought samples of all the fabrics," Lucinda said, unzipping the case deftly. "And pictures of everything else. I can't wait to show you. Did I tell you the color scheme? Lavender and blue. I'll wear sky blue, and so will you. The other attendants will wear lavender. My bouquet will be violets and blue hydrangea. Doesn't that sound heavenly?"

Kitty nodded numbly. The open suitcase overflowed with photo albums, swatches, bits of tulle and lace, silk flowers and ribbons. It was as if Lucinda had stuffed in all her girlish dreams and brought them across the country for Kitty's inspection.

As she watched her mother's manicured hands sift through the rainbow box, Kitty felt an unexpected twinge of pity. Lucinda had been a young mother, about twenty-three, which, Kitty realized with a shock, was three years younger than Kitty was now. That meant she'd been only about thirty-three when Kitty's father died. Young to be married to a sick, tired older man. Young to be a widow.

Was it so unnatural that she would have craved stimulation, an outlet for all her robust energy? Maybe Kitty had judged her too harshly.

But her foolish, self-centered behavior hadn't ended then. Even though she had just turned fifty, being the belle of the ball was still so important to her mother. Lucinda always seemed half afraid that, if she weren't the most beautiful, desirable woman in the room, she would dry up and disappear.

What could have created such a hungry ego? For the first time, Kitty wondered what her mother's childhood had been like. Had she felt loved? Had she felt safe? Had anyone ever told her that her value wasn't measured in boyfriends, compliments and jewels?

And then she had another startling thought. Why had she spent so many years rebelling against Lucinda's pretension and vanity? The green hair, the eyebrow ring, the rejection of conformity...all designed to spit in her mother's face.

Yes, her mother had let her down. But that was eight years ago. Kitty hadn't even seen her mother for the past two. At this point, wasn't she fighting ghosts?

"Yes, it sounds perfect," Kitty said, hoping she wouldn't regret this momentary relaxing of the guard. Hoping it wasn't just the hormones making her soft. She picked up a satin ribbon and held it out toward her mother's face. It matched Lucinda's eyes exactly. "Gorgeous."

Lucinda turned toward the mirror, so that she could enjoy the view, as well. She smiled at her reflection. No one could doubt that the color would be beautiful on her. Kitty, on the other hand, had inherited her father's eyes: green, with gold and brown flecks. Particularly with her green hair, this piece of summer-sky material would look horrible on her.

But it wasn't her wedding.

That's when she knew it had to be the hormones, because her eyes began to sting. Like tears. Like...like it was sad that she would never have this kind of wedding.

Nonsense...stop that...what's the matter with you? She hadn't ever wanted a wedding of any kind. She hadn't lived her life waiting for the prince.

So what *had* she spent her life doing? Proving that she wasn't her mother?

Seemed like a damned empty goal.

The room felt too hot. The silk flowers had been sprayed with some kind of perfume. Kitty's stomach roiled slightly. She hadn't slept all night, pacing the floor, dreading today. Suddenly it was all too much for her. She stretched out her socked feet, rested her head on the pillow and let her eyes drift shut.

"Yes," she murmured, knowing a token response was all Lucinda would need to go on for hours. "It will be lovely, Mom."

CHAPTER NINE

FOR THE FIRST DAY OR TWO, David had been pleasantly surprised by Lucinda. Before the woman's arrival, he'd carefully read between the lines whenever Kitty talked about her. His mental image of Lucinda Hemmings had been a cross between Marilyn Monroe and Medusa.

But in reality Kitty's mother was a well-kept, well-heeled, very early-fifties cougar whose worst fault was that she was…a little too much of everything. Too good-looking, too gussied up, too flirtatious, too rich. Too concerned with what others thought of her. David had represented a dozen women just like her in divorce cases when he first got out of law school.

Not a monster, then. That was something, and he breathed an inner sigh of relief. Maybe he'd been right to insist that Lucinda stay here. Maybe she and Kitty could work some things out.

But it wasn't long before he saw the signs of real trouble. The two women were trying too hard. A good relationship flowed easily, like a river. But this one kept breaking on rocks just below the surface, rocks you couldn't see except by reading the ripples and foam in the water.

Their past was obviously fraught with problems. Kitty's father never came up, even once. Whenever Lucinda mentioned her fiancé, Kitty clammed up. And the topic of the baby, and David and Kitty's plans, seemed equally verboten.

Rather than reminisce for a single moment about her childhood, or speculate a single minute into the future, Kitty doggedly encouraged her mother to ramble on about the relative merits of satin and silk, or the subtle but apparently important difference between lilac and lavender.

David stifled one yawn after another, but whenever Lucinda flagged, Kitty asked a new question to keep the fashion homily going.

It was a long three days.

When David arrived home Monday evening, very late and weary, he saw a new rental car parked out in front of the house. Oh, right…this was Lucinda's last day, so the notorious yet never-mentioned Jim Oliphant must have arrived to retrieve her. David's spirits lifted at the thought that soon he and Kitty would have the house to themselves again.

Plus, he'd been dying to get a look at Oliphant. He hadn't forgotten, of course, what Kitty had said that night in the Bahamas. She'd said her mother was planning to marry a "very bad man."

So what made Oliphant "very bad"? David had tried not to jump to conclusions, but he had a feeling Kitty wasn't talking about anything as simple as Oliphant's designs on her mother's money, or a propensity to cheat on his taxes. When she had mentioned him, her voice had sounded like an open wound. And David had a feeling that only one thing could cause that kind of angry grief.

Something sexual.

But what? How bad? Just a come-on? A touch? An attempt…or something far worse? David was almost glad he didn't know the details yet. If this guy had… if he'd actually…

Better not think about it too much. Not until the guy was safely gone, and Lucinda with him.

David entered in the back, as always, through the kitchen. The first thing he saw was Bettina, her ear pressed against the door that led into the dining room. Not that she needed to be so close. The voice coming from the other side was deep and forceful and easily heard.

"—some freaky, green-haired brat! And if you keep lying about this, if you keep trying to turn your mother against me, I swear I—"

David didn't even think. He moved past Bettina, who had backed up, embarrassed, and he shouldered through the door.

The bastard had his hand wrapped around Kitty's wrist, which she had lifted in order to try to pry it free. Her cheeks burned beet-red, and she looked angrier than David had ever seen her.

"Let go of her," David said.

He didn't raise his voice. He didn't need to. Oliphant had begun to release Kitty's wrist and back away the minute he saw the door open, if only in his peripheral vision. And he had instantly arranged his face into a blandly civilized mask.

He was that kind of bully, then. The kind who would arm-wrestle and insult a woman, but turned all slippery and innocent the moment anyone his own size showed up.

Kitty took two steps back, rubbing her wrist, but she didn't say anything. Her breath was coming fast.

David took a minute to size up Oliphant. The man was tall, athletic, good-looking and expensively dressed—but it was easy to see he hadn't been born to it. For people like the Malones, who'd been dropped in gold-plated clover by the stork, being sophisticated was as easy as being brown-eyed. It was in the DNA. But for people like Oliphant, it was a costume they put on every day.

David knew it because…well, as the saying went, it took one to know one.

But where the hell was Lucinda? Wasn't this her pet monkey? Shouldn't she have him on a leash?

Oliphant seemed to decide to brass it out.

"Sorry. Just working out some family stuff. Nothing serious." He extended his hand. "You must be David Gerard. I hear congratulations are in order."

David flicked a glance toward Kitty. Still scowling, she shook her head. The message was clear. She didn't want him to do anything. She didn't want, or need, rescuing.

"Kitty—"

But she wasn't looking at him anymore. As if David had never interrupted, she had wheeled back toward Oliphant, her green gaze laser sharp.

"I'm not trying to turn Mom against you, Jim. It wouldn't work, and frankly I've decided the two of you deserve each other. I hope you live happily ever after. But if you ever touch me again, for any reason, I won't go to her. I'll go to the cops."

"The cops!" Oliphant flushed. He glanced at David, and shook his head, as if to say, "See what I have to put up with?"

When David remained poker-faced, Oliphant turned back to Kitty. "No one would ever take your word over mine. Look at you! You're just a dysfunctional—"

"That's enough, Oliphant," David began to say, but he could have saved his breath.

Kitty stepped forward and slapped Oliphant so hard it sounded like a gunshot. The man's face flushed a deep, congested red, against which the pale imprint of her palm lay like a scar.

Oliphant practically wheezed with fury. "See what you've gotten yourself into, Gerard? That girl's crazy, and she's dangerous. You're a lawyer. You know that's assault."

Kitty narrowed her eyes. "That's just a fraction of what you deserve. But by all means, if you want to call the cops, do it. Let's hash this out in open court."

Oliphant opened his mouth to retort, but, as the reality sank in, he deflated like a pricked balloon. If it hadn't been so serious, David might have laughed.

The older man obviously knew he'd been checkmated. He tried to wither Kitty with a long, contemptuous stare. When that didn't work, he did a stiff about-face and moved toward the dining room door.

At the last minute, he turned toward David, ostentatiously ignoring Kitty.

"Let me give you some advice, Gerard," he said. "I can see she's trying to weasel a wedding ring out of you. But don't be a sucker, man. Make the bitch take a paternity test."

God. David was almost speechless. Could the jackass get it any more wrong than that?

He glanced at Kitty. Their gazes held for a couple of seconds, and then Kitty began to smile. He smiled. One of them chuckled. And then, like naughty children, they broke into helpless laughter that was, in its way, far more of an insult than Kitty's slap.

Disgusted, Oliphant left the room.

By MIDNIGHT, Kitty knew she'd never sleep. Not until she talked to David. Colby Malone had called right after Jim and her mother drove off, asking whether David could help an employee who had run into legal trouble. David had left immediately, and he hadn't returned until late.

So she hadn't had time to offer him more than a quick, superficial "thank you" at the kitchen door.

He deserved better than that. She should go down right now and thank him properly.

Problem was, she hadn't ever been good at this kind of thing. Needing help in the first place felt weak. It felt vulnerable. In her experience, people who "helped" you ended up believing they owned you.

But, to be fair, David hadn't shown any signs of being overly controlling. In fact, he seemed to bend over backward to give her space, to allow her to make her own decisions, good or bad. He'd been more generous and patient, she suspected, than most men would be. He never lost his temper, never sulked when she didn't take his advice.

He'd been darn near perfect.

Maybe that was part of the problem. No one really *was* perfect, so, to one degree or another, he had to be pretending. Trying to win her over. She'd only been living here a week. Anyone could fake it for a week.

Still, she wasn't going to get any rest until she did the right thing. Leaving Murphy asleep in his crate, she walked down the one flight of stairs and rapped softly on David's door.

She knew he was still awake. When she had taken Murphy out just fifteen minutes ago, she'd seen David's foot shadows pass through the strip of light under his door.

He was a night owl, anyhow. She'd learned that this week. If he wasn't reading some massive law book, he was restoring and hand-sanding the porch's broken gingerbread trim. So she wasn't sure why knocking on his door and saying one simple word, "Thanks," felt so hard.

He answered within seconds. "Hey," he said. "Everything okay?"

"Everything's fine. It's just that we just didn't get a chance to talk, after Jim left. I wanted to thank you. For being so…supportive."

"You're welcome." David smiled. "Come on in."

He stepped back from the door and swept his free hand in invitation. Though the room was of course configured just like hers, it was so much more masculine. It actually looked more like a study than a bedroom, with bookcases and a couple of cushy leather armchairs facing the fireplace. The large four-poster bed hadn't been turned down, and, though he'd removed his work suit, he was still fully dressed in jeans and a T-shirt.

Even so, she hesitated. "I didn't mean to interrupt you."

He waved the heavy red-leather book he held. "You can't imagine how I welcome an interruption. Come on in."

He touched the back of one of the armchairs, offering it to her. She took it, sinking deep into its luxurious warmth. She'd come down only in her jeans, sweatshirt and socks, so she tucked her feet up under her. It smelled just like her father's armchair in his library back at Lochaven, and she felt a sudden wave of homesickness.

David dropped his book on the coffee table, then settled himself in the other chair. With the fire burning in the hearth, the arrangement was surprisingly comfortable.

"So, anyhow. I really did appreciate what you did tonight," she said. "Harry…then Jim. It seems as if you're always having to save me from some jerk or another, aren't you?"

"Save you?" He laughed. "Looked to me as if you had this one covered. I didn't do a darn thing—except maybe provide an appreciative audience."

She shook her head. That was nice, but…what had he really thought? Anyone who so studiously avoided losing his temper had to have been appalled by the bare-throat hostility he'd witnessed.

"I'm sorry we caused such a scene. I don't know why I couldn't just ignore him. That's how I used to handle it." She lifted her shoulders. "Well, either ignore him or run away."

"Is that how you got to the Bahamas? Running from Oliphant?"

She tugged one corner of her mouth up. "The road twisted and turned a bit, but basically, yeah. I wanted to be somewhere he wasn't."

For a moment, the only sound in the room was the wood cracking and spitting as the tongues of fire licked it. But in the silence she felt David's unspoken question.

Why? Why had she needed to run, and keep running for so long?

She looked at him, wondering whether maybe she owed him an explanation. It wouldn't be easy. She hadn't ever talked about this to anyone but her mother. And look how that had gone. But Jim had said some ugly things tonight, in front of David. He'd called her a liar. He'd called her crazy.

She wondered, suddenly, whether David harbored some doubt.

"It's really not a very remarkable story," she said, keeping her gaze on the fire. "Just the usual cliché, without a single interesting twist. Mom's scumbag boyfriend decides it would be entertaining to climb in her daughter's bed and see whether she's any fun. She's not. She's flaming mad, and she's got fingernails. He has to slink away, bloody and disappointed."

"Disappointed?"

"Yes." She shrugged, assuming that said enough. No rape. Just…horror. "But when the girl tells her mother, the scumbag denies it, and Mom believes him."

Though David didn't respond in words, she felt his tension. The firelight played over his features, giving them the illusion of movement, but his body was unnaturally still. His fingertips were pale where they gripped the arms of the chair.

"In Mom's defense," she went on, "the girl wasn't very reliable. She'd been rebellious and angry, a troublemaker for years, ever since her father died. So she didn't have a lot of trust banked, if you know what I mean, when the time came for a withdrawal."

Finally he looked at her. "That's crap. How old were you?"

"Just turned eighteen."

"Then baloney. A rebellious teenager is one thing. An accusation of assault is different. You take that seriously. Every time. No matter what."

"No." Kitty smiled ruefully. "That's how it should be, maybe. But that's not how it is in the real world."

"How did Oliphant explain the scratches?"

"He said I'd been having a nightmare. I did, sometimes. He said he went in to see if I was okay, and I went all Rambo on him. He made it sound as if I had deliberately set him up because I resented his sleeping in my father's bed." She bit her lower lip. "Which I did. My father died in that bed. Slowly."

"Did you consider going to the police?"

"Not for a second. The D.A. is a regular at my mom's parties. He plays golf with Jim on Thursdays, and they go to the same church. They never miss a Sunday. It's all so civilized."

She heard the bitterness in her voice, so she tried to tone it down. "Plus, I wasn't exaggerating when I said I'd been a troublemaker. The police and I weren't exactly strangers. And the real problem wasn't Jim, anyhow. He really was just the cliché scumbag, so how much could his betrayal hurt? It was my mom. No matter how rocky things had been between us since my father died, I still couldn't believe that she didn't…that she wouldn't…"

She couldn't quite finish the sentence. It was so stupid, so embarrassing, that she could still be reduced to tears by this. Eight years was a long time. If these pangs of shame, anger, betrayal hadn't died in eight years, was she going to be stuck with them for life?

She wrapped her arms around her knees. "You can't put a woman behind bars for being a crummy mother. Even if I could have gotten him locked up, she would have kicked me out anyhow. So I just saved her the trouble, packed my bags and never looked back."

David's face was still composed, but he stood abruptly and began to stir the fire. His shoulders were rigid, his movements tight.

"It's amazing either one of them can come here and look you in the eye."

She'd thought that, too, at first. "I think Jim's told his version so many times he's begun to believe it. When he got here tonight, he seemed shocked that I was still angry and unwilling to admit I'd been wrong. It went downhill from hello. And that's when you showed up."

He turned. "I'm glad I did. I enjoyed watching you scare the tar out of the bastard."

"You should have seen him that night eight years ago." She smiled, hoping it looked lighthearted and not as tremulous as it felt. "I bet he never takes off his shirt in public. I left some scratches on his chest that aren't going anywhere."

On his chest…

His naked chest, muscles bunching, his forearm pressing into her throat.

The memory was too much, all of a sudden, and she squeezed her eyes to make it go away. The weight and heat of his body over hers, the feel of his skin coming off beneath her nails. The terror that had made her kick and scratch like a cornered animal.

"Kitty."

When she opened her eyes, David was kneeling in front of her. He had reached out to push her curls out of her face. "Don't think about it anymore. I shouldn't have asked."

But he hadn't asked. She'd volunteered. And now she was shaking all over, almost as badly as if it had happened yesterday, rather than a lifetime ago.

David leaned in and put his arms around her softly. No pressure. Just an enfolding warmth that, paradoxically, made her feel like crying. Made her feel as if, after battling the storm alone for so long, she'd finally reached a safe port, somewhere she could relax and not have to be strong anymore.

But it wasn't true. In the end, all harbors, all havens, all ports in the storm were mirages. They would lure you in and disappear right when you needed them most.

Her father hadn't wanted to leave her, but he had, nonetheless. Nobody stayed, in the end.

And her mother…

If she couldn't trust the woman who had borne her,

nursed her, shared her DNA, how could she possibly trust a man she'd known only a few weeks? A man who, according to his housekeeper, was still in love with another woman?

She couldn't.

David seemed to be a very nice man, and she was glad of that, for her baby's sake. But she wouldn't dissolve in his arms. She wouldn't hand him her heart and her life to take care of, just because she was tired. Tired didn't matter.

She wasn't a weeper. She wasn't a clinger. She was a survivor. She stood on her own two feet, relied on her own guts and determination.

It was, in the end, the only thing that could really keep her safe.

"This is ridiculous." Swallowing hard, she drew her head back so that she could look into his face. "You said you wanted to get to know me. Well, this isn't me. That moment doesn't define me. I don't blame you if you think I'm weak. Between the Bahamas and all this, you probably think I'm a pathetic stereotype of the fragile female. But I promise you, I'm not normally the damsel in distress type."

"I know." He smiled. "You're a lot more like the green-eyed, fiery dragon."

"Right." She realized they were almost whispering, and that their faces were only inches apart. She glanced at his lips. She knew exactly how they would taste, how they would feel against her skin.

Impulsively, she leaned in and kissed him. Lightly— though her whole body seemed to be tugging at her, longing to lean in and press against him.

She meant it to be brief. Just a quick thank-you, a gesture of goodwill that surely wasn't out of place between people who had once been lovers.

But his lips were so warm, so intriguingly hard around the edges, tender in the center. She lingered, despite her best intentions. She touched his shoulder and felt the tight muscles humming under her palm. He, too, was clearly fighting the need to go further, take more.

Common sense battled desire. They'd made so much progress toward becoming friends. Becoming allies in this precarious situation. Wasn't that enough? Wouldn't it be foolish to throw away the security of friendship, the promise of a lifetime of harmony, for a quick thrill?

Finally, she found the willpower to pull away.

He lifted one corner of his mouth, a wry smile that was devastatingly sexy. He tilted his head a fraction of an inch. The minute motion was a question.

But it was a question she couldn't answer. Not the way he wanted her to.

Not yet.

Reluctantly, she stood. If she didn't go now, she might never go at all.

"I'm sorry," she said. "I'm tired, and I don't think that we…"

She paused, realizing that she'd expected him to interrupt her, to argue, to coax or persuade.

But he didn't. Obviously he'd decided that he wouldn't take the decision out of her hands.

That meant she had to be sensible. She had to be wise.

"I guess I should go back upstairs."

CHAPTER TEN

KITTY HUMMED as she stirred the bourguignonne, skimming the fat that had risen to the top. The aroma of the stew was mouthwatering, and she inhaled deeply—thrilled that she could actually do so without feeling nauseated.

When she'd woken up this morning to let Murphy out, she'd realized something was different. Or rather something was normal. She didn't feel sick. Her head didn't swim, and her stomach didn't roil. She felt almost like herself again.

It was like being reborn. She'd scooped Murphy up and danced him around the room. Even that hadn't set off any waves of nausea. She rubbed her chin luxuriously against the puppy's glossy back and thanked whatever fates controlled these things. She wasn't going to be like her mother.

And then the manager at Punch and Judy had called and told her a scheduling glitch left them overstaffed, and she didn't need to go in that afternoon. She almost shouted for joy. Bettina was off, finally visiting her sister. David was at work. For the next eight hours at least, the whole beautiful house belonged to her and Murphy.

This was her lucky day. And she knew exactly what she was going to do with it.

She was going to make dinner for David.

The choice of menu was easy. Beef bourguignonne was the first recipe Kitty had ever mastered, and it had always been her favorite. She decided to substitute red grape juice for the wine. She knew everyone said the alcohol cooked off, but the responsibility for the life inside her was overwhelming, and she didn't want to take the slightest risk.

She still had the rental car, so even scooting up to the grocery store had been easy. She could get used to this kind of life.

By seven o'clock, the time David usually got home, the stew had been simmering for nearly three hours. The table shone with china and silver. The mashed potatoes, over which she'd serve the stew, were as fluffy as clouds. Maybe another ten minutes, and she'd light the candles.

She glanced out the bay window over the sink, wondering if she should bring Murphy in. The puppy loved the chilly weather and had been busily hunting imaginary things through the bushes for the past hour.

The floodlights illuminated the fenced yard thoroughly, but it was fully dark by six these days, so the contrast created sharply angled shadows. If Murphy darted out from one of those just when David opened the gate, he might get loose. That might well be how he'd ended up lost in the first place.

She grabbed her sweater and went out onto the back porch. She snapped her fingers—Murphy was such a smart little guy, he'd been easy to train—and he came romping toward her.

Just as David's car swung into the drive.

Kitty hurried out to meet him. Murphy beat her there, equally excited by the idea of a new arrival. With her hand on the latch, she bent and scooped up the puppy, then swung the heavy wrought-iron gate free.

He killed the engine. Then he opened his door. He looked surprised to see her. Of course, he'd thought she was working at Punch and Judy tonight.

But he also looked...uncomfortable. Almost...guilty.

"Hi," she called. "Murphy and I decided to form a welcoming committee—"

She stopped abruptly as she saw the passenger door open, too. David wasn't alone? She couldn't see much through the tinted windows, but soon enough a graceful young woman emerged, one slim leg at a time. She was beautiful. She wore a navy suit that epitomized understated elegance. Her round, radiant eyes, her bright smile and her blond hair shone in the floodlights as if she were a celebrity arriving on the red carpet.

"Kitty, I don't think you've met Belle Malone," David said, bridging the awkward moment smoothly. "The work ran long, so we decided to finish up here, where we could grab a sandwich."

Belle shot David one quick, questioning glance before she moved up the stairs, her arms outstretched. "Kitty! David's told me so much about you! I can't believe it's taken us this long to meet!"

Kitty didn't know what to do except let the other woman hug her, with Murphy caught in the middle.

They were both about the same size, except that Kitty was skinnier, five times as badly dressed and a hundred times more awkward. Belle was like a princess out of a fairy tale. All that perfect hair, those perfect teeth, perfect curves and clothes and perfume.

She did PR for Diamante, Bettina had told Kitty recently. A job where image was everything.

Kitty felt like a freak just standing next to her.

She wondered what David thought, looking at the two of them on the porch, hugging as if they were friends. The golden princess he'd lost and the mixed-up urchin he'd found.

He had pulled a stack of files out of the car and joined them by the door. He started to speak, but Belle interrupted, giving him another of her quizzical glances.

"David Gerard. This can't be true. You have a dog?"

He frowned down at Murphy. "No. This is just a stray. We're combing San Francisco, trying to find out where it belongs."

"Not *it,* Grinch. *He.* And he's adorable." Belle tugged playfully on Murphy's ears. He trembled ecstatically. "I think you should keep him. Don't you, Kitty?"

"*He* belongs to somebody, Belle," David said firmly. "We just need to find out who." Then he turned to Kitty. "I'm sorry. I thought you worked tonight. We'll just get a snack and try to stay out of your way."

Suddenly, Kitty remembered the carefully set table, the flowers she'd impulsively bought from the grocery store and arranged in a small vase. Thank God she hadn't lit the candles.

"Actually, you're in luck," she said, trying to think quickly. "I just made a huge pot of stew. A friend from work was going to come by, but—"

She stumbled over which pronoun to choose. Candles and flowers for a "she" didn't seem quite right, but would it look strange to have invited a "he"? Suddenly she wished she hadn't been juvenile enough to try to invent a lie. She wasn't good at it.

"They couldn't make it," she ended lamely. "So there's lots of food here, if you're hungry."

If David knew she was spinning a bunch of nonsense, he didn't let on. "Enough for four people? Matt's coming, too, as soon as he gets free."

"It's okay if there's not enough," Belle interjected with a reassuring smile. "I'll just tell Matt to bring some pizza with him. Lord knows there's always plenty of that around Diamante. I've had to train myself to believe the scent of pepperoni is an aphrodisiac."

David and Belle laughed, in that way only special, old friends can do, as if every joke had ten layers, nine of which were invisible to outsiders.

And Kitty was the outsider.

"I think I made enough to feed the whole neighborhood," she said brightly. "Come on in. I'll set another couple of places at the table."

In spite of being spoiled by a housekeeper, David wasn't one of those guys who kicked up his feet and let the ladies wait on him. In the pleasant chaos of providing extra place settings, dishing up the food, taking drink orders, and, yes, even lighting the candles, he was always there, working as hard as Kitty and Belle.

Kitty made a point of not being in the room the first

time he saw the table. She didn't want to know what he thought. If he figured out that she'd originally intended it for the two of them, she didn't want to know. That way, it would be easier to pretend.

It was quite pleasant, really, the big old house ringing with activity, thanks mostly to Belle, who was easy company. Witty, smart, bubbly, kind. Kitty had been prepared to dislike the other woman intensely, partly because she'd so often felt Belle's ghost hanging in the air. She would pull down a book from the library shelves, and see Belle's inscription in it. Bettina would set aside a pile of pictures she'd found while cleaning, and Belle and David would be in all of them, arms around each other, laughing.

Kitty had even glimpsed the ring, once, when David sent her to his library desk looking for a pen that worked. A huge diamond solitaire, rocking and bumping at the back of a drawer without a box or a case or even a shroud of cotton to protect it. Oddly, such careless treatment didn't really strike Kitty as indifference. It felt like unresolved disappointment and loss.

So, yes, Kitty had expected to pretty much hate the reckless blond heartbreaker who had so much she could afford to throw away a man like David.

But Belle the ghost and Belle the woman were very different.

By the time they sat down to eat, Belle's easy camaraderie had won Kitty over. And when Belle took a forkful of potatoes and stew, closed her eyes and moaned ecstatically, she absolutely sealed the deal.

"Kitty, this is fantastic." Belle's blue eyes opened,

still unfocused with bliss. "Quick, let's eat it all so that Matt doesn't get any. That's his punishment for being late."

But just then her cell phone chirped. She excused herself, and went to the library to answer it.

That left David and Kitty alone for the first time. After the easy banter of the trio, the intimacy was strangely awkward. Just for something to do, she held out the covered tureen that held the stew, which was stupid, because he hadn't eaten a bite yet, and his plate was full.

"No, thanks," he said. He seemed uncomfortable again, too, and glanced toward the library door, which Belle had shut behind her.

"Matt is a bit of a workaholic. He's probably just leaving Diamante now." He smiled, as if affectionately amused. "Belle will be chewing him out, no doubt. She isn't a fan of holding things in. If she's really mad, we'll probably feel the fire from here."

David and Belle must have been a seriously bad match. Kitty couldn't imagine David, the man who never let a rogue emotion slip free, happily engaged to a woman who didn't believe in holding back.

Or maybe he'd been different with Belle. Maybe, with Belle, he'd been willing to get angry, go wild, let loose. Maybe it was only with Kitty that he kept his emotions under lock and key.

The thought was surprisingly painful.

Sure enough, when Belle returned, her heart-shaped face was flushed, and her blue eyes were bright with disappointment.

"He's not coming at all," she said without preamble. She sat down and snapped the napkin across her lap. "He says he can't get away. Something about a power failure over at Horseshoe Bay."

David put his hand out and closed it over Belle's. "It's the expansion," he said. "You know it's a heavy weight to carry."

Belle looked up into his handsome, concerned face. She took another moment, then squeezed his hand and smiled. "You're right. I'm being a dork. Smack me if I get like that again, will you?"

"With pleasure," David said. They were still holding hands across the snowy white tablecloth. Both smiling that gentle, goofy smile.

And then, as if a bullet entered both their minds at once, they seemed to remember Kitty. It was almost comical, how quickly they jerked their hands back.

"Well, it's not as if he was going to be any good with the Drivers' Fund party plans anyhow," Belle said, her voice a shade too animated. She reached for the bowl of green beans. "And just think. If he doesn't come, that's more of this delicious food for us!"

They kept at it, like good little society soldiers. But for Kitty, the party was over. She bumped along for another twenty minutes or so, playing the third wheel. David and Belle never touched again, not even as they handed around platters. They never let eye contact linger for more than a second or two.

It was worse, somehow, seeing them work so hard to avoid the simple touch of a finger.

Kitty held her chin up, though. She wasn't going

to expose how redundant she felt. She plucked at her mashed potatoes with the tines of her fork, and she even swallowed a couple of mouthfuls, though her appetite had completely vanished.

Finally, the meal was over, and she could almost hear a collective sigh of relief.

"I guess we ought to get to work, or I'll be here all night." Belle smiled, but her glance toward David implored him to lead the way, to show her the appropriate words.

He nodded and turned to Kitty. "She's right. We've got a lot to do. You look as if you might not feel all that well, anyhow." He glanced at her nearly full plate. "You didn't eat much. Please don't worry about the dishes. I'll do them before I come upstairs, and if it gets too late Bettina can handle them when she gets back in the morning."

Kitty nodded. It was gracious, but there was no mistaking it as a dismissal. They would be working—or whatever—and they didn't want Kitty hanging around the kitchen where she might be able to hear them.

"Sounds great," she said, making her voice as hearty as she could. She didn't intend to slink away as if *she* had anything to be ashamed of. She didn't want to give them any more to talk about when she was gone.

She held out her hand. "It was lovely to meet you, Belle."

Belle hesitated a fraction of a second, and then she surged forward to wrap Kitty in another hug.

"Get some rest," she said. "We'll see each other a lot, now that we've finally met. I'll call you soon, okay?"

"That sounds great," Kitty said, aware that she

sounded like a hollow echo. She knew Belle didn't mean it. People in public relations always said the "right" thing convincingly.

Another few polite good-nights. The long climb up three floors. And then she was finally alone again. Alone with her thoughts.

Alone with the awful new awareness that hummed through her like an electrical current. David really had been in love with Belle. He probably still was. Kitty had allowed herself to hope that maybe Bettina's grim warnings had been a power play, that the housekeeper had exaggerated the importance of Belle Carson Malone in David's life.

But it had all been true.

She felt a pain, digging hard between her ribs. Though Murphy was sound asleep, she opened his crate and pressed his warm, floppy body to her heart. She sat on the bed and stared at herself in the vanity mirror.

What was wrong with her? What kind of madness was this?

She wasn't tired, and she wasn't sick. The misery that welled up inside her had nothing to do with pregnancy, or long hours on her feet. It was far, far worse than that.

It was a terrible, primitive fear.

Because she'd done the one thing she had told herself never to do.

She'd allowed herself to dream. She'd allowed herself to hope.

She'd allowed herself to care.

DAVID GOT THE CALL about the dog the next afternoon, while Kitty was at work.

It was a middle-aged woman, maybe in her late fifties. David had just barely been able to finish saying "Hello" before her story spilled out in half sentences, panicked, tearful, rambling.

She'd lost her dog, she said. She'd been on a cruise. It was the anniversary of her husband's death, and he'd wanted his ashes scattered at sea. Her grandson had been watching the house, he wasn't a kid, he was eighteen, he should have known better. The puppy must have dug out under the back fence the very first night. Rick had thought it would be better not to tell her until she got back, because he was afraid she couldn't take it, not with her husband's ashes and everything.

So stupid, the young don't understand. But then she'd seen David's ad in the paper. Was it possible, oh, she prayed it was, that the puppy he'd found was her Rooney?

It wasn't easy, getting past the generic, doting descriptions like cuddly, sweet, beautiful, but finally David extracted enough details to feel fairly certain the dog belonged to her. Only one way to be sure, though. She had to come take a look.

He tried to stall her until Kitty returned, but Kitty worked until ten tonight, and clearly the woman was too overwrought to wait that long. She almost broke into tears again, just thinking about waiting another six hours to see her darling Rooney.

Plus, she had a suspicious streak, and even when David offered to meet her in a public place, she didn't like the idea of a night-time assignation with a strange man.

They settled on four o'clock. He hung up the phone with a mild, but manageable, sense of misgiving, and stared at the dust motes that danced in the sunbeams. He'd better put on his mask before he did any more sanding.

He tried to make the niggling feeling go away. Kitty would be disappointed, no doubt. It had been a long time—even David had begun to wonder whether the dog's real owner would ever show up.

"You're going to give that dog away without letting Miss Kitty say goodbye?" Bettina stood in the library doorway, her hands on her hips. She'd obviously been listening to the whole conversation.

David finished jotting down the woman's particulars, and tapped the space bar to wake up his computer. He wanted to check her out, just to be sure. "I'm not giving the dog away, Betty. If it belongs to this woman, she has a right to it. Kitty will understand."

"She won't understand not getting a chance to say goodbye."

"Don't worry about it, Betty."

But he wasn't really listening. He had found the woman instantly. Eleanor Pritchard. Retired school-teacher. On the library board. She even had a Facebook page, with heavy privacy settings, but a profile picture he could click on. A pretty, slightly dumpy lady holding a very small Irish setter puppy. Yep, there it was. The dog had even been tagged, which meant it had its own page. Rooney Mahooney. David grimaced. In the picture, Rooney Mahooney licked Eleanor's face so uninhibitedly David grunted and exited the program.

Well, so much for that. He stood, ready to get back to his sanding. He had taken down the trim from the south second-story gable this morning, and he wanted to finish it today.

"I *am* worried," Bettina said stubbornly. "And you should be, too. Miss Kitty loves that dog. It's going to break her heart."

Bettina was such a drama queen. If she didn't keep this crazy old house in such perfect order, he would probably give her to Mrs. Pritchard, too. He picked up his electric sander and left his finger on the trigger, indicating that he hoped this conversation wouldn't drag on very long.

"It will not break anyone's heart. Kitty has known from the start that the dog probably had an owner. She's enjoyed it, but she'll be fine. She might even be glad to be spared the ordeal of saying goodbye."

Bettina shook her head darkly. "Men," she muttered.

David ran his hand over the thin, twisting curlicue at the tip of the trim. It wasn't going to be easy getting the layers of paint off without sanding the little piece down to nothing. It would take a very light hand.

"No, not men, generally," Bettina corrected herself. "Just you. You're so good with the house, with the wood, with the tools. How come you're so bad with the dog?"

He laughed. "I'm just a cold-hearted beast, I suppose."

"Seriously. What? You got bitten by a dog? Your mom wouldn't let you have a pet?"

"Betty." He let his voice drop down to serious. "Stop psychoanalyzing me. I've got a lot to do. And so do you."

But when the housekeeper stomped away, unmollified, he still didn't start the sander. He kept thinking about tonight, when Kitty got off work. The first thing she did when she got home was race up the stairs to release the dog from the little play pen she'd bought— play palace, David called it privately. It was big enough to hold a bed, a bowl of water, half a dozen of the dog's favorite toys and, Betty told him, even one of Kitty's old shoes, on which the dog always rested its chin before falling asleep.

He tried to imagine stopping Kitty at the foot of the stairs, and telling her Murphy was gone.

No. For once, Bettina was right. That wasn't going to work.

He went to the computer again, looked up Punch and Judy, then called its listed phone number.

"Punch and Judy Puppets, Kitty speaking. How can I help you have fun today?"

He winced at the script, at the artificial lilt she added to her voice, which was lovely enough without any extra saccharine.

"Hi," he said. "It's David."

She paused, clearly shocked. He had never phoned her at work before. He had worked enough hourly, minimum-wage retail jobs in his life to know that employees at such places were discouraged from taking personal calls.

"Is everything all right?" Her voice was cautious.

"Yes," he said. "I just thought you might want to

know. A woman called a little while ago. She thinks Murphy may be the puppy she lost a couple of weeks ago."

The silence this time was longer, heavier.

"Tell her I'll call her when I get home," Kitty said, finally, and all the Punch and Judy music had died out of her voice.

Hell.

"No. She doesn't want to wait that long. She's pretty upset. She's coming at four."

"But I can't get there by four…. And how do you know she's even telling the truth? People do terrible things with little dogs. I know you've read about it. They take any dog they can get for free and—"

"I think it's hers, Kitty. She's bringing the papers, and vet records, and everything she has to prove ownership. I've already checked the dates and markings, all the facts we could nail down. Plus, I looked her up and found her Facebook picture. She's holding a dog." He took a breath. "It's pretty clear it's Murphy."

He heard a muffled rustling sound, as if she had closed her palm over the speaker. Then she came back. "I can't talk right now. My boss won't allow personal calls. But listen. Can't you just tell her we'll let her look at Murphy tomorrow?"

His chest tightened strangely. Something in her voice… "I can't, Kitty. I've already set it up. If the dog is hers, we don't have the right to keep it from her."

"David, I—"

"Think about it, Kitty. It'll be easier this way." He couldn't stand the way her voice sounded, as if she wanted to say *please,* wanted to beg him, but wouldn't allow herself to do it. "If it really is her dog, you wouldn't want to keep them apart, and saying good-bye might be hard. Emotional. Messy."

He heard her take in a breath. And then he heard the dial tone. He stared at the phone a minute, as if it might possibly have malfunctioned. But he knew it hadn't. He slipped the phone in his pocket and picked up his sander again.

He shouldn't have called. He should have known he'd only make it worse. It was just like Bettina had said. He was okay with wood and windows, but he sucked swamp water with dogs.

And women.

The sanding took his mind off things for a while. Time passed without his registering every tick.

He almost forgot about it. Almost.

At five minutes to four, he looked through the library window and saw Kitty arriving, parking her rental car at an awkward, rushed angle in front of the house. He saw her dash up the steps and fling open the door. She let it shut with a bang behind her.

She didn't look right or left, didn't see him standing in the library doorway, sander in his hands. She just stampeded up the stairs faster than he'd ever heard her run before.

Bettina emerged from the kitchen, and impaled David with one long, dark spear of a glance. Then she stomped back into the kitchen.

When Eleanor Pritchard rang the doorbell at four o'clock sharp, Kitty was already walking down the stairs, carrying a tote overflowing with Murphy's toys and the half-empty sack of puppy food under her arm. Murphy, freshly brushed and gleaming, pranced beside her on his leash.

David turned the knob, and Eleanor Pritchard almost fell in, as if she'd been leaning on the door.

"Where is he?" She folded her hands, pressing them against her breast nervously.

The puppy's reaction to its long-lost owner put all doubts to rest. It almost strangled itself on the leash, trying to leap into her arms.

The next few minutes passed in a weirdly numb blur. David registered with amazement how sweet and gracious Kitty was to Mrs. Pritchard. She handed Murphy over with grace, accepting the woman's effusive thanks modestly, and even walked her out to the car to say goodbye.

David watched in awe. But in the back of his mind he noticed that Kitty never once looked his way or responded to a single comment he made. He might as well have been invisible.

When Mrs. Pritchard and Murphy drove off, Kitty walked, spine straight and chin high, back into the house. She didn't go much beyond the door, and stayed just long enough to pick up her keys from the hall table.

"I think I need to be alone a little while," she said. "I'll see you later, okay?"

"You aren't going back to work?"

"No."

"But…" He looked at his watch. "How did you get off so early?"

She paused, then turned. Her eyes seemed to be carefully devoid of expression.

"I quit my job," she said.

And then she exited, strode down to her rental car, and was gone.

CHAPTER ELEVEN

FIVE HOURS LATER, Kitty had a new job. One that was simultaneously exciting and scary.

She always watched the want ads, just in case. And recently she'd noticed that a women's craft cooperative only three miles from David's house had been advertising for a receptionist/clerk.

It was called The Three Swans, and its charming logo of silver, blue and white called to her in a way she couldn't explain. She knew the area—a two-block-long strip of quirky stores that faced a small park heavy with oak trees. It was low-key, soothing to the spirit, beloved by the locals and completely undiscovered by the tourists.

She'd been carrying around that ad for three days now, unsure whether she ought to apply. Since she ran away from Lochaven eight years ago, she'd taken only what she called "warm body" jobs. Jobs where any relatively bright, smiling human would do. Jobs she could quit without regret on either side, as long as she gave enough notice to let them find another warm body.

Like Punch and Judy, for instance. The owner hadn't been willing to give Kitty an early dinner to say good-bye to Murphy, even though the store had clearly been overstaffed. She hadn't been at all upset to accept Kitty's resignation instead.

The Three Swans felt different, somehow, though the pay wasn't any better, or the education requirements any more stringent. It was just filing, helping customers, running a register. But it felt like a job she could care about. Maybe make friends. Maybe even make a difference.

It felt, in short, like a commitment. And commitments scared her.

But today, after she left the house, she had gone anyway. And she got the job. When she mentioned that she might like to have a booth of her own to bring in baked goods, the owner, a brisk older woman named Maeve McDermott, had seemed thrilled.

By the time Kitty finished talking to Maeve and taking an impromptu tour of the shop, it was almost nine. She decided to grab something to eat at her favorite sandwich shop. No point annoying Bettina by messing up the kitchen. And besides, she wasn't eager to face her tower room, which she knew would feel empty without Murphy.

It was a moonless night, and the streetlamps cast pale circles of white light at intervals down the street. On this block, the deli was the only store still open—a busy island of illumination and noise in the otherwise deserted retail strip.

She'd come here so often in the past couple of weeks that the waitress knew her. She brought Kitty to a booth in the back corner, then just said, "The regular?" They both knew that meant an egg salad on pumpernickel, with fruit instead of chips.

Kitty took her time with the sandwich, looking over the literature from the co-op. Maeve's enthusiasm had been contagious, and Kitty felt less depressed than she'd thought possible, so soon after losing Murphy.

She'd be doing two jobs until she worked off her notice at the puppet store, but that was okay. Work had always been her best therapy. She thought about the little booth Maeve had pointed out, the one Kitty might be able to use for her cookies and cakes. She mentally went through her recipes, trying to decide which ones were both healthy and affordable.

Maybe it was all meant to be. Mrs. Pritchard needed her puppy back, and Murphy had been ecstatic to be claimed. It hurt, but it was right, which meant the hurt would eventually go away.

She was so absorbed that she didn't notice someone standing beside her until a gray shadow fell over the page. She looked up with a smile, assuming it was the waitress.

Instead, she saw David. His windbreaker was turned up at the collar, and his hair was disheveled, as if he'd been out in the night wind a long time.

His expression was sober.

"We need to talk," he said.

Kitty wasn't sure what to think. "How did you find me here?"

"It wasn't the first place I looked," he said. "But I've seen you bring home takeout often enough to know it's a favorite of yours." He gestured to the empty side of the booth. "Do you mind if I sit down?"

She hesitated. She wasn't as upset as she had been when she first handed Murphy over to his owner, but still…for some reason she wasn't ready to be alone with David. She didn't want to talk about Murphy—that would just make her cry. And she didn't want to talk about the new job. If he disapproved of it, she would be angry and hurt.

She definitely didn't want to play any more of his "Three Questions" games. When he asked questions, she found herself giving far more revealing answers than she'd meant to.

Even when she kept her mouth shut, he seemed to know what she was thinking. It was as if he could slip into her mind and look around at his leisure. She wasn't used to that. She'd learned to protect herself quite well with most people, even her own mother. But this man threw her off. He had done so from the moment he'd come up to her on the beach.

She kept her hands on her brochure. "Can it wait until morning? I imagine we're both tired."

"No." The blunt answer surprised her. "No. We need to talk right now."

The egg salad suddenly felt heavy in her stomach. She'd never seen him this…cold. This must be what his version of anger looked like. More civilized than most…though equally wounding, she suspected.

But what choice did she have? She nodded and set down the brochure.

He ordered coffee from the curious waitress, then shrugged off his jacket and dumped it on the booth beside him.

"I was worried about you," he said bluntly. "It's been five hours since you left, obviously upset. When it got dark, and I couldn't get you on your cell, I didn't know whether I should start checking the hospitals."

She frowned. "That's ridiculous."

"Is it?" He leaned forward, unsmiling. "You're pregnant, and you've only recently stopped vomiting in every trashcan you pass. You were upset, trying to drive the streets of an unfamiliar city. The idea of some kind of mishap wasn't entirely far-fetched. It would have been more considerate to call, to let me know you were all right."

He was right, of course—it would have been polite to call. Or at least to be sure her phone was charged. She hadn't heard it ring. If he'd been calling, that must mean she'd let the battery die.

And yet the idea of having to check in rankled. When she agreed to live with him, had she given him power over her? Did she have to register her itinerary for every moment of every day?

"I'm sorry," she said, but she heard the grudging quality of the apology. "I'm accustomed to living on my own. I hadn't thought of our arrangement as—"

"The kind where people are thoughtful to each other?"

She flushed. "The kind where people have to account for their whereabouts every minute."

"It isn't." His words were clipped. "But we're going to have to come to some better arrangement. I know your independence is important to you. I've tried to respect that. I haven't pushed for any kind of commitment, not even a legal contract. But you're not the only one who…" He hesitated. "I just need to know that you're safe. I need to know that you…"

Somewhere during that speech, he'd picked up the paper napkin wrapped around the fork and knife, and he'd begun turning it end over end against the red-checked tablecloth, a sharp, edgy motion.

She watched a minute, mesmerized. Then she prompted him. "You need to know that I what?"

He looked up at her. His blue eyes were almost navy in the shadows of this back-corner booth. "I need to know that you aren't going to do anything stupid."

She felt herself recoil. "Stupid? Like what? You think I'm going to kill myself?"

"No." He almost smiled. "No. Of course not."

"Well, what, then? What stupid thing are you afraid I'm going to do?"

He set down the bundle of silverware and gave her a straight gaze. "You don't know?"

Her skin felt hot. "No. What?" She put her hand against her stomach. "No—I—you couldn't think... Look, if you honestly believe I would ever do something to hurt—"

"I don't think that." He shook his head firmly. "I may not know you well, but I know that's not a possibility."

"Well, then, what..."

But suddenly she knew.

"You thought I had run off?"

His face was stony. Unmoving. "I considered the possibility. I would have been a fool not to. You've just ditched your job without blinking. The dog is gone. What's left to hold you here?"

She considered whether she should explain about the new job, but decided not to. It all led back to Murphy, and she didn't want to talk about that. He'd figure it out soon enough, when he realized she was still working out her two weeks at the puppet store.

She also could have reminded him that *he* tied her here. He was her baby's father. But apparently he didn't consider that a big deal.

Besides, she was still angry. How could he have been so unfeeling? How could he have agreed to give Murphy away without even giving her a chance to say goodbye?

"And what if I had left town? Would that have been a bad thing? Tell the truth, David. In your heart of hearts, wouldn't you have been a little relieved not to have to worry about me, or the baby, or any of this anymore?"

Something very dark flickered in his eyes, and his fingers twitched on the tabletop.

"No," he said tightly, his jaw clenched. "No. I would not have been relieved."

For a minute the intense vibes rolling off him confused her. His famous control seemed about to slip. For the first time, she watched him struggle with his emotions.

And then, in a flash, Kitty understood. Under the wintry disapproval lay true fear. David had been afraid. He'd been terrified that she'd driven off into the darkness, into another state, another life, leaving no footprints for him to follow.

It shocked her to realize that the prospect had affected him deeply. The man across the booth from her wasn't cold—not even close. He was a boiling volcano of emotions covered over with a thin layer of ice.

What did that mean? Could it possibly mean he cared about her?

She felt strange, unsure what to say or feel. She could fight back against anger, scorn or bullying. But she didn't know how to handle this carefully camouflaged vulnerability. She might not even be reading him right.

She repressed the urge to put out her hand. "David," she said, her voice oddly meek. "I wouldn't do that. I'm not going to disappear on you."

"I hope not," he said. Ironically, his voice was matter-of-fact, as if to prove how wrong she was about his emotional state. "But today, when I was looking for you, I finally realized that I've been imprudent. We both have an investment in this child—emotional and biological. We both have rights. But you carry your rights around with you, inside your body. While mine…"

He drew a breath and narrowed his eyes. "Mine need protecting."

He tilted to the side and dug into the front pocket of his windbreaker. She knew how soft and deep those pockets were. For a minute her fingers curled into her palms, remembering.

He drew out a long, mustard-colored envelope and extended it across the table. "Colby drew these up last week, but I thought—I thought maybe we wouldn't need them. After today, I can see that we do."

Her mind told her hands to accept the envelope, but her hands weren't listening. They remained in her lap as she stared at the ugly yellow-brown paper, comprehension slowly dawning.

In her peripheral vision, the activity of the diner

continued, with customers holding up their hands for refills or checks, and the waitress scurrying about, trying to keep up.

But none of that seemed real. Only this piece of paper and the truth it told her about David's feelings seemed to exist in her world.

Her inner voice repeated her earlier naive thoughts back to her, snide and mocking. *Could he possibly have started to care?*

What an idiot she was! Would she never stop trying to clutch at any wisp of a fantasy that floated by?

He'd started to care, all right. But it wasn't the thought of losing her that had frightened him.

It was the thought of losing his child.

LATER THAT WEEK, in Lily Jensen's small office at The Three Swans, Kitty took a seat next to the beautiful walnut Queen Anne kneehole desk, and waited for Lily to speak.

Lily had given her a cup of tea with a cookie in the saucer when she first arrived, but Kitty had set it aside, too edgy to eat. She kept her hands braided tightly in her lap, so that she wouldn't wring them, or bite her nails, or do anything that looked weak or sophomoric. She felt foolish enough, just having asked this graceful older woman, one of the three owners of the co-op, to read through the contract David had given her.

But Lily, who had spent thirty years as an attorney for Legal Aid before retiring to paint gorgeous Victorian teacups, hadn't seemed a bit fazed by the story Kitty had told her. She'd simply nodded, as if no tale of the complicated relationships between men and women could surprise her, and asked if she could take the document home overnight to study it.

Kitty had agreed gratefully, without reservation. She'd worked at the co-op only a few days, but she had no secrets from anyone here. Before she'd accepted the job, she'd told Maeve about the baby—and at least the bare facts about living with David. It had seemed only fair, and, besides, she didn't feel like keeping up a facade of "normal."

She'd given Maeve permission to tell the others. So they all not only knew that Kitty was pregnant, but they also knew how strange the circumstances were. To her surprise, no one had even blinked, much less judged her. She'd long since stopped wearing the eyebrow ring, but no one mentioned her green hair, either, or even seemed to notice it.

The tightness inside her began to relax, and she realized she had already come to think of The Three Swans as a safe place. All shapes, sizes, colors and personalities coexisted comfortably here.

But now that she was in Lily's private office awaiting her verdict on the contract, she felt suddenly nervous and embarrassed. It wasn't, in the end, a flattering document. It was sordid to be in this position, pregnant by a stranger who obviously didn't trust her. A stranger who demanded a contract to spell out the things that should have been taken for granted between two people. Things like under which conditions they could have sex, and how far and long she could wander off without calling home.

Worst of all, Colby Malone, who had written the contract, wasn't exactly a member of Team Kitty, and she feared that his contempt could be read between almost every line.

She fought the urge to gabble questions at Lily, as the older woman gave the pages one last glance-through. She leaned against the back of her silk-covered chair and breathed evenly, trying to appear relaxed.

Finally Lily looked up, her silver reading glasses perched elegantly on the tip of her chiseled nose. She sighed, resting her pen against the paper. "Well, there are a few small details I'd suggest you change, but overall I wish I could have negotiated a contract like this for the young women I represented when I was practicing law."

Kitty frowned. "You do?"

"Absolutely." Lily lifted off her glasses, folded them neatly and slipped them into the case she kept on her desk. "This is a very thorough document. His lawyer isn't taking any chances. But it's also a very generous one."

"How so?"

Lily flipped through the pages, then tilted the paper toward Kitty. "Well, obviously he's very patient, particularly when it comes to the custody arrangements. Many men would require a custody commitment before offering anything. He seems willing to work that out later, after the baby is born, as long as you remain in San Francisco."

Yes. Kitty had noticed that.

"And here." Lily turned the page. "The amount he's offering as living expenses until the baby's born? That's maybe twice what's considered standard. Especially since you're living in his house, rent-free."

"But—" Kitty hardly knew how to express how uncomfortable David's generosity made her. She could work. She wanted to work. She had always intended to support herself. If she took this money…didn't it end up looking as if she'd come here just to extort money from him?

After the baby was born, it might be fair for David to contribute money. Diapers and food and maybe, since he seemed comfortably off, even half of a college trust fund.

All she'd been asking for right now was help making sure the baby got the best medical care, right from the womb. But, as David had said from the start, a demand that he share the medical expenses could easily have been accomplished by way of a registered letter, her lawyer to his.

Instead, she'd flown up here…for what, exactly? She felt like such a fool, having to admit that her plans had been so nebulous. In all this time, since the minute she realized she was pregnant, she'd never organized her needs and fears and demands as carefully as this contract did. She wanted her baby to be safe. She wanted good medical care. She wanted—

It made her stomach feel cold to admit it. But she was tired of lying to herself. She had wanted to see David again. She had wanted him to know she was carrying his child.

"I know how it looks," she said, shifting in her chair. She glanced through the small office window and saw that the store was beginning to fill with customers. She would have to clock in soon and start helping people find flower arrangements, knickknacks and earrings.

She turned back to Lily. "But it really isn't about the money. And, as you say, what he's offering is too much, given that he's made sure I don't really have any living expenses."

"Nonsense." Lily tapped the contract with her pen. "He has asked you to agree to remain in San Francisco until after the birth of the baby, at which time you'll negotiate the terms of the final custody arrangement. He and his lawyer understand that, under these circumstances, you must have independence. You have chosen, for the moment, to accept his offer to live in his house, but you must be in a position to choose otherwise whenever you wish. The provision is exactly as it should be."

"But now it looks as if I just wanted—"

"Kitty." Lily put out her hand and touched Kitty's hand. The other woman's fingers felt so warm, and Kitty suddenly realized her own skin was clammy. "Don't start buying into the ugly old notion that real women—loveable, *feminine* women—shouldn't think about money. And for heaven's sake don't fall into the trap that says women are somehow more responsible for an unplanned pregnancy than men. It took two of you to make this baby, and you have every right to expect him to participate in raising it."

Kitty smiled. These were things she'd said to herself back in the Bahamas, as she'd stared down at the pregnancy test and tried to keep from fainting. But the reality of David, and the complex emotions she felt when she was around him, had muddied everything up until she hardly knew what she thought.

"I know," she said. "I really do know."

"Good. But maybe what you don't quite understand is how incredibly lucky you are."

"Yes, you're right. I probably have lost sight of that." Kitty touched her stomach softly. "Sometimes I get all mixed up, and I focus on what could go wrong, instead of appreciating what's already gone right."

"Exactly." Lily's face was intensely feminine, under its cloud of silky silver hair, with a rosebud mouth and china-blue eyes. But her jaw was firm and square. "I wish you'd seen what I've seen. I wish you knew how many women in your situation can't even *find* the fathers. Or if they do find them, they're worthless. Less than worthless. I don't think you understand how rare it is to find a man who is willing, even eager, to accept his responsibilities. Not to mention *able*."

Kitty nodded. For a minute, she let herself imagine. What if David had been married, or a drug addict, a playboy, a bum? What if he'd offered her money to make the baby go away? What if she had carried the child of a man she couldn't respect or trust?

The vision was almost unbearable...bleak and hopeless.

She reached out for the contract. "You're right. Of course I'll sign it."

SATURDAY NIGHT. Exactly three weeks after Kitty had moved in, and she was as tense and insecure as she'd been the very first day.

Her interactions with David had been tense all week. She'd handed him Lily's list of changes to the contract that night, and by the next afternoon Colby Malone's office had called to say the revised copy was ready for her signature. She'd driven over, signed three copies and then gone home. A courier had come that evening, with David's copy, and he'd taken it into the library.

But they hadn't discussed it since. Once or twice, she'd wondered whether he might bring it up, but neither of them had seemed to know what to say.

Oddly, instead of making everything easier, it had thrown up a new wall between them. In a way, they'd gone back to square one. Now it was official, down in black and white. They weren't lovers, and they weren't parents. They were polite strangers, legally bound by their one, inescapable mistake.

It wasn't bad, exactly—David might be remote, but he was never anything less than courteous. She told herself she should welcome the clarity. But in spite of her better judgment, she missed the small steps they'd taken toward friendship. She missed working with him on the house. She missed his company in the kitchen.

Now, at seven o'clock on this Saturday night, they were on their way to a company Valentine's Day party at Diamante Pizza. In fact, they were late. But, even though the silence in the car was awkward, Kitty wished the drive could last forever.

Even better, she wished she could go back in time and withdraw her promise to attend at all. What had she been thinking? David had broached the subject more than a week ago, long before the whole mess with Murphy and the contract.

Besides, with a week to spare, the party had seemed safely…distant.

But now the night had arrived, and she was stuck. David had to be there, because he represented the

Malone brothers in some charitable fund they had set up for their drivers. But surely no one would care if he didn't bring a date.

She wouldn't know anyone in the room. Well, no one except Colby Malone, the snobby lawyer who thought she was a devil woman who had spawned a baby the way a fisherman would bait a hook—to help reel in a big one.

Oh, and of course Kitty would know Belle. The blonde princess David still pined for, even while he made babies and played house with another woman.

Great. This should be a barrel of laughs.

She should have pointed out that the contract hadn't stipulated that she had to attend social functions with the party of the second part.

But she wasn't that petty. She'd said she'd go, and she would keep that promise. When David brought the car to a stop, she sneaked a glance in the side mirror. Yep. She looked every bit as awful as she felt.

She had gone back and forth all week, toying with the idea of dyeing her hair back to its natural mousy brown. She was tired of the attitude implied by the green. In the end, though, she had decided to leave it as it was. The timing was too obvious. She didn't want anyone—especially David—to think she was desperate to fit in with his rich friends.

But now that she saw her Grinch-green Dr. Seuss curls springing out from every side of her head, she knew she'd made the wrong decision. She didn't look creative and interesting, or even tough and empowered. She looked like a dork.

"You look great," David said, suddenly opening her door and holding out her sweater.

She flushed, horrified that he had caught her checking. She got out, straightened her spine and smiled.

"Thanks," she said with all the casual indifference she could muster. She tossed the sweater over her arm. It was pink, about the color her cheeks must be. It had seemed a good Valentine's Day choice…but now she saw it would only make things worse.

Even from halfway down the block, music spilled out of the pizzeria doors, and Kitty could tell that the interior was bulging with people. As they moved across the sidewalk, two balloons, one pink and one red, escaped into the open and floated up into the deepening blue sky.

She tracked the flight, wishing she could slip free, too, and float away.

As if he sensed her anxiety, David took her hand. "They're a nice group," he said.

But before she could assure him she wasn't worried, a breezy, beautiful couple swept past them, apparently eager to reach the restaurant. The man smiled when he saw David and slapped him on the shoulder.

"Find me when we get inside," the man called back as his gorgeous date dragged him laughingly forward. "You've been dodging that rematch, and I'm going to take you this time if it kills me."

"It will, Red," David responded, chuckling easily. "It will."

And then there was no more time for jitters, because they were inside, and everything was laughter, smiles, hugs from people she didn't know and introductions she couldn't quite hear over the music.

David seemed to know everyone, and the atmosphere was relaxed and informal. The guests spanned all ages, sizes and income levels. Kids weaved in and out, giggling as they dodged between the grown-ups' legs. A few guests must have come straight from work—they still wore red, white and green uniforms embroidered with the Diamante diamond of a delivery driver.

Okay. Kitty took a breath. This wasn't going to be so bad. Diamante had spared no expense carrying out the Valentine's Day theme. While David chatted with friends, Kitty sipped from a tumbler of pink punch in which a pair of cherries floated and accepted a red carnation from a passing waiter wearing a headband of springy heart-ears.

David finally pried himself free from the others and brought her a piece of heart-shaped pizza. Though she'd thought she was too nervous to eat anything, the aroma was irresistible. She took one bite, and then another until the whole piece was gone.

David, who had already put away two pieces, licked his fingers and grinned. "Pretty good, huh?"

She nodded, then stood still as he took a napkin and wiped at her lower lip. "The purest olive oil this side of heaven," he said. "And honey. Those are the secret ingredients."

His hand lingered at the edge of her mouth. She parted her lips to speak, to say she was sorry she had been so stilted all week, sorry she'd refused to see reason about Murphy. Maybe she'd even tell him she planned to give up the green hair, first thing tomorrow.

But before she could say a word, a man on the other side of the room jumped up onto a platform that probably housed bands when they came to play, and began calling out for quiet.

Only the people nearest him seemed to hear, so he grabbed a knife and a goblet, then rang the crystal like a bell.

"Attention!" The man reached down and lifted a laughing Belle Malone up beside him. She fussed, pretending to be afraid, but anyone could see that she was as light as a feather in his hands.

So that was Matt Malone. Now that Kitty looked more carefully, she could see the resemblance to Colby. Both were tall, dark-haired, blue-eyed, handsome… but their kinship was even more than that. They both moved with rippling animal energy.

Belle smiled up at her husband with an adoring glow. Whatever petty trouble had come between them the other night, when she'd had dinner at David's house, was obviously ancient history.

Suddenly Kitty felt a little safer.

Until she glanced at David. As he watched the two on the stage, his face had gone dark, closing in on itself again. So…no reason to relax. Belle might be deeply, passionately in love with her charismatic husband, but that didn't mean David's feelings were dead.

Matt Malone had everyone's attention now. "Please gather round, ladies and gentlemen, because my beautiful bride has a few words she'd like to say to you!"

Applause went up for the "bride," who wore a darling pink dress trimmed with hearts all the way around the flattering princess neckline. Belle's public relations job must have given her an opportunity to make friends with the workers. They seemed delighted merely to glimpse her up there, smiling down at them.

"First, I want to thank everyone for coming," she said, blowing kisses at several of her most vocal admirers. "We thought Valentine's Day was the perfect time for our party, because we have the best employees in the world, and we absolutely love you guys!"

The cheering rose to the rafters until Kitty's ears hummed from the din. There was a little more sweet talk about how well the company was doing, and how the employees were responsible for every great thing that had happened since the invention of apple pie.

Belle was good. Not just beautiful and charming, but really, really good. Kitty was almost ashamed to admit what a pang it gave her to acknowledge it. But Belle Carson Malone was just one of those lucky people who did everything right.

And Kitty, who was eternally clumsy and uncertain, was jealous. No denying it. As green with envy as her own ridiculous hair.

She stole a glance at David. In spite of his earlier darkness, even he was smiling. That's how good Belle was.

And then Matt took over again.

"There's another reason we're glad you're here tonight," he said. He reached out and pulled Belle close to his side. She was so small, she fit like a fairy in his embrace. "Belle and I have some very exciting news to announce."

Kitty heard David inhale.

She felt something streak through her like an arrow of fire.

Oh. Please, no. The contrast would be unendurable.

She took a step backward, instinctively trying to avoid the blow she knew was coming. Ironically, David took an equally automatic step forward. Perhaps his subconscious believed he could intervene and stop the words from coming.

"I am the luckiest man in the entire world," Matt Malone was saying. His voice was suddenly ragged. "Because Belle and I…" He bent his lips to her hair. "Belle and I—"

Belle put her hand softly against her husband's cheek. Their love and joy were almost visible, tangible things, and everyone who saw it was transformed, at least for an instant.

Finally, Belle turned to her audience with a beatific smile and glistening eyes. "What Matt is trying to say is that we're going to have a baby!"

As if the word itself were magic, dozens of pink and white and red balloons fell from nets that swagged along the ceiling—nets Kitty hadn't even noticed until that very moment.

She couldn't help it. She tried to control her face, but she failed. She looked at David, who had turned to look at her. Even as the crowd surged past them, pressing toward the stage to offer their congratulations to the royal couple, their gazes held for a minute.

And in those few seconds, a thousand thoughts were exchanged. He knew. He knew how second-rate she felt. He knew that she ached for her baby, who would never be celebrated this way, who would never be wholeheartedly embraced as a perfect, joyous blessing.

And, on her end, she knew he was in pain. If he had clung to hope that Belle might someday come back to him, the arrival of these two babies, one wanted, one merely accepted and endured, sounded the death knell for that.

But there was nothing either of them could do to make it right. They were all trapped in their roles in this sad, ridiculous farce.

"Kitty," he began.

She shook her head, silently asking him not to say anything. He glanced at the stage, then back at Kitty, torn.

"Go," she mouthed, and then she turned around and made her way blindly to the ladies' room.

This just wasn't her night, though. On the way, she encountered a cluster of young men with expensive suits and arrogant faces, who watched her covertly as she passed. Her back tingled, with the uncomfortable awareness of their piercing stares.

And then, just as she opened the door to the bathroom, when they probably thought she was out of earshot, they began to speak.

She heard only one sentence. But it was enough.

"Yeah, poor Gerard—after Belle? He certainly traded down."

CHAPTER TWELVE

"David? Well? What do you think?"

Belatedly, David realized he hadn't been paying attention to the prospective client across the desk from him. He'd been like this all day, preoccupied, his mind full of personal things.

Like Kitty. And Belle. And what the devil his feelings really were for either of them.

Problem was, J. P. Borisse, the prospective client, was getting impatient.

"David?" Marta Digiorno, who sat next to Borisse, kept her voice more polite. She had brought Borisse here, hoping she could hand him off to David, and she was treading lightly, obviously afraid he might say no.

That was part of David's dilemma. He would have liked to oblige her. He and Marta hadn't seen each other much since the night Kitty arrived, just the occasional quick chat in the courthouse hallways or a wave at one of the downtown lunch spots. The date they'd been planning that night obviously hadn't ever happened, and now that everyone knew Kitty was carrying David's baby, Marta was too smart to hold out false hope.

She'd been calm and understanding. Their "relationship" hadn't ever gotten off the ground in the first place, so no real harm had been done. She'd been dating someone else within a week.

But they both knew that she'd been handed the wrong end of the stick that night, and he owed her one.

Taking this difficult client off her hands would be one way of settling the debt.

"Are you even listening to me, buddy?" Borisse ran his finger under the rim of his collar, rearranging the neck skin more comfortably. "I need to know if you think I can win these cases. If I can't, I want to settle."

The man, who owned an upscale department store, was being sued by two female employees. They contended he had terminated them because one was too old and the other too fat. He insisted he'd fired them for poor sales performance.

"But if I have to settle, I'll be damned if I'll give those banshees a cent more than I have to." Borisse leaned back and irritably tugged at his belt, trying to find another inch for his belly. "You should see them, Gerard. Damn weird women."

Borisse was the kind of client David had always disliked—complacent, demanding and convinced that they were the center of the known universe. If their cause was just, he tolerated them. They paid the bills so that he could also represent underdogs who couldn't afford good lawyers.

But this case stank. Marta or no Marta, no way was David going to touch it. The only issue here was whether he could find the patience to turn Borisse down diplomatically. He tried to think of some other attorney he might suggest, someone he could hand Borisse off to in this game of legal hot potato.

"Damn it, Gerard. Answer me. Can I win?"

"No," he said, choosing the direct route. "You can't win." He might have the time for tact, but he didn't have the focus.

"David!" Marta obviously hadn't expected the frontal attack.

Casting her an apologetic glance, David picked up the spreadsheet his paralegal Amanda had brought in five minutes ago. "I'm sorry. I know you don't want to hear this, but it's true. The problem is the numbers. They don't support your contention that the plaintiffs' sales were below par."

He ran his finger down the "old" plaintiff's figures. At the creaky age of forty-nine, she had still been outperforming the whole pack. "Ms. Colvin was your best saleswoman, and Terri Ammerman was right behind her."

"Ammerman!" Borisse grunted his disgust. "Have you seen her? She's one-eighty buck-naked, and blowing up like a balloon every day. Fat women can't sell expensive clothes. Ask anyone in retail. They'll tell you."

David held back a scowl. "And yet she does."

Marta sighed, settling back against her chair, evidently aware that she wasn't going to get any help from David. One side of her mouth went up, as if to say she couldn't really blame him.

But Borisse wasn't ready to give up the ghost. "Okay, fine. She sells well. Then find me something else I can use."

"There isn't anything else." David tossed the figures

onto his desk. "Well, there's one other course available to you, but you're not going to like it."

"I don't like any of this. What's your idea?"

"You could reinstate them."

Marta's eyebrows went up, but she didn't speak. She'd clearly decided to just sit back and enjoy the show.

Borisse, on the other hand, didn't get it. He laughed, obviously assuming David was joking.

It grated on David's last nerve, and he felt diplomacy flying out the window. He might regret this tomorrow, or next month, when his bankbook didn't balance. Today, though...

He glanced over at the bust of Thomas Jefferson for a little extra inspiration.

But the image that rose in his mind was, surprisingly, Kitty. She wouldn't let this blowhard intimidate her. She wouldn't dream of pretending that his attitude was okay. She'd probably haul off and punch him.

The thought made David smile.

"It's not such a crazy idea, really," he said. "You could accept that the women who work for you are human beings, not merchandise. They can eat too much or get older. They can even be, as you say, *weird*."

Marta closed her eyes helplessly and touched her fingers to her forehead. David thought it was possible she was holding back a laugh.

Borisse obviously didn't see a single damn funny thing about it. He scowled hard. "You're serious?"

David nodded. "Completely. In my opinion, you'll lose both suits. You haven't got a single detail to back up your claim that you fired these women for cause. They're going to take you to the cleaners."

Borisse stared into the middle distance, drumming his fingers on his armrests. For a minute, David thought he might actually be considering the idea.

But he should have known better.

After a short silence, the older man turned his focus back to David, and his gaze had become hard and shrewd.

"I hear you've got a new girlfriend," he said, as if starting a new, unrelated conversation. "Living with you, they say."

David wasn't surprised. San Francisco was a big city, but it still had an active rumor mill. "Yes."

He didn't say more. If Borisse had any sense, he'd let it go.

"Pretty, they say, but not quite as classy as your last gal. Belle Carson, right? We all thought you were going to marry her."

Marta quickly folded her files into her briefcase. "Mr. Borisse, maybe we should—"

Borisse held out a meaty hand. "In a minute. I'm trying to remember what I heard about the new girl... picked her up in the Bahamas, didn't you? And there was something..." He pretended to search his mind. "Oh, right. Green hair. Piercings, too. Regular counterculture queen."

He smiled. "Sounds as if she's a little...*weird* herself."

For just a split second, David saw red. He wasn't sure anything could satisfy him right now except the sight of Borisse flat on his ass...

It was only thanks to long years of practice that he clamped down on the surge of emotion. No, damn it. He wouldn't hit the guy. He wasn't worth it. There was always a better answer than violence, if you took a minute to find it.

In this case, it took only about five seconds.

Though his temples were pounding, David continued to smile. He gently pressed the speaker button on his desk phone.

"Amanda," he said in his smoothest faux-Pacific Heights tones. "Mr. Borisse is leaving. Ms. Digiorno may decide to stay." He flicked a glance toward Marta, who nodded. She clearly couldn't stomach this bastard any better than David could.

Borisse's fat face was red and splotchy. He started to sputter, but David didn't wait to hear it.

"And, Amanda," he added. "After you see Mr. Borisse out, please get Terri Ammerman and Carol Colvin on the phone. Tell them Marta and I would like to help them sue the jackass who fired them."

"THAT'LL BE two-ninety-eight-ten," Kitty said, passing the well-groomed customer her bag, which held a gorgeous handmade wreath from Maeve's booth. Maeve was one of the owners, one of the three "swans" who had opened the co-op ten years ago. Even after a full week of working here—and a decade of working retail—Kitty was still a little shocked by how much disposable income some people seemed to have.

The neighborhood of The Three Swans wasn't that glamorous, but the co-op had a reputation, apparently. It had started just as a way for women to help other women make money they could call their own. But the crafts were clever, beautiful and unique—and drew customers from all over San Francisco.

Maeve wandered to the counter after the customer left and gave Kitty a half-hidden thumbs-up. That wreath had been her most expensive. Maeve was almost seventy years old, but she still got as giddy as a kid when someone bought her creations.

Maeve hoisted herself up to sit on the edge of the counter, where she could comfortably pluck M&M's from the candy jar they left out for the customers. "So," she said around one of the chocolates, "how are you liking the job?"

"I love it," Kitty said. "The only hard part is stopping myself from spending all my pay on the merchandise."

Maeve laughed, recognizing the truth. Everyone adored Maeve's wreaths and flower arrangements, Lily's hand-painted teacups, Carla's earrings and necklaces of colored crystal beads. And those were just the owners. Kitty lusted after the clever crafts made by all twenty co-op members.

"Nope, can't let you do that." Maeve popped another M&M. "I remember all too well what it's like when there's a baby on the way. Never enough money to spare."

Kitty agreed ruefully.

It was easy to be honest with Maeve. Because of that, and so much more, the store had already become her comfort zone, an oasis where she could forget the stress of living with David.

Not that he wasn't kind to her. He was. Unfailingly—especially since the party at Diamante, and the announcement from Belle and Matt Malone.

He offered shoulder massages at night and surprise omelets in the morning. He got Bettina to stock all Kitty's favorite foods, and he added a CD player and television to her room. He had arranged for a long-term lease on her rental car, so that she'd find it easy to get around, then kept it filled with gas when he noticed it was running low. He asked her advice on colors for the outside trim, proclaiming himself hopeless at that kind of thing, though all evidence was to the contrary.

Once, he had even talked to her about the work he did for Diamante. He had been reading a few of the applications for need-based disbursements, and he'd been uncertain about whether to qualify one of the employees. There wasn't enough money to help everyone, unfortunately, and this case was right on the line.

She liked hearing him think it through out loud. As he spoke, she recognized true compassion, and she felt his distress at the thought of saying no to anyone. He wanted to make a donation himself, to help stretch the money just a little further. To her shock, he asked her what she thought…as if she actually had a say in what he did with his money.

She'd told him she thought he should make the donation. Of course.

But the nicer he was, the harder it got to keep her head on straight. It was far, far too easy to slip into a cozy domestic routine. Far, far too easy to forget that it wasn't really about her. It was about the baby. Once you weeded out all the legalese of that contract, you could see that it required him to treat her with kid gloves, giving her no cause to complain of anything that smacked of emotional or physical neglect.

"Hey, I think it's your lunch time." Maeve broke in to her thoughts with a smile. "I refuse to let you work through it again. Go outside, sit in the park. Soak up some sun. It's an order."

Kitty nodded. She reached for her purse, which she'd tucked under the desk. She accidentally grabbed just one strap, and as she hoisted it, the purse fell open onto the desktop, scattering odds and ends across the computer's keyboard.

Including her box of brown hair dye, which she'd picked up at the health food superstore on the way in to work this morning. She'd checked with Dr. Tapia's office, and they'd told her which natural brand was safe for the baby.

Maeve couldn't help seeing it, of course. But in her usual way, she just smiled easily, as if every woman in the store probably had a box of hair dye in her purse.

"Time for a change?" She held up the box. "Yes. It'll suit you, I think."

Kitty had thought she'd be embarrassed. In fact, pride was the main reason she hadn't already gotten rid of the green. She dreaded the questions, dreaded having to explain her decision to everyone she met.

But Maeve's easy acceptance erased any hint of awkwardness.

"Thanks," Kitty said. "It'll take some getting used to. I've had this green since I was a teenager."

Maeve laughed. "Oh, then it's *definitely* time for a change. Creative people have to grow. The outside needs to keep up with the inside."

And that was it in a nutshell. Her hair color wasn't a matter of conforming or not conforming with the outside world. It was a matter of making her external reality fit her internal truth.

And the truth was, in the past few years she *had* grown up...maybe not gracefully, and maybe not completely. But the green hair, which had once felt like a statement of independence and a thumb in the eye of all petty bourgeoisie hypocrisy, had clearly outlived its usefulness.

"Right." She wondered whether a week was too short an acquaintance to give Maeve a kiss, then decided she didn't care. She came around the counter and pressed her lips against her boss's softly wrinkled cheek. "Thanks, Maeve. See you in an hour."

It was a gorgeous afternoon, not too chilly, not too windy, and the park was full of families eager to enjoy the weather. The modest neighborhood was lovingly tended, clearly on the rise. The children playing on the sun-dappled equipment were rosy-cheeked, clean and well dressed.

She wasn't hungry, so she set her sandwich aside and watched for a while, trying to imagine the day when she might sit on one of those benches beside the monkey bars, chatting with the other parents. She imagined her own child running up on chubby legs, hands outstretched to show her a treasure—an acorn, a braided pine needle, a caterpillar on a leaf.

The image was fuzzy. And a little frightening.

In about five months, ready or not, she would be a mother. She didn't have a very good map to motherhood—

her own would have to serve more as an example of what not to do.

But she did still have something to navigate by. She had her father's voice in her heart.

Once, when she had complained to him about her mother, about how mean it was for Lucinda always to be going out, leaving her father behind while she went dancing, boating, playing tennis, he had shaken his head firmly.

"Your mother has a marvelous *élan vital,* Kitty. That means she has a powerful life force. You have inherited it from her. Now you just need to learn to use it with sensitivity and love."

At the time, she'd thought she understood. The way her mother used her energy was careless and dangerous. She wounded people, especially Kitty's father.

Kitty had hated the thought that she was like her mother in any way.

But now, sitting here in this park, Kitty realized that she'd oversimplified what her father had been saying. She'd heard what she wanted to hear. Perhaps her father's message had been more subtle, more complex. Yes, in some ways her mother's vitality had hurt him and had left him behind. In other ways, though, he had enjoyed it, had lived vicariously through her adventures and had been happy because she was happy.

Maybe that profound loyalty and selfless love had been his own *élan vital.* He might have been trying to tell her that if you had this energy, if you felt things deeply and longed for passion and joy, it didn't have to be a flaw.

You just had to find a way to channel it into something that mattered.

Maybe The Three Swans was Kitty's first step toward doing that. Tonight, she decided, she'd make a couple of cakes, and she'd bring them in tomorrow. Not for sale, not right at first. She'd just give them to Maeve and Lily and Carla and the others, and see what they thought.

One step at a time. And maybe, by the time the baby was born, she would be a mother worth having.

KITTY HAD officially signed on as Dr. Tapia's patient and had seen him at least a couple of times already, but today was the first time David had been allowed to tag along for a prenatal appointment. It wasn't as if Kitty had invited him of her own free will. Colby had been smart enough to stipulate in the contract that David should have an equal say in all medical decisions.

Still, miraculously, Kitty didn't seem resentful.

In fact, she seemed different in so many ways today. Of course, the biggest external change was her hair. When he first saw her coming down the stairs, with those soft brown curls bouncing around her shoulders, David had been so surprised he didn't quite know how to react. She looked wonderful, but, then, she had looked wonderful with green hair, too.

He didn't want to make too big a deal of it. So he'd just said, "You look nice," which was an understatement, but at least had the virtue of being true. It seemed to be the right note to hit, because she had smiled with genuine warmth, and what could have been an edgy morning got off to a good start.

They had chatted easily on the drive to the doctor's office. Just trivial things, like whether he preferred her apple strudel or her blueberry muffins. He loved them both—she was an amazing cook—but he chose the strudel because she really seemed to want a verdict.

Anything to keep her so relaxed and friendly. She had seemed satisfied with his answer, though she grinned and said, "Tomorrow I'll make you guys an almond swirl. Even Bettina will like that one."

They had both laughed, enjoying the thought of Bettina and her perpetual scowl.

Maybe, in their own stumbling way, they were making progress.

When they got into the examining room, though, and the nurse arranged Kitty on the table next to the ultrasound machine, David almost had second thoughts. The intimacy of the moment was overpowering.

A contract might be able to get him into this room, but it couldn't make him belong here.

Colby wasn't married, had never fathered a child, so he couldn't possibly know the intimidating reality of the clause he'd written. "Full responsibility for all prenatal expenses, and equal participation in all prenatal care and decisions."

Colby had no idea how awkward it would be to walk into this scenario, maybe a full partner on paper, but in real life a weird hybrid of DNA donor and interfering stranger.

David wasn't the typical father-to-be. There would be no kissing, nuzzling, whispering of private joy. He couldn't add to her comfort or hold her hand.

He'd researched pregnancy for hours, as if it were

a legal case he couldn't afford to lose. But now that he was here, he didn't even know where to stand or what questions to ask.

"Okay, let's get you ready."

As the nurse folded Kitty's blouse up over her belly, David's heart thumped in double time. Her naked skin was just as he remembered—creamy and pale, healthy and firm.

But her body was different.

Below the lift of her breasts, there was a new curve. Subtle, but definite. A small, rounded swell.

The swell that was their baby.

He stared. It seemed so soon. He hadn't understood, hadn't known…

She always wore loose tops or swingy dresses. He never touched her anywhere but on the arm, or maybe the back. She'd never stood so close to him that her body grazed his.

It was as if this physical change had been her most carefully guarded secret. And, with his lawyers and his contracts, he'd pushed his way into this room, forcing her to reveal it.

And yet, he couldn't take his gaze away.

"Sixteen weeks is a little early for any guarantees," the nurse said, smiling at David as she bustled about getting strange wands and gels and instruments prepared. "But if we can see the sex of the baby, do you want to know?"

"Yes," Kitty said. She didn't look at David. Her eyes were trained on the ultrasound, though naturally it showed nothing yet. "Yes, please."

The nurse was still looking at David, as if his vote counted. He nodded. "Yes, of course."

"Some people like to be surprised," she explained. "So, are you hoping for one or the other?"

The woman was obviously just making small-talk. Doing the warm-up routine before the doctor arrived. She couldn't know she was asking a question he couldn't answer.

"No," Kitty supplied for him. "No, it doesn't matter."

"As long as it's healthy," he said. And when he heard the nurse laugh he knew he'd just uttered one of the most pathetic clichés in the book.

But it was simply the raw truth. *Please, God, let the baby be healthy.* He suddenly wanted to kneel beside Kitty and put his hand on that small, vulnerable, swollen place. He wanted somehow to transmit his strength to the tiny heart that beat in there.

He didn't, of course. He didn't because he had no idea whether she would push his hands away.

For a miserable moment, he imagined this same scene playing out in Belle Carson's examination room. He imagined the laughter, the kisses, as her arrogant playboy husband gladly turned into a lapdog just for the chance to share this miracle with the woman he loved.

Once, David had felt that way about Belle, too. He had loved her. And until the other night, when she and Matt had announced their pregnancy, he hadn't been entirely sure he wouldn't love her forever.

Hopelessly, and from a distance, of course. But permanently.

That night, though, when he saw how happy she was, he had finally been able to let go of the dream. A bittersweet moment, but in the end he felt an odd sort of relief, as if he'd set down a heavy burden he'd carried so long he'd forgotten exactly what was in it.

And, best of all, it left him free to deal with the pregnant woman who *was* his responsibility.

What he felt for Kitty was different. He wasn't sure what to call it, even. It was about seventy percent lust, and the remaining thirty percent was a mixture of bewildered curiosity and protective tenderness.

The nurse tugged down Kitty's waistband, then tucked a towel around the edge to shield it from the goo. Now David could see the complete contours of the baby bump, and the sight made his mouth go dry.

Yes, his feelings for her were definitely different. But powerful, nonetheless.

"Hello, Kitty!" Dr. Tapia entered the room with a smile. He put his hand gently on Kitty's shoulder. "How are you feeling today?"

"Fine," she said with an answering smile. Obviously their relationship had warmed since the difficult CVS testing day.

The doctor turned to David, handling the moment with the aplomb that obviously had helped earn his reputation as one of the best ob-gyns in San Francisco. "And David. Good to see you."

They shook hands, and then Dr. Tapia settled himself on a little wheeled stool, and rolled it up to Kitty's side. "Anything going on?"

Kitty shook her head. "Nothing I'm worried about. I thought I might have felt the baby move the other day. But I guess it's too early, isn't it? I must have been imagining it."

"No, not at all." He laughed. "My skinny mothers are always the first to know. After the pros, of course. Once you've done this a few times, you know exactly what to watch for."

"Oh." Kitty's face glowed. "I'm glad." She put her palm over her stomach and shut her eyes briefly.

David would have liked a photograph of that split second, when every muscle in her body emanated a sheer, uncomplicated bliss.

After that, a tech came in, and they got down to business. The ultrasound machine was like a big, white rolling robot, but the pictures it offered were...

There was no word.

Right before his eyes, his baby formed on the screen. In a strangely beautiful approximation of amber marble, the features, the feet, the fingers, the little bowed head, all came into focus. The nurse was fussing with the buttons, and the tech was narrating, but David was absolutely speechless.

Kitty seemed similarly struck dumb. As the wand swept over her belly, she raised up on her elbows for a better look, her newly brown curls spilling down her back. Her eyes were wide and her lips parted, but she didn't utter a sound.

"He has my mother's nose," David said, the words startled out of him by the sudden recognition.

The tech laughed. *"He?"*

David shook his head. "I...I just meant..."

"That's all right," the tech said, still smiling. "We can't always tell at this stage, but I'd bet the bank on this one." He manipulated the wand a couple more times, as if double-checking. "Yep. No mistaking this guy. Congratulations, Mom and Dad. Your baby is a boy."

CHAPTER THIRTEEN

THE NEXT AFTERNOON, Kitty had just pulled a tray of Easter egg-shaped cookies out of the oven when her cell phone rang. She took a minute to inspect the cookies before answering. It was almost six weeks till Easter, but she had picked that holiday to open her booth at The Three Swans, and she and Bettina were trying recipes out.

Somewhere in the past couple of weeks, the housekeeper had abandoned her sullen hostility and inexplicably decided she liked Kitty. When she heard about the co-op booth, she had jumped on the idea, and now she was Kitty's biggest ally, joining the cooking experiments with her low-key version of excitement.

Kitty saw that the caller was her mother, and she almost let it go to voice mail. But her conscience won out in the end. She caught the call on the last ring.

"Oh, Kitty, I'm so glad you're there."

Lucinda sounded as if she'd been sobbing or had a horrible cold. She was congested, and her tone was patchy and uneven.

Kitty stifled a sigh, wedging the phone between her chin and shoulder so that she could take down the frosting bottles. She held them up for Bettina's approval.

The housekeeper scowled at the pink, but then nodded vigorously at the yellow and blue.

Kitty smiled and handed them over, then righted the telephone. "Is everything okay, Mom?"

Bettina shook her head ominously as she set out the offset pastry spatula Kitty had bought for this project. Kitty knew the negativity wasn't about the spatula. It was about Lucinda. All the disapproval Bettina had once exhibited toward Kitty she now directed at Kitty's mom. The three days Lucinda had stayed here, subtly complaining about the house and Bettina's meals, had sealed her fate.

Right now, listening to the tears that kept Lucinda from forming a coherent sentence, Kitty shared Bettina's annoyance. Her mother had been back home in Virginia less than two weeks. Could there possibly be a new emergency already?

"Mom, slow down. Start from the beginning."

"It's Jim." Her mother's voice broke on the name. "I had to tell you, honey. I wanted you to know he's gone."

Kitty froze in place. "Gone?"

Bettina looked up, her radar telling her something was amiss. She frowned and pointed the spatula at the phone. The overhead light flashed along the stainless steel blade, accentuating the impression that she would use it to run through anyone who bothered Kitty.

"Sorry," Kitty mouthed. She gestured that she'd go into the dining room. She probably would need privacy to deal with this. Her mother had started crying again, and her words were almost unintelligible.

Bettina nodded, then, growling under her breath,

returned to the cookies and began switching the tips on the frosting bottles. Resigned, Kitty wandered into the dining room. From here she could see the front yard. It had rained all morning, and now a low-hanging fog obscured the grass. She wondered whether that meant David and Colby would cut short their afternoon of sailing.

She hoped he wouldn't come home right now, not while her mother was staging one of her scenes. But, as always, the only way to end the scene was to let Lucinda play it out. She did love her drama.

Kitty forced herself to focus on her mother's voice, which thankfully was beginning to sound calmer.

"And I just don't know how to say I'm sorry, Kitty. I'm so sorry I didn't believe you all those years ago."

"Wait." Her fingers turning suddenly cold, Kitty plopped down onto one of the straight-backed chairs. "I couldn't hear all that, Mom. Are you saying you've called off the wedding because of *me?*"

Lucinda hiccupped softly. "Not you, honey. Him. I couldn't go through with it. He was so angry when we left San Francisco. He said things, such ugly things—"

Kitty could imagine. Jim had always said ugly things. But he used to be smart enough to say them only where Lucinda couldn't hear. If he'd let down his guard around Lucinda, he must have been rattled. Was it because of David? Jim wasn't accustomed to having another alpha male around to challenge his view of the universe.

"But then…he just kept at it. He couldn't let it go." Lucinda paused, as if reliving the moment. "That's when I knew something was wrong. I asked him, flat out, whether you'd been telling the truth back then."

"And?" Kitty put her hand, palm down, on the tablecloth and tried to remain calm. It wasn't likely that Jim had actually admitted it, not when he was so close to the ultimate goal.

"He denied it, of course." Her mother inhaled raggedly. "But I could see it on his face. The guilt. The—the lies. I don't know why I couldn't see it before. Maybe I know him better now, or maybe he isn't as good an actor as he used to be. But I knew."

For a long, numb moment, Kitty couldn't think of a single thing to say. She heard her mother sniffling, waiting for Kitty to speak, to jump in and….what?

Did she expect Kitty to commiserate with her for the loss of her dream wedding?

Or perhaps she thought Kitty might applaud her courage.

Did she expect Kitty to thank her?

Didn't Lucinda realize it was years and years too late for any of that?

Kitty watched the fog swirl through the banister of the porches, restless gray fingers probing the scrolled woodwork. The world looked like the fuzzy landscape of a dream, which fit this moment perfectly. Nothing she heard her mother say sounded real.

"Kitty?" Her mother's tremulous voice broke through the silence. "Honey, are you still there?"

"Yes, I'm here," Kitty said, hoping her voice didn't sound as cold as she felt. "I'm not sure what you expect me to say, Mom. If you want me to say I'm sorry about your wedding, I'm not. As far as I'm concerned, you've had a narrow escape."

"Yes, I know. You never wanted me to marry him. But still, it feels so… I don't really know—" She stopped, clearly fighting tears again. "I'm not like you, Kitty. I'm not very good at being alone."

Kitty almost laughed. "No one is, Mom, until they get some practice."

"But now we don't have to!" Her mother's voice brightened. "Don't you see? That's the one good thing about this. Your baby doesn't have to be born halfway across the country, in some ramshackle old house. Jim was the only thing that stood between us. Now that he's gone, you can come home again."

THE DAY HAD STARTED OUT cool and sunny, the perfect Saturday for boating. The Malones knew how to have fun, and they always mixed just enough business in with their pleasure to keep everyone from feeling guilty. Colby would wave his hand toward the sky, and laughingly say, "This is our out-boardroom." And sure enough, when they got back, they realized they'd accomplished more out there than they ever did at a desk.

David hadn't done much sailing before he met the Malones, but he'd developed a taste for it dangerously fast. He wondered if there was any point in buying a sailboat of his own, considering he had a baby on the way. You couldn't take an infant out into open water, could you?

He'd thought about asking Matt what he planned to do after he and Belle had their baby. But the green water, the blue sky and the streaky silver clouds were mesmerizing. Pretty soon, talking about anything halfway deep seemed like too much work. The Malones' twenty-six-foot MacGregor handled beautifully, and except for the rare occasions when Colby and Matt stirred to trim the sails, the four men had spent about three hours tacking lazily back and forth along the bay.

Even when the rain began, the Malone brothers weren't daunted. They had a stash of storm jackets below, and once everyone was covered up, they just kept sailing. It wasn't until the rain stopped and the fog slid in that Colby yawned and said they'd better call it a day.

By the time they got back to Angelina's house in Belvedere Cove, everyone was cold and wind-whipped, so it made sense to sit around in the boathouse, sipping a beer until their faces thawed out. And then, of course, they had to tramp up to the house to get some coffee and make sure everyone was fit to drive before Angelina would let them have their keys back.

Consequently, David got back home a lot later than he'd expected.

He pulled into the back slowly, careful not to plow over his landscaping now that the fog had erased the outline of the driveway. He killed the engine and got out of the car, the opening door creating a swirl of gray mist.

As he gathered up his wet things, he heard footsteps, and, looking over to the house, realized that Kitty was coming down the porch stairs. She wore casual clothes, just jeans and a T-shirt, but she had her purse over her shoulder. She must be planning to go out.

"Hey," he called with a smile. "If you have to go get something, how about if I drive you? The fog's getting thicker by the minute. But at least I'm used to it."

She had come close enough now for him to see her face. *Uh-oh.* Her cheeks had the scarlet stain that said she was upset about something. His mind scanned the possibilities. Her job? The baby? Bettina? He had thought Kitty and the housekeeper were getting along better these days, but…

"Thanks, but I need to get out by myself for a little while," she said, and her voice was tense, strung tightly in that way he'd come to recognize as trouble. "I won't be long."

"Why?"

She paused stiffly. "Why what?"

"Why do you need to be by yourself? What's happened?"

"Nothing," she said, then apparently realized how ridiculous—and rude—that sounded. "Nothing serious, I mean. I just got a call from my mother."

"Is she okay?"

"I guess so." Kitty ran her hand through her curls, wincing as her fingers caught on a tangle. "No, not really. Apparently, after all these years, she's decided that Jim is a bad guy, after all. She's kicked him out, and she's called off the wedding."

David frowned. "I must be missing something. Surely that's a good thing, right? Why does that make you need to take off, driving God knows where, alone in a pea soup fog?"

For a minute he thought she wasn't going to answer

him. Her gaze cut to her rental car, as if she were a trapped animal plotting a dash to her escape route.

God, Kitty, he wanted to say. *Why do you see me as your enemy?*

But, with effort, he managed to strike a more neutral note. "It's really not safe out there, unless you know what you're doing. Why would it be so bad to wait until the fog clears?"

"Because…" Kitty's register rose a note. "She's trying to lay a guilt trip on me about the whole thing. She's trying to make me feel responsible for the fact that she's lonely." She took a deep breath, and he knew they were coming to the crux of the matter. "She's trying to make me come home to have the baby."

If she'd slapped him, she couldn't have surprised him more. His jaw and his shoulders tightened instinctively, and his voice hardened. "So just tell her no."

"It's not that easy."

"Of course it is."

"No. It isn't. Look, I know you're trying to be helpful, maybe even trying to be protective, but I really need to be alone right now."

"Why?"

She made a small sound of frustration, as if he were being deliberately obtuse. "I need to think."

"Maybe you need to *talk.* To me."

"No. Later, maybe. Not yet." She tried to move around him. "Right now I need to be alone to think it through."

And suddenly, just like that, he was angry as hell. Thirty years of rigid control forgotten.

He reached out and took hold of her arm.

"God damn it, Kitty. Why? Why do you always take off whenever anything goes wrong? Why can't you ever talk to me? Just stop running for a minute, for God's sake, and let us see if we can work it out together."

"I can't—" She shook her head. "This isn't about us. It's about me and—"

"The hell it isn't. You're going to take insane risks, driving around in this godforsaken fog, to *think through* whether you should leave me and have our baby in another state? And you have the nerve to tell me that's not about us?"

She paled. But then she lifted her chin. "You need to let go of my arm," she said frigidly. "It's clearly stipulated in the contract, *your* contract, that any physical contact must be voluntary, initiated only after both parties have given verbal consent. If this, or any clause, is violated, the contract can be declared void."

He shook his head. "Damn it, Kitty, this isn't—"

"Yes, it is." Her cheeks were flaming red. "Did you think I'd sign it without even reading it, David? Without getting my own lawyer to explain the ramifications to me? I know your opinion of me is pretty low, but did you really think I was that stupid?"

No, he didn't think she was stupid. But there were times when she was so cold, so unwilling to let him in, so determined to push away any hope of intimacy, that he thought she was one damned unfeeling bitch.

He managed to stop himself from uttering that word, though he was knotted up inside, made half insane with a mixture of fury and fear. If she went out there…

If anything happened to the baby…

"I have never for one minute thought you were stupid, Kitty."

He let his hand drop, then forced himself to climb the porch stairs, putting some distance between them before he said something he could never unsay. When he was safely at the kitchen door, he turned back.

"But if you get in that car and go out in that fog today, I will *know* you are."

KITTY SAT in the car almost half an hour, fighting tears. She sat till it was dark, and the cold seeped into the little tin box, along with the fog. She sat until the lights blinked on in houses all up and down the block.

But as time passed, her head of steam fizzled out. Her thinking cleared, and she was left with only the misery of knowing she'd been an idiot. She'd said horrible things, and she wasn't sure she could ever make him understand.

She wasn't even sure she understood herself.

He'd been one hundred percent right about the weather, of course. It would be reckless for a newbie to cruise around, going nowhere but in pointless circles, on a day like this. She didn't even really want to be out there on those dense, eerie roads. She never would have considered it if she hadn't been so wrought up, so busy trying to prove she didn't need anyone, not for advice, not for comfort, not for anything.

She put her hands over her face. What was *wrong* with her?

She heard David's angry voice in her head again. "Why do you always take off whenever anything goes wrong?"

And there it was. The one question she couldn't answer. The one question that could change her life forever.

Why did she flee whenever he tried to get close? What was she so afraid of? Was this how she would live the rest of her life? Was she always going to assume that everyone would hurt her, just because her mother had?

She remembered an old adage her father had told her long ago. Something about a cat that learned the wrong lesson after sitting on a hot stove. The cat couldn't think it through. And so the cat never sat on any hot stove again. But it also never sat on a cold one.

Yes, her mother's call had hurt. It had, surprisingly, brought a resurgence of the old pain. Hearing her mother finally say, "I believe you"—well, it had brought the whole terrible experience back.

There had been a time when those words would have meant the world. Years after Kitty had consciously given up hope, she'd caught herself praying for them. Dreaming about hearing them.

And yet…coming eight years too late…they held no healing power now. All they could do was remind her how much pain her mother's betrayal had brought. All they could do was open the scars and let the wound bleed again.

It was like learning the bitter lesson all over again. Don't depend on anyone. Don't need anyone. Don't love anyone.

Not even David.

And yet.

God help her. She did. She did love him.

He was a very special man. An honorable, stoic man who was carefully bringing his battered old house back to life, plank by plank. A man who had, from the very start, tended her scrapes and touched her body with gentle fire. A protector and a gentleman.

The father of her child.

But those were just the logical things. Those were the character traits her brain had sense enough to value in a life partner. That was respect. Admiration. Esteem.

Love was not nearly as rational. It simply existed because her soul thrummed when he was around. Her heart sang, even when she was frightened or defensive or angry. Love was beyond the reach of common sense.

The realization sent chills through her body that had nothing to do with the weather. She curled her fingers into her palms to keep them from trembling. She had no idea what to do with this new and terrifying awareness.

She could run, of course. That old life path had deep grooves, and she could easily fall into them again.

Or she could stay and fight. Fight for the chance to have a real life. A real family. A real future.

The problem with staying to fight, though…

You couldn't fail at running.

But a fight was something you could lose.

She caught a glimpse of her pale face in the rearview mirror. She hardly recognized that lonely woman with bedraggled brown curls falling into her forehead.

Apparently it took more than a new hair color to make a person grow up.

It also took self-awareness, honesty and, most of all, the courage to take a leap of faith.

Kitty opened the car door and stepped out into the fog.

Time to see if she had any of those things.

CHAPTER FOURTEEN

DAVID WISHED he could light a fire to banish the pressing chill of the incoming fog. But unfortunately, the flue, which was ancient, had jammed and would need to be replaced. If he lit a fire now he'd probably set the whole house ablaze.

So he took a cup of coffee up to his room, pulled out some depositions he needed to review, got comfortable in one of the armchairs and tried to take his mind off the fight with Kitty.

It didn't work. He kept reading the same sentence over and over, until it looked like a string of Egyptian hieroglyphics. With a mutter of frustration, he dropped the files onto the floor by his feet.

He couldn't see a damn thing through these fog-blind windows, but he hadn't heard her car start. He was pretty sure she'd never left the driveway, thank God. She might be cold and damp and furious, but at least he didn't have to imagine her careening over a guardrail or crushed beneath the indifferent tires of a semi out on 101.

She might be too ticked off to come inside and get warm, but at least she was alive.

That meant he was free to use all his mental space to berate himself instead.

Why had he allowed himself to lose his temper like that? That wasn't the man he believed himself to be. David Gerard never raised his voice or let his fury get the better of him.

Except tonight.

And then, in an ultimate loss of control, he had actually grabbed her. He would never forget the look on her face when she realized he wouldn't let go of her arm. It had mirrored his own shock. He'd looked down at his iron-clamped fingers and wondered who they belonged to.

He'd been angry before. He'd been lied to by clients, frustrated by coworkers, deeply disappointed by the woman he loved.

Yet never once, in his entire life, had he ever touched a woman in anger. In his mind, that was the final boundary, the edge of the civilized world, and he had been only ten years old the day he vowed he would never cross it.

He never had. Until tonight.

He heard the back door open, then shut again. He heard her slow footsteps on the staircase.

He almost stood. He should go, stop her on the landing and apologize to her. But he stayed in his chair. He didn't trust himself, not yet. He still felt this edgy, unfamiliar hum of tension. He still felt as if all his nerves were held together with metal thread stretched so tight and thin it could snap at any second.

He tossed back the last of his black coffee and picked up the depositions. Tonight, he'd stick to work. He'd get a good night's sleep. And then, tomorrow, he'd pull himself together, and they'd find a way to start again.

Suddenly, someone rapped, gently on his door.

"David?" It was Kitty. Her voice was low and soft. "David, it's me. May I come in?"

He should have pretended to be asleep, but he didn't. Who had he been kidding? He didn't want to wait until tomorrow. He wanted to see her now. He wanted to tell her he was sorry, and be sure she would forgive him. He wanted to see if her arm was bruised where he'd held her.

He wanted to kiss the hurt away, from her arm, from her eyes, from her heart.

He was at the door in seconds. When he opened it, his heart twisted at the sight of her tired, ivory face. Dark circles smudged the delicate skin beneath her green eyes. Her shirt was damp from the clammy air, and for once he could see the swell of her stomach beneath the clinging cotton.

"Come in," he said, taking her hand and drawing her into the room. "You're half frozen."

Her gaze went to the coffee, the scattered papers in front of the chair. "You're working," she said. "I'm interrupting again."

"No. I've been sitting here trying to work, but instead I've been writing apologies in my head."

He ran his hand through his hair. "I'm sorry about what I said out there, Kitty. I shouldn't have lost my temper. I'm not sure why I did, but I promise you it won't happen again."

To his surprise, she shook her head vehemently. "Oh, no. No, please don't say that." Impulsively, she took a step closer. She put her hands on his chest. They were ice-cold. "Please don't go back to the old ways, David."

"The old ways?"

She looked anxious for a minute, as if she feared she couldn't find the right words. Or perhaps she simply feared she wouldn't have the nerve to say them.

"Don't go back into that shell, where you never show emotion at all. You're always so controlled. Nothing ever…it doesn't feel natural. It feels as if you're a million miles away. As if you're not emotionally involved with me—with any of this."

"Kitty, that's ridiculous. I—"

"Please. Let me try to say this while I still have the courage. I'm the one who should be apologizing. You were right to be angry with me tonight. I was being a bullheaded fool, and I—"

"No, you were upset. You needed to be alone, and I should have let you."

"I was being stubborn and childish. Running isn't the answer, not ever. It's my lifelong failing, and I know it. I'm impulsive and emotional, and I have a chip on my shoulder that always gets in my way. But you…"

She floundered again. "It's not that I liked the fact that you were angry. I didn't. I was hurt, and I was angry, too. But even so…I was glad. Because you finally seemed to feel something real toward me. Any emotion, anything real, is better than that…that blank wall that always shuts me out."

He didn't understand. "You think I'm shutting you out? But you're the one who—"

"I know," she said. "I lash out, and then I run. We're such a bad match, aren't we? Whenever things get difficult, you turn to steel and I run away. But you're right.

How will we ever find our way? How will we ever get to know each other if neither of us will take a chance?"

She looked so beautiful, her pale face so earnest, her chestnut curls so easy and natural, spiraling down to touch the tips of her breasts. Oh, he would take a chance right now, if only he had the right. He'd lay her down on his bed, and he'd show her that he wasn't made of steel.

He put his fingertips in his jeans pockets, to keep himself from reaching over to touch her. "I'm not trying to shut you out, Kitty. That's just who I am—with everyone. It's how I cope. I always keep my emotions under control."

"But why?" She wrinkled her brow. "I want to understand. But it's so different from the way I cope…"

He backed away a step or two, and leaned against the carved walnut foot post of his bed.

"It's a long story," he said. "And not a very pretty one. It's getting late. Maybe tomorrow."

She shook her head. "No. That's not fair. You owe me, remember? I never got my three questions."

He smiled. "I see. Caught in my own net."

"That's right." She came over and sat on the edge of his mattress, apparently unaware of how tempting she looked there. He had only to press her back and…

"So that's my first question," she said. "Why do you think you have to be controlled all the time?"

He wondered whether he could fob her off with some half-truth. But he remembered how honest she'd been with him, the night he'd asked his questions, and he knew he'd be ashamed to offer any less.

Still, it wasn't an easy topic to talk about. He didn't

want to sound bitter, or melodramatic. He tried to think of the simplest terms possible, ones that would eliminate any hint of hysteria.

"My father was a very violent man," he said. "I guess the bottom line is…I've always been afraid I might have inherited his temper."

Her eyebrows drew together in instinctive compassion, but she didn't speak. She waited, just as he had waited for her. Funny, he thought, how much harder it was to be the one on the hot seat.

"It's strange," he went on. "I've always wanted to reinvent my past. I didn't want this sordid violence to be my story. I don't want it to be any part of my son's heritage. I guess I thought that if I didn't talk about it, it might just disappear. But it doesn't work that way, does it?"

She shook her head soberly. "No," she said with feeling. "Unfortunately, it doesn't work that way."

He girded himself emotionally, then started at the beginning. "My father never married my mother, though they had two children. Me and my little brother, Ernie. He was two years younger than me. He died when he was seven, of pneumonia."

Just speaking Ernie's name, he felt the old ache, remembering his little brother's snub nose and silly red-gold eyebrows. Remembering how, the night after Ernie's funeral, David had lain in his bed, listening to his father beat his mother to make her stop crying.

"I'm sorry," Kitty whispered, looking up at him with eyes unnaturally bright. "That must have been almost unendurable."

"It was roughest on my mother," he said. "I was only

nine. I was really too young to understand how final it was. Or how unnecessary."

He stirred and cleared his throat. No more about Ernie. That was far enough down that particular dark and treacherous memory lane.

"Anyhow, my father was a brutal bastard, and I swore I'd never be anything like him."

Kitty was silent a moment, absorbing it. He wondered whether she might forfeit the other two questions. Surely, after an answer like that one, she wasn't eager to lift the rocks that covered any of his other secrets.

But he was wrong.

She looked up at him, a small line between her brows. "What about Murphy?"

"Murphy?" For a minute he didn't recognize the name.

She wrapped her palm around the bedpost, just inches from his elbow. "I mean…why wouldn't you ever love him, or even hold him? Bettina says you have never owned a pet. Was that your father's doing, too?"

God, he'd rather face a firing squad than these questions. He knew how his answers would make him look. Pathetic, stunted…fixated on the past. Damaged in spite of all his efforts to rebuild and repair. Forever weak at the broken places.

But it wasn't that simple. Learning from the past didn't make you weak. He wasn't broken. He was just careful. Forewarned and forearmed. Determined not to repeat the tragedies.

"Yes," he said, forcing himself to be honest. He couldn't help what she thought. The truth was the truth. "I suppose that's my father's doing, too. We had a puppy once, when I was maybe six. It wasn't quite housetrained yet and that infuriated my father. When he came to visit, he kicked the dog to teach it a lesson. It was just a little thing. He broke its neck."

Kitty's eyes blazed, hot coals of green fire in her pale face.

"I hate your father," she said.

He nodded with a half smile. "So did I. When I was nine, I decided I would kill him when I grew up. By the time I was ten, I decided he wasn't worth going to jail for. I vowed instead to change my stars and maybe even my DNA. I vowed to be a huge success, a paragon of serenity and benevolence, and nothing like him at all."

"That's when you decided to be a lawyer?"

He laughed. "No. I think I decided to be the King of Siam. But when I figured out the small issue of reality, I settled for the law. I thought maybe I could do something for the little guy."

Her hand shifted slightly, and he felt her fingers wrapping around his. He looked down, his skin tingling where she touched him.

She tilted her face up toward him, a half smile playing at her full lips. "I know what you're thinking."

"You do?"

"Yes. You think I'm going to feel sorry for you because you had such a crummy childhood."

He smiled, too. "But you're not?"

"Not one bit. Because that childhood, even the bad parts, made you who you are. It made you one of the strongest, most honorable people I know."

His throat tightened. He tried to loosen it with a

joke. "Yeah, well, I've met your family, so I'm not sure that's saying much."

She laughed softly, then nuzzled her fingers up between his, until they were palm to palm. She tugged softly, and he didn't hesitate. He left the footboard and moved to stand in front of her.

"David," she whispered. She reached up with her other hand, and pulled him to his knees.

He felt something twist inside him, and his heart pounded like a quick, secret drum message.

"You have one more question," he said. "Unless you've had all the Jerry Springer stories you need for one night."

She shook her head. "You know what my last question is," she said, still in a half whisper, as if she were afraid a loud noise would scare the moment away.

He held his body very still. He searched her face for clues, and found them. Her eyes were brilliant. Her lips were soft and parted, her breathing shallow. Her cheeks were flushed as her heartbeat pushed blood faster through her veins.

"I need you to say it," he said.

She leaned toward him, at the same time pulling him toward her. She captured his hands against her breast, and he could feel that skipping heartbeat against his knuckles. He tried not to groan, but every inch of him was pulsing and pushing, wanting more.

"David," she said, her lips so close he could smell the sweetness of her breath. "Do you want to make love to me?"

"Yes." He inhaled sharply. "Every time I see you."

She smiled. "Good answer," she whispered.

They both laughed softly. And when he kissed her, he felt the curve of her smile tremble, open and soften, her laughter dying away to a warm, dove-like murmur of joy.

He picked her up, and laid her carefully on the bed. He didn't turn off the lights. Darkness was too anonymous, too safe. He wanted to see everything, learn everything about her. He wanted to take all the hours and care he hadn't had time for in the Bahamas.

He knelt on the bed, too, between her legs. He held himself with the heels of his hands so that he could just look at her. Her brown curls spread out against his white pillows, and her eyes caught the overhead light, sparkling like emeralds.

She reached for his belt buckle, but he stopped her and coaxed her hands gently back to her sides.

"Me first," he said, and claimed her lips for another kiss.

When he released her, she nodded. She watched him as he undid her blouse slowly, taking another sweet-honey kiss for every button. It took forever, rocking back onto his knees, ducking his head down to her breasts, then rising up to drink from her lips. Every time he moved, he felt the fire between his legs, aching and burning and begging to be set free.

Soon, she was panting, and she was laughing, begging him to hurry, and he felt her wriggling beneath him. He reached under her, and cupped the silken curve of her buttocks, tilting her up to him. He rubbed his mouth against her jeans, sensing the heat beneath. She groaned and tugged at his hair.

"David, don't. If you don't hurry, I'll go mad."

"Good," he said. "You've already driven me insane. Now it's your turn."

But he released her, reluctantly, and turned his attention to her shirt again. When the last button was open, he peeled the shirt away. Her breasts were bare...and below them, the sweet, firm slope of her belly.

His breath stopped. He bent his head and kissed each breast until the tips pebbled under his tongue. She moaned softly, and ran her hands through his hair, touching his ears, his forehead, pulling him closer as if she couldn't get enough.

He took both hands and cupped his palms against her stomach. He stroked the satiny flesh, up and down, until he knew it with his own skin, until his hands had memorized every inch of this change in her.

He'd had other lovers, of course. But this was new—these feelings were new. He'd never wanted to touch a woman like this, endlessly, carefully, as if her body were a poem only his fingers could read. He didn't even think in terms like that...terms like honey and silk and poetry. What was happening to him?

It was as if she were changing the very way he saw his world.

And then, with her panting beneath him, he knew he was losing control. He dragged her jeans down, over one leg and then the other. She kicked to help free herself more quickly. He nipped at the absurdly sexy white panties, nearly undone by their elegant, see-through lace, which reached just barely to the bottom of the baby mound, but didn't try to cover it.

Oh...no...

For all his famous control, he wasn't going to make

it. He was going to climax right here, long before he entered her, spilling helplessly without a touch…just because she was so beautiful, so round and full with his child.

He clenched every muscle, but there was no hope. He had been wanting *her* for so long.

He was lost. Lost in the thrill of her. She was wet and sweet, and she smelled like flowers and lace and honey and heat.

He groaned, and she seemed to understand. She pulled him up onto his knees, until he was off center and had to grab the headboard with both hands just to keep from falling.

She folded herself forward, and, quickly opening his zipper, she tugged his jeans down an inch, and then another, just far enough to free the hard, thrusting heat of him.

Before he could protest, she'd taken him into her mouth and begun to suck gently. She wrapped her hands around his hips to hold him safely against her, and moved her lips over the rigid length of him.

He cried out, rocking into the dark rhythm. One, two, three…she owned him, she controlled the spasms and the heat, and he no longer had any power over what happened to him.

And then he came, with a cascade of shuddering fire. Still she wouldn't let him go.

When it was finally over, his head dropped between his arms, though somehow he kept hold of the headboard, so that he didn't collapse on his drained and trembling legs, and crush her.

When his heart calmed, he rolled to the side and

threw his arm over his head, to open up his panting lungs. He dug for breath, and tried to speak.

"That wasn't what I meant to happen," he said. "I wanted for this…for you—"

"Shhh." She smiled, her green eyes half shut and dreamy, like a kitten's. She laid her soft fingers on his chest. "This is just the beginning. We have all night for that."

CHAPTER FIFTEEN

KITTY WOKE VERY LATE. She could tell how late it was even before she opened her eyes, because the sun streamed so brightly through the windows that the insides of her eyelids were warm and golden.

Her first thought was a muddle of anxiety and confusion.

Where was she? What day was it? Was she late for work?

And then, when she felt the unaccustomed, lovely soreness between her legs, she remembered. She was in David's house, in David's bed. Just hours ago, she had been in David's arms.

They had become lovers last night. Lovers. At least, that was how it seemed to her. The experience in the Bahamas hadn't really been lovemaking. It had been—painkilling. They had been two shipwrecked people who found each other, lost and bleeding, on the beach. They had taken steps to make the misery go away.

But they hadn't made love.

Last night…last night was different.

She stretched, luxuriating in the feel of stubble-burned skin and kiss-swollen lips. She stretched out her hand and ran it over his side of the bed. The sheets were cool. He was gone—he probably had been at work for hours.

He must have gotten ready very quietly, so that he wouldn't wake her. He had worn her out last night, and he knew it. She smiled into her pillow, wondering whether the knowledge of his own prowess pleased him in that silly, macho-guy way.

He had every reason to be proud. It had been wonderful. He had been amazing. He had never seemed to give out. Even as she fell asleep, she'd felt his hard body pressing against her, ready to take her flying again, if she wanted it.

Her heart had wanted it—but her body was completely drained. She'd reached back and touched him with a sleepy regret. He'd hardened more, just at that simple contact, and she'd heard herself laughing softly as she drifted off.

And now she had come back to consciousness in a sun-dappled room, a man's room, with hints of David everywhere, in the smells, in the colors, in the patterns of light against the dark wood of his bed.

She stretched again and laughed out loud with delight.

This was what it felt like to wake up in love.

Finally, she forced herself to get up and shower. She checked his bedside clock—it was almost noon. She would have to face Bettina eventually. She wondered whether this new development would bring out one of the housekeeper's rare smiles—or one of her infamous frowns.

Not that it would matter. It would take more than a cranky Bettina to take the shine off Kitty's mood today.

When she was dressed, she loped down the stairs two at a time and went straight into the kitchen, suddenly ravenous. By now Bettina must know that Kitty's bed hadn't been slept in, so no use pretending this was just another day.

But Bettina wasn't there. The stove gleamed, pristine and freshly cleaned, which showed that breakfast had been put away long ago.

Kitty grabbed a banana and wandered a bit. She finally found the housekeeper in the garage, bent over the washing machine, hands deep in the suds, making sure the laundry was properly distributed.

Kitty smiled. Only Bettina, the perfectionist.

"Hey," Kitty said, waving. "Sorry to get up so late and miss breakfast." She felt herself flushing, her smile deepening, as if the very fact of missing breakfast proclaimed how she'd spent the night. "I was wondering— do you know whether David had lunch plans today?"

Bettina looked up. She was frowning, but that didn't mean anything, of course.

"Yes," she said. She scowled harder, then rushed into an unnatural flood of explanation. "I think he said he had a deposition that went straight through lunch. Very busy day. He said to tell you he'd be home late."

Kitty felt a low sinking in her midsection, a childish sense of disappointment. Late meant eight o'clock, maybe even nine. So many hours before she could see him again. Touch him again…

But she shook herself mentally. Had she really thought he'd be able to play hooky with her all day? How greedy was she? He'd given her the entire night.

She wished she was scheduled to work at The Three

Swans today. A long, busy shift with lots of demanding customers would make the time go faster. She wandered back into the house as disappointed as a teenager.

She caught a glimpse of herself in one of the shiny new mirrors. She frowned. Maybe she'd let herself go a little bit...maybe she should get a manicure. Some new clothes. Underclothes...

She brightened. Maybe she'd go shopping to pass the time, and surprise him when he got home. She hadn't bought a single maternity outfit, and her jeans had begun to pinch hard around the middle.

For the first time, she felt like flaunting her baby bump. She knew David found her new shape beautiful...sexy, even. She'd felt it in the reverent touch of his exploring fingers.

And that changed everything.

She chose a maternity boutique downtown, not far from David's office. She told herself it was because she'd heard some of women at The Three Swans raving about it. But who was she kidding? Deep inside, she just hoped she might find an excuse to stop by and see David. Maybe he'd call, to say hi, and she'd casually let it slip that she was nearby.

But she was too impatient to wait even for that. She phoned him, just as she drove past his office building.

She got Amanda.

"No, I'm sorry, Kitty. He's not here. He...um..." Amanda sounded odd. Distracted, maybe. "He's at the courthouse, I think. A trial. But I'll tell him you called."

Not a deposition, then, as Bettina had thought? Kitty had a momentary squiggle of anxiety. Why did everyone sound so strange when she asked about David? Was there something wrong? Something they thought she shouldn't know?

For a split second, she was reminded of the first day she came looking for him, and Bettina and Amanda had stood in her way like loyal, ferocious guard dogs.

Her cheeks burned with the memory. Was there any chance he was avoiding her? Was it possible he regretted last night already? Maybe she'd misunderstood—maybe he'd considered it just another one-night stand.

Maybe he was afraid she might read too much into it, and might become a clingy, mushy pain in the neck who wanted a kiss or a compliment every few hours.

The blood rushed suddenly to her feet, and she grew weirdly light-headed for a second. *Oh, my God.* That was exactly what she *had* become.

She parked the car in the first space she found, which was still a couple of blocks down the street from the boutique. Downtown parking, she'd learned, was like that.

She didn't get out right away, waiting for the dizziness to pass.

Nonsense, she scolded herself. This was ridiculous. This was that same demon of insecurity she'd been battling for years. She had no reason to think David was sorry about last night. He couldn't possibly have been faking all that passion. Nights like that might not be as unique and miraculous for him as they had been for her. But they couldn't be exactly common for anyone.

She was definitely imagining things. She banished

the thoughts with a shake of her head. She would not fall back into these old patterns. A new Kitty had been born last night, and she wouldn't let that brave woman disappear the minute she hit a bump in the road.

The boutique's windows were still decorated for Valentine's Day—a "baby love" theme carried out in all kinds of cute pink jumpers and white leggings patterned with red hearts. Most of the clothes were a little cutesy for Kitty's regular style, but maybe the new woman needed a new look. That red tunic was lovely. It would be perfect, in case she got invited to any more of those fancy Malone parties.

Still, she dawdled, studying the window, well aware that clothes this trendy came with crazy high price tags. Besides, most of the women going in and coming out were farther along than she was—their baby bumps were much more pronounced.

Maybe she should go home. Maybe she was jumping the gun a bit.

After dithering a couple more minutes, she had to laugh at herself. She was being a neurotic ninny. She really could make mountains out of the smallest molehills. She hoisted her purse higher on her shoulder and put her hand on the boutique door.

As she did, she glanced to her right. One of the majestic, old-time San Francisco hotels was on this block, just two doors down. And coming out of the revolving lobby doors was a handsome, laughing couple—a pair so strikingly attractive, with their glamorous blond good looks glowing in the sunlight, that no one could help noticing them.

Especially Kitty.

She stopped breathing.

She knew those happy people, who were walking briskly in her direction, their heads bent together intimately. Their bodies lined up so closely their shoulders touched and their fingers brushed as they swung along.

One of them was David.

And the other one was Belle.

For a fraction of a second, she was frozen in place. And then all the pieces came together. Bettina's rambling explanation of a deposition. Amanda's vague references to a trial.

None of that was true. Not even close. The loyal guard dogs in David's life had been covering for him because they knew he was in the one place Kitty must never, ever find him.

He was in a luxurious hotel with a married woman.

A married woman he had always loved.

She felt slightly sick.

What was she really seeing here? Had he been in a hotel? Or a hotel room?

In the nick of time, she snapped to. She yanked open the boutique door, sending a blast of potpourri-scented air billowing into the street. The chimes rang out, and she let the door fall shut behind her. She stepped to the side quickly, her heart pounding, just before David and Belle passed by, still engrossed in their conversation.

She saw her pale face reflected in the mirrored walls. Just a nondescript, hollow-eyed nobody. Thank

God she didn't have green hair anymore. It would have marked her as vividly as a neon sign.

"May I help you?"

The saleswoman was about nineteen years old, and her pencil-thin eyebrows were drawn together suspiciously. And why shouldn't she be concerned? Kitty had ducked into this store like a convict with the cops hard on his heels.

Kitty frowned. Something about the simile bothered her.

Like a *convict?*

Yes, that was the problem. She was acting exactly like a criminal. Like someone who had done something wrong.

But she hadn't. She hadn't done a damn thing she should be ashamed of.

Okay, she'd fallen in love with a man who couldn't be trusted. A man who didn't love her. She'd made love to him all night long, and foolishly believed the magic would last even when the sun rose.

But stupidity wasn't a crime. A million women the world over were probably waking up to the same broken dreams.

She didn't have any reason to hide. And by God she wasn't going to.

"Miss?" The saleswoman came closer. "Is there something I can show you?"

Kitty stepped out of the corner, chin up.

"Yes," she said. "I'm here to buy your most expensive maternity dress."

"I'm not sure I understand." The young woman's eyebrows shot up. "The most...*expensive?*"

"Yes." Kitty smiled tightly. She watched through the window as David helped Belle into her car. "Oh, and, if you've got one, I'd also like to purchase a good strong backbone."

AMANDA, DAVID'S PARALEGAL, was a sweetheart, a simple Midwestern schoolteacher's daughter, born honest and kind. Every time Kitty saw her, she was wearing a yellow ribbon in her hair and a wide brown innocence in her eyes. She was also, Kitty had learned, exceedingly smart about numbers and details and forms.

But apparently she was not great at reading body language.

When Kitty appeared in the anteroom of David's elegant office, girded in her new bronze-colored designer maternity dress and her new bronze-plated spine, Amanda looked up with a welcoming smile.

"Hi, Kitty! Great timing! He just got back. He's got a client coming in about ten minutes, but I know he'll be glad to see you." Amanda let her hand hover over the telephone. "Shall I let him know?"

Kitty nodded grimly. "Yes, by all means. Warn him I'm here."

Amanda frowned for a second, but then apparently decided to take it as a joke. She picked up the intercom and put a chirp in her voice. "Kitty's here. I told her you have a client in a few minutes."

The adjoining door opened, and David appeared, looking fantastic in his medium blue suit and maroon tie. He'd combed his hair since walking through the gusty San Francisco wind.

He looked so fabulous Kitty felt a kick in her gut—

almost as if she hadn't seen him in a month, instead of less than half an hour. He was smiling, just as warmly as he'd been smiling twenty minutes ago, when leaving his tryst with Belle.

But he was more intuitive than Amanda, and he seemed to sense immediately that Kitty hadn't come merely for the joy of seeing his handsome face. Though he continued to smile, his expression turned wary.

"Is everything all right?"

"No." She couldn't seem to put any inflection into her voice. It was all one dead and dull note. "No, actually, I don't think it is."

He took an anxious step forward. "Is it the baby?"

"No. The baby's fine. The problem is with us."

She glanced at Amanda, who had finally caught on and was staring hard at her computer, pretending to be deaf. Kitty would just as soon have this out in front of the whole world, on stage at Carnegie Hall, if necessary. But this was David's place of business, and though she was hurt, embarrassing him wouldn't make it better.

He let his gaze flick over her, putting the details together. In half a second, she could tell he understood just how serious this moment might be.

"Let's talk in here," he said, putting out a hand, as if to guide her into the office. Avoiding his touch, she walked ahead of him with all the dignity she could manage. Out of the corner of her eye she saw him make some kind of sign to Amanda.

Hormonal girlfriend alert, it might have said. *Hold the calls.*

Or maybe... *If I'm not out in five minutes, buzz through and say I'm needed urgently on the moon.*

He shut the door with a restrained click. Kitty had already made her way to the window, and was staring down at the miniature dollhouse world below. From up here, you'd never know that half of those brisk and purposeful people probably walked around with broken hearts.

"Kitty, what's wrong? I was sorry to have to leave this morning without saying goodbye, but you clearly needed your sleep. I asked Betty to tell you I'd had to come in early and might be home late." He hesitated. "It's been a busy day, but I was just about to call you."

She turned at that, laughing without mirth. "You think *that's* why I'm upset? You think I'm pouting because you were gone when I woke up, and you didn't send flowers by noon?"

He frowned. "I don't know what it is. All I know is that the woman who was in my bed last night is gone. And in her place is a stranger whose very angry face says she hates me."

She tightened her jaw. "And you have no idea what might have caused that transformation?"

"I've been at work, so no. I have no idea what's happened." His voice had taken on an impatient edge, and he folded his arms in front of his chest. "Since you're here, I assume you want to tell me."

To her dismay, she felt tears pricking at the back of her eyes, and the overhead fixture grew fuzzy in a halo of rainbows. She was afraid that if she spoke Belle's name, her voice might break, so she stalled. "I think you already know."

He made an annoyed gesture toward the mantel clock. "Kitty, I have five minutes before my next client arrives. If you want to play this out as a guessing game, you'll have to wait until I get home tonight."

The dismissive tone stung, and it helped her find her voice.

"But you'll be home late, remember? And why is that? Is it the deposition Bettina told me about? Or the trial Amanda insisted kept you busy?" She inhaled a steadying breath. "Or is it that you need to see Belle again? Your lunch tryst wasn't enough?"

His studiously blank face said it all. The total lack of expression was the last ploy of a poker player with a hopeless hand.

He knew what had happened, and he knew there was no way to deny it. He leaned back on the edge of his desk, resting the heels of his hands behind him on the glossy mahogany surface.

"Ahhh." His frown deepened. "I take it you saw us at the hotel?"

"Yes. I wasn't spying on you. I went out shopping. To buy some maternity clothes. It was pure dumb luck. The boutique is only two doors down from the hotel. It was hard to miss the two of you as you came out." She swallowed. "I wish I had."

"We didn't see you."

"Obviously."

He studied her a moment, as if trying to identify all the elements of the emotions that were storming through her right now.

"So all this anger...it's because I was with Belle?"

"Yes. And don't say it like that, as if I'm crazy. It's

not just because you were with another woman. I'm angry because just a few hours after—after being with me, you were with your former fiancée. A married woman, by the way. The woman Bettina told me from the start was the only woman you'd ever really love."

He tilted his head. "Let me get this straight. You think I'm committing adultery with the wife of one of my best friends?"

She flushed. She'd tried not to believe it could have gone that far. Surely…surely the relationship with Belle was just an emotional bond, a connection he couldn't quite give up. After all, Belle was pregnant, and she seemed to be in love with her husband—when she wasn't mad at him.

But Kitty knew lots of married women who kept former lovers on the hook. The pining exes made lovely ego boosts. It was probably comforting to know they hovered faithfully nearby, a safe haven for when married life hit its inevitable rocky spots.

And if, during one of those rocky moments, the emotional affair suddenly became a physical one, as well…

Well, Kitty had no intention of waiting around for that.

She set her jaw. "I don't know if it's a full-fledged affair, but I know you're meeting her at hotels, while everyone does a smoke-and-mirrors dance to keep me from finding out. That's enough to look pretty darned suspicious to me."

He looked thoughtful, which somehow just made her angrier than ever. It wasn't natural. Why wasn't he more ashamed? Why wasn't he backpedaling madly, trying to convince her she hadn't seen what she saw?

She suddenly realized she'd been secretly hoping he'd try something. Anything. Sweet talk, counterarguments, indignation. A lie. Yes. Why didn't he come up with a brilliant lie that she could believe, a lie that would make all this disappointment and pain stop?

He'd convinced her that he hadn't slept with Jill, that night in the Bahamas. Now she wondered whether that had been a lie, too.

How had she ever believed that a man as desirable, as smart and sexy and successful as David Gerard, could ever be satisfied with mixed-up little Kitty Hemmings?

And yet she had believed it, and a part of her wanted desperately to go back to believing it. She had a crazy impulse to go over to him and beat her fists against his chest—to force him to stop her by folding her into his arms while he explained it all away.

"Kitty, we probably should talk about this at home tonight. I promise you, it's not what you think."

"I don't care what it is," she said fiercely. "I just want it to stop."

"You want what to stop?"

"Belle. I mean, you and Belle. I don't want you to see her again."

She knew she was contradicting her own thoughts, doing an emotional about-face in that illogical, hormonal way that had become a habit since she got pregnant. Or since she met David…she wasn't sure which.

But she couldn't help herself. He turned her upside down and inside out.

His eyes widened. "You want me to stop seeing Belle completely?"

"Yes. At least if you want me to stay in your house and in your bed. In fact, maybe we should get Colby to rewrite that contract to exclude any contact with Belle Malone."

"Kitty, that's irrational, and you know it."

"Maybe. But I won't be the spare female you have sex with at home because the woman you really want isn't available. I won't sit around every day, wondering whether you're sneaking out to see her. I won't live in fear that someday she'll want you back."

She wondered if he was even listening. He couldn't be…not and look so calm.

But then she remembered. Of course he could. Showing no emotion was his specialty.

"Don't do that," she said impulsively, her voice heated. "Don't retreat behind that wall. I thought we had finally moved beyond that. I thought maybe we could actually communicate. Be honest with me. I'm trying to be. When I saw you with her…"

She shook her head, as if she could shake away the memory, and the lance of pain that came with it. "I could have just run away right then—and believe me, I considered it. I just wanted to get out of there. I even considered taking my mother's offer to go home."

"No," he interjected quickly. "You know running away isn't the answer."

"Yes, I do know that. I said I *wanted* to run, but I didn't. I can't compete with Belle. She's accomplished and educated…and so blissfully normal. She's all the things you would naturally want in a wife. I've spent a lifetime avoiding that kind of normal. And yet—"

She squared her shoulders. Saying this was going to be the hardest thing she ever did. It would leave her defenseless in front of a man who had already hurt her badly.

"And yet, in spite of all the obvious ways I'm the wrong woman for you, and you're the wrong man for me, I've fallen in love with you. That would have scared the hell out of me in the best of times. But loving you, while you love her—I can't do that. It just hurts too much."

She took a breath. "If you can't give her up, David, I'll have to go."

Throughout the whole incoherent speech, he'd said nothing. His clear blue gaze rested lightly on her face. When she stopped, he opened his mouth to speak, but at that moment they both heard the outside door open.

Two seconds later, Amanda buzzed the intercom.

"Terri Ammerman is here, David. And Marta Digiorno. For their three o'clock?"

He reached back without even looking and punched the correct button. "Thanks, Amanda," he said smoothly. "Tell them I'll be right out."

He had never taken his gaze from Kitty. With the overhead light shining on his gold-and-bronze hair, and his unruffled, even features, he looked as glossy and perfect as a picture in a magazine.

Powerful, conservative, confident, controlled. Athletic, upwardly mobile, a social lion in the making. If she'd made a handwritten list of all the things she didn't want in a man, David Gerard would possess every one.

And yet, this was the man she loved. The man she could hardly imagine life without.

"I won't work late tonight," he said. "I'll cancel things here, and I'll be home by eight. I just need you to—just stay, okay? Just promise me you won't run away before then."

The voices in the outer room were muted, but Kitty could hear every word Amanda and the client spoke. Amanda was being nervously charming, and the client was assuring her she didn't need coffee.

No doubt Kitty and David could be heard, equally well, on the other side of that door. So she swallowed the acidic frustration that rose in her throat and lowered her voice.

"Eight o'clock," she repeated. "No later than that?"

"No later than that."

And, with that, the conversation was over.

Suddenly her adrenaline wore off, and every muscle in her body ached. Though she had foolishly believed they could work this out right here, right now, she saw that she was going to have to be patient.

Some detached, objective piece of her mind even understood why he wanted to buy time. Belle had been important in his life a lot longer than Kitty had. Of course, a personality as controlled and deliberate as his would need to think it over. To decide whether he wanted the crazy bartender enough to give up everything else.

Maybe he even wanted to talk to Belle. To see whether he had any hope of getting her back for more than a stolen hour now and then.

Weighing his options, like a good lawyer.

The baby would undoubtedly weigh heavily in Kitty's favor. He wanted his child. There was even a good chance he might want the baby even more than he wanted Belle.

But that hurt, too. Maybe Kitty was being unrealistic, or even greedy. But she desperately didn't want his decision to be based only on the baby.

It was out of her control now, though. All she could do was wait.

Not, unfortunately, her strong suit.

She put her hand on the doorknob.

"I'll wait," she said. "But not forever. If you come home late—if you decide to go somewhere else first—I can't promise I'll still be there."

CHAPTER SIXTEEN

KITTY WENT to four more maternity stores, just to kill time, though she bought nothing. She dropped by The Three Swans, and worked a couple of hours free. She camped in a booth at the diner and called her mother, though that meant listening to half an hour of weepy recriminations against Oliphant.

She even scanned the rental ads, looking at apartments. She found one inexpensive efficiency that sounded possible, and she drove to Mission Hills to check it out. She hated it.

She went everywhere but home.

She couldn't. She just couldn't sit there, wandering through those lovely, unfinished rooms, waiting for David to come back with his answer. She wondered if this was how he felt when he waited for a jury to return with a verdict.

Restless. Impotent. Scared as hell.

And yet, somehow, she didn't run. She told herself that was growth. But it didn't feel like much.

Finally, at five minutes to eight, she pulled her car around the shadowy side of the house and up the back drive. To her surprise, David's car was already there, its sleek black curves shining under the porch light.

She wondered how long he'd been home.

As she climbed the porch steps, she clenched her keys so tightly they grew hot in her palm. The workers had attached the freshly restored and repainted gingerbread on this part of the house today. Though the work had been done offsite, at David's insistence, she could still catch a faint whiff of the clean scent of new paint.

Zero Volatile Organic Compound paint, of course. David's first priority was always the safety of the baby.

She thought of her mother's subtly disapproving glance at the mottled, dingy walls of the foyer. That was the kind of judgmental snobbery Kitty despised. It hadn't occurred to Lucinda that David refused to paint any interior rooms, even with zero VOC paint, until after the baby was born.

No one in his right mind could think David didn't care about order and grace in his home. In the past few weeks, they'd spent hours poring over paint chips, looking for great combinations. At first she'd just thought it was neutral territory, a topic they could talk about that wasn't awkward or personal. But gradually, she'd come to care as deeply about the restoration as he did. She had endlessly researched old Victorian interiors online, so that they could be sure to remain authentic.

She had a feeling he'd want to hold off on the painting, though, even after the baby's birth—maybe as much as a year, he'd said once. He'd been looking into things like that. No need to take chances with an infant's fragile developing brain.

She wondered if she and the baby would still be here when the house finally bloomed with color.

The idea of leaving this house was like a knife. How

could she live anywhere else now? Every other scenario she could imagine, even the long-pined-for Lochaven, felt strangely dreary.

David's home had become her home. His dreams had become her dreams. And, with a pang, she realized just how much she'd begun to rely on the safety net of his quiet, careful protection.

The kitchen was dark, except for the light that always burned over the stove. The rest of the house seemed unnaturally quiet, too.

How angry would he be, she wondered? She hadn't exactly sugarcoated her words. Anyone would bristle at being issued such a bitter ultimatum. She tried to remember how exactly she'd put it. Had it sounded horribly bitchy? Pushy? Jealous?

Of course it had. She'd been hurt and upset. And she wasn't controlled, like David. She didn't know how to stay cool and diplomatic on the outside, when she was bleeding and frightened on the inside.

He must be upstairs. But when she passed his landing, his door was firmly shut. She paused there. She thought about knocking, but decided against it. It was his move now. When he was ready to talk, he would know how to find her.

She wanted to get out of this foolish bronze dress anyhow. This frothy haute couture confection belonged to the pampered Belles of the world. Not Kitty. She wanted to get back into her old, baggy sweatpants and a simple T-shirt, and stop trying to pretend to be someone she wasn't.

She changed, then plopped down onto the seat of the little vanity table between the two center windows.

The brown-haired woman who looked back at her was still a bit of a shock. This person looked prettier than the green-headed, metal studded troublemaker she used to see. But the new woman also looked younger, softer and much more vulnerable.

She looked like a woman whose heart could be snapped like a twig.

She stared, her chin in her hand, and eventually she lost track of time. It might have been a few minutes, or just a few seconds later, when she heard David's quiet rap on her door.

Her heart jumped into her throat, and she glanced out at the night sky, which was a clear, glassy black, studded with stars.

She had a crazy thought that perhaps, if she wished hard enough, she could freeze time right now, this very second. It would be better to sit here, endlessly staring at her own wide-eyed reflection, and let him remain like a statue outside her door, one hand raised, than let them both be propelled into a future that might change everything.

But outside her windows the night wind continued to comb through the tree limbs, shivering the leaves so that they made the stars behind them appear to wink and flicker.

The world didn't care what she wanted. The world moved on.

She glanced once more at the pale woman in the mirror. Then she crossed the room, inhaled deeply, and opened the door.

For a minute, she couldn't speak. She simply couldn't make anything at all come out of her mouth.

Standing in her doorway, with raised eyebrows and a roguish smile on his face, stood the sexiest…goofiest man she'd ever seen. It was David. But he had shockingly blue hair, the color of a puppet she'd seen once on Sesame Street. He wore a track suit that must have come from some Valentine's Day bargain bin, because it was bright red with a heart on the pocket that proclaimed him the World's Best Daddy.

And, as if that weren't enough, he wore a cluster of diamonds in his left earlobe.

She opened her mouth, but only air came out.

"So here's the thing," he said casually, leaning one shoulder against the door jamb, as if he'd just stopped by to say howdy. "I was listening to you today when you came to the office. I was listening very carefully, in fact, though I could tell you thought I wasn't."

"I—" She still couldn't find any words. "I—"

"No, don't bother denying it. You have a really bad poker face." He chuckled. "Anyhow, you weren't making a lot of sense, as you have probably figured out by now."

She frowned.

That made him chuckle. "Now don't go getting all prickly until you hear me out. Anyhow, because what you were saying wasn't making any sense, I started listening to what you weren't saying. I started trying to read between the lines. And what I decided you were really saying is that you think I'm too uptight, stuffy, boring and conventional for someone like you."

She made a small, startled sound. "I never said anything of the—"

He put out one finger and pressed it gently against

her lips. His fingernails were painted as blue as his hair. It was so inexplicably sexy to think of those fingers against her skin that her heart did a swooping dive in her chest.

"Sure you did. You said, 'I've spent a lifetime avoiding that kind of normal.' Your words exactly."

"But I meant—"

"So anyhow," he went on conversationally, as if she hadn't interrupted. "I decided that I was going to have to take some drastic measures if I didn't want to lose you."

He stepped slowly into the room. She backed up, hypnotized by the blue hair, the twinkle of starlight at his ear.

"And I don't," he said.

"Don't what?"

"I don't want to lose you."

He kept approaching, steadily, and she kept retreating blindly. She stopped only when her legs hit the foot of the bed.

Her mouth was dry. She licked her lips, realizing she'd let them fall open. "Why?"

He smiled. "Is that a real question?"

"I mean…is it because of the baby?"

"Yes." He touched her face again, chuckling softly as though the idea amused him. "Of course it's because of the baby. But the baby exists in the first place because of the way I feel about you. Because of the way I've felt about you from the moment we met."

"But you see…" She knew she was being pushy, forcing him to spell it out. And maybe she was being stupid, but she desperately needed something to hang on to. She wanted—oh, how she wanted—to believe that when he said "the way I've felt about you" he meant *love.*

But doubt had become second nature to her. It was so powerful it almost drowned out the sound of his words.

"That's the problem," she said. "I *don't* really know what you feel. I don't know why you want me."

"I don't just want you. I *need* you." He smiled. "I need your crazy moods and your fire. I need your honesty and your courage. I need you to tell me when I'm full of crap. I need you to yell at me, and make me laugh, and teach me to understand my own feelings."

"You don't need me for any of that. I'm just a gypsy, David. I'm…I'm what your friends call 'trading down.' I can change my hair color, but—"

She wasn't sure how to put any of this. It was beneath words, below logic. She had brought chaos into his orderly life, and she suspected she always would.

"You've got your life exactly the way you want it," she said, trying again to articulate her fears. "You already have so much, so many people who—"

"If I don't have you," he said, "then I don't have anything."

His voice had dipped low, and its tones were somber, an unnerving contrast to his quirky appearance. She felt her pulse quicken as confusion, fear and hope all battled for the upper hand.

He touched her cheek. "You don't ever have to change in order to please me, Kitty. Look at me. This is my way of saying I'll come to you. If you don't want normal, I'm finished with normal. I'll dye my hair every color of the rainbow, if it'll prove to you that we belong together."

She had to laugh, despite her confusion and the lingering traces of fear. She reached up and fingered the spiky blue tips. It was wonderful, laughable, perfect.

But the biggest obstacle was still out there, standing between them.

"What about Belle, David? If you choose me because of the baby, but you love her…"

"I will always love her," he said.

She inhaled sharply. She hadn't expected him to state it so baldly.

"I know that makes you uncomfortable right now," he said. "But you'll see, soon enough, that you have no reason to be threatened or jealous or afraid. She's a fantastic woman. But I love her only as a friend."

"A friend." Even she could hear the doubt in her voice. "But then what about today? The hotel? Why were you there? Why was everyone lying to me about it?"

He sighed in exasperation, but he was still smiling, so she knew he wasn't truly angry.

"Because we're planning a party for you, that's why. It's scheduled for March first, all rush-rush and hush-hush. At that hotel. Blue and white balloons and blue punch. A happy-baby party, or a shower, or whatever women call these things. I told Belle the baby is a boy. You'll probably get fifty pairs of blue booties."

"A party?" She shook her head. "But that doesn't make sense. I hardly know her. Why would she—"

He tucked a curl behind her ear gently, his eyes warm. "Because, as I said, she is a wonderful woman.

She's a very kind person. She saw your face the other night, when she and Matt announced her pregnancy. She was furious with herself, because she hadn't considered how it might make you feel. So now she's going to make the biggest fuss over you that the Western world has ever seen. And, by God, you'd better look surprised, because I vowed I wouldn't tell you."

A surprise party. Kitty tried to hold her thoughts together, to put them into some logical order. Could that really be all it was? It seemed so convenient, almost too plausible. And yet, something tight inside her chest relaxed instinctively. Convenient or not, it had the ring of truth.

Still. She shook her head again, unwilling to let herself believe. "But, even if that explains today, what about the rest of our lives? Will I always be second-best for you? Bettina said…she said you've always loved Belle, and always would."

He groaned. "Please. If I have to defend myself against every crazy thing Bettina has ever said, we'll be talking all night." He wiggled his eyebrows. "And I'm in sort of a hurry to get this explaining-with-words part done, so that we can move on to the other part."

She laughed. "The other part?"

He stepped in closer. "Yes. You know. The part where we explain things with our bodies. It works much better, actually. There's much less room for misunderstanding."

He put his fingers beneath her chin. "For instance, I kiss you like this—"

He nipped at her lower lip once, twice, and then closed

in for a hot and hungry kiss that seemed to go on forever. She shut her eyes and saw stars behind her lids.

Finally he drew his head back slowly. "See? I kiss you like that, and you know it means I love you."

"I do?" She took in a deep breath, but she still felt dizzy. "I mean…you do?"

"Kitty." He smiled and bent his head once more, until his lips tickled warm against hers. "Maybe I'd better try that again. I don't think you were listening."

This time, he claimed her lips with a vengeance and let his arms come around her, his hands cupping her hips so that he could tilt her into him. It seemed to go on forever, as if they were becoming one breath, one moist, intimate warmth. He drove his tongue into her mouth, and tiny fireflies began blinking through every one of her veins. Her knees went weak and liquid, and she had to drop back onto the bed.

"Yes." He let out a low, wolfish growl of triumph, and followed her onto the soft sheets. "I think the signals went through much better that time."

She didn't answer. She was still trying to catch her breath.

He knelt before her, placing his hot lips against her neck. "I love you." He touched his mouth to her breast. "*Always* you."

Finally, he kissed the swell of her abdomen. "*Only* you."

And it was, in the end, as simple and as illogical as that. He loved her, and their bodies could get the matter sorted out in a tenth the time it would have taken their brains to do it.

He loved her.

Not just for the baby. For herself. He had lived with her. He had learned her, with all her flaws. And maybe, just maybe, he had seen what her father had seen. Her *élan vital*. Her powerful life force.

And he wasn't afraid of it, or ashamed of it.

He didn't want to tame it. He wanted to share it.

A wet warmth spilled suddenly from the corners of her eyes. She didn't even recognize it at first. It couldn't be tears. Not when she was so happy...

He leaned over her, brushing each tiny trail of moisture away with a gentle finger. "Hey," he said, smiling down at her. "You're not crying, are you, sweetheart? I know what's bothering you, but you really don't need to worry. I know I look pretty darned ridiculous in this god-awful tracksuit, but it does come off, you know."

She laughed, even as the warm tears continued to seep. She had too many intense emotions to hold them all inside.

"Yes, I know it does," she said, putting her fingers over the tab of the zipper and creating a slow downward pressure. "But maybe we'd better make absolutely sure."

He kissed her while she removed his clothes, and she kissed him, which made the whole process take forever. Neither of them minded a bit. It was awkward and wonderful and silly, twisting and laughing and nearly falling off the bed as they tried to reach the best spots, blue fingernails and pink ones twined, blue hair and brown tickling against flushed and panting bodies.

She ended up with her shirt dangling from one wrist, and he never did get his left leg quite out of the sweatpants. Somehow everything came to a stop with his head burrowed between her legs.

She cried out in helpless bliss.

Her climax was intense and unstoppable, like the arrival of a thunderstorm, all light and release and exploding heat. As she came drifting back to reality, she ran her hands through his soft, dreamy hair, and stroked his beautiful seashell ears...

And came away with a palmful of diamonds.

She looked at the sparkling things, like ice chips in her hand.

"Why, David Gerard, they're fake," she said, laughing. "You didn't really pierce your ears!"

He lifted his head with a feigned air of indignation. His lips were swollen, and she almost melted again, thinking about what they'd been doing.

"Hey, cut a guy some slack, would you? I had a lot to accomplish in five hours. I had to get my hair dyed blue, not a color every barber shop in town stocks, by the way. I had to acquire a whole new wardrobe. And I had to pick up your engagement ring. So excuse me if I fudged a bit on the earrings."

She sat up, at least partway, and clamped her palms on either side of his head, holding him in place. "What did you say?"

"I said excuse me if—"

"No, no. What did you say you had to pick up?"

He grinned. "Your engagement ring."

She fell back against the pillow, laughing. He climbed up and put his head beside hers, so that their faces were only inches from each other.

She arranged the little rhinestones on the inch of

open white sheet between them. "I don't see any engagement ring."

"I think we just tossed it halfway across the room, in my sweatshirt."

She smiled. "It's not made of rhinestones, is it?"

"No."

She wriggled a little closer. "What does it look like?"

"It's an emerald, exactly the color of your hair." He laughed when she softly chuffed his shoulder. "I mean your eyes."

She raised up on one elbow, leaned over his arm, and tried to locate the discarded sweatshirt. She leaned farther, until her breasts pressed into his chest. But the shirt must have slid under the vanity bench.

She fell back onto the sheets. "I don't see it. Should we go get it, do you think?"

He leaned in and kissed the tingling tip of her breast. He made a low, ecstatic murmur, like someone who had just discovered chocolate.

"If you want to," he said. Then he kissed the other breast. "If you really feel you must."

"Well, I'd like to see the ring, but…"

He tongued her gently, and she groaned. She arched her back and shut her eyes. "I suppose it'll still be there later."

"Yes," he said. He let his lips move down her skin, dragging a comet trail of stardust in their wake. "Much, much later."

CHAPTER SEVENTEEN

Valentine's Day, three years later

"MAEVE, HUSH!" Kitty had lost count of the money in the register for the third time now, and she let loose a noise that was a cross between a laugh and a groan. "You're driving me mad. Go home."

"No way. I'm going to get this wreath right if it takes all night."

Maeve McDermott had officially retired from The Three Swans as of January first, and Kitty had bought the older woman's share of the co-op. But now that Maeve was free of all boring responsibilities, she spent more time than ever at the shop, puttering about, rearranging booth displays and creating ever more gorgeous flowers and wreaths.

And driving Kitty insane, chitchatting as she tried to close up for the night.

"If it takes all night, you'll be here alone," Kitty said firmly. "David will be here in fifteen minutes, and we've got dinner reservations."

"Ah, young love."

Kitty laughed, and tried one more time to count. Irrepressible, Maeve plucked a red silk rose from the wreath she was designing and tucked it behind Kitty's ear.

"Red," she said, leaning back to consider it. "Green was nice, but I think you should go red. With those eyes, you'd look like Christmas all year-round."

"Shh!" Kitty shook her head and went back to counting. Maeve hummed a love song from the Twenties, but at least she didn't sing the words. Kitty finally got the same result twice, made up the deposit slip and entered the amount into the computer's spreadsheet.

Now she could relax. She settled back in her comfy desk chair and sighed happily.

"Business was fantastic today," she told Maeve. "I sold every single cake, and all but one of the Valentine's cookies." She jiggled the heart-shaped basket they'd put by the register, loaded with her creations. "Your idea of giving samples away was brilliant."

Maeve smiled smugly. "Well, I just thought…it works for the drug dealers, doesn't it?"

The chimes over the front rang out, and Kitty closed her eyes in frustration. "Oh, dang. I forgot to lock the door."

But it wasn't a customer, thank goodness. It was David.

"Hey," he called. "Hi, Maeve! Still here, I see. Like every night."

Maeve chuckled, waving his comment away airily. "They'll carry me out of here feetfirst," she said. "And no time soon. McDermotts are too ornery to die young."

Kitty stood, her spirits lifting at the sight of David. His hair was tinted slightly pink from the light of the

Valentine's Day tree by the door. It reminded her of the brief blue phase, which automatically made her midsection pinch with desire.

He was...amazing. She wondered whether she would ever be able to look at her glorious, glamorous husband and not melt just a little inside.

But it was a double delight this time. As she stood, she saw that he had Kevin with him. The little boy was dressed in his brand-new navy blue suit, and his hair, which was even blonder than David's, was still damp and slicked down.

He looked very sedate right now, but as soon as his hair completely dried, it would be springing up like a crazy wig. He had inherited that from her.

He held his shoulders back and his chest puffed out, feeling very important in his dress-up clothes. He clutched his daddy's hand obediently, but he moved his feet up and down, dancing in place, trying to get Kitty's attention.

"Mommy! Mommy! I'm coming to dinner!"

Kitty kissed David hard on the lips, then bent down to scoop Kevin into her arms. Even though it had been two and a half years since he came into the world, he still fit there like a warm, squirming extension of her own body.

"Hey, there, little man. You and Daddy look very handsome tonight!"

"It's Valtime's Day," Kevin announced. He plucked at his jacket's lapels proudly. "I'm coming to dinner!"

She glanced up at David, who tilted his head with a smile. "Bettina has a cold. Kevvie's revved up. Someone gave him too many cookies." He blinked innocently. "If we leave him with her all evening, she'll be dead before we get home."

Kevin knit his eyebrows together and nodded his head in a broad, exaggerated arc.

"I am *too much* for her," he said, in a hilariously apt imitation of Bettina.

"Yes," Kitty agreed solemnly, tweaking his nose as she set him down. "Yes, indeed you are."

And darned if she didn't suddenly feel happy tears behind her eyes. Honestly. Where had this sentimental streak come from? Remember when she used to be a badass? So much for that. That old attitude felt as artificial now as David's Blue Phase. The real Kitty, it seemed, was this sappy, giggling homebody who loved to bake cookies, refinish wood paneling and build forts out of Legos.

And that was fine with her.

She rose to her feet. Kevin grabbed her hand, so that he was bracketed between his parents. He lifted his knees to his chest, turning their arms into a swing.

"Do you mind?" David touched the red rose she'd forgotten was still behind her ear. "We'll have to scale down a bit, not quite McDonald's, but not quite the Ritz, either. And we'll have to postpone the X-rated part, but—"

"Mind?" She caught her lower lip between her teeth and tried not to go all mushy right here in front of Maeve. "Mind having dinner anywhere with my two favorite men? Not likely. But you'd both better have brought me a present."

"I have one," Kevin said, letting his feet touch the floor again. He reached into his pocket, then stopped himself with cartoon drama. He squeezed up his face, forcing himself to remember the rules. "But I can't tell you, or Daddy will be pretty doggone mad."

David tried to scowl at his son, but he just couldn't. As their gazes met, David began to laugh.

So of course Kevin did, too. "Pretty doggone mad, right, Daddy? That's funny, isn't it, Daddy?" He doubled over, cracking himself up. "You don't get it, do you, Mommy?"

She shook her head. "I never get it with you two, kiddo. Never."

"You guys go on," Maeve said from behind them, her mouth full of the last of Kitty's cookies. "I'll close up. It'll be fun. Like old times, only without the stress."

"Thanks," Kitty said. She gave the older woman a kiss. "Really, thanks."

Maeve winked at her. "Just call me in the morning and tell me how it goes."

Kitty nodded, and then both women grinned at the look on David's face.

"Tell her how what goes?" His mouth was hanging open, his eyes wide with mock shock. "You give her morning-after reports?"

Kitty took his arm. "Get your mind out of the gutter, darling."

And Kevin whooped, obviously liking the sound of that. "Yeah, Daddy. Get your mind out of the gutter!"

He mimicked everything they said—so they'd learned early to watch what came out of their mouths. Kevin had talked even before he walked, and by two he'd been so good at expressing himself that they sometimes had to invent "quiet contests" just to get a minute's peace.

Kitty insisted that his precocious verbal skills meant he was going to be a lawyer, like David. David had countered that it meant he would be a professor, like her father. Secretly, that had pleased her. Her father would have loved Kevin, who had been named for him.

Even Lucinda adored the little boy. They traveled back to Virginia whenever they could, so that Kevin could feel at home at Lochaven. And when Lucinda was between boyfriends, which happened frequently, she flew out to San Francisco to get a dose of what she called "grandbaby medicine."

Once, such a sappy term would have irked Kitty. But now, she knew exactly what her mother meant. Kevin truly was like a dose of medicine—with his energy, his honest sweetness and his goofy slant on the world.

Tonight, he kept Kitty and David laughing all the way to the restaurant. Sometimes he was actively trying to be funny. Sometimes he was just so adorable that it was impossible not to smile when they looked at him.

They settled on Diamante's, which was upscale enough to feel like a celebration, but had the advantage of being super family friendly. Plus, the Malones were their best friends, and Matt and Belle's little Sarah, who had been born only a few weeks after Kevin, was his constant playmate.

So, considering they were practically family, the odds of getting tossed out of Diamante when Kevin did something outrageous were diminished.

Not eliminated, because Kevin could get creative, but low enough to be worth the risk.

Kitty didn't care where they ate. She wasn't very hungry, anyhow. As long as she was with the two of them, she was completely satisfied.

She had never imagined she could be so happy, and every day she thanked the fates that had sent these wonderful, loving, laughing men into her life.

Kevin hated all kinds of pizza, which hurt his Nana Lina's feelings terribly. But the little boy had been born with a love of spaghetti, even the canned baby food kind. Recently, repeated viewings of *Lady and the Tramp* had sealed the deal.

Only after he shared a strand of pasta with each of his parents would he allow David to cut his meal up into fork-sized pieces. From that moment on, though, he was all business. Not a straw of the pasta would escape uneaten, even if he had to lick it off his cuffs.

By dessert time, his lips were as big and red as a clown's, and Kitty was extremely glad she'd decided on a dark color for his new suit.

As she wiped his sticky mouth, he suddenly yawned.

"Hey, buddy, you can't go to sleep yet," David said. He pointed to Kevin's pocket. "Remember?"

Kevin frowned. "Yes, I can," he said. "Because it's already night."

"Yeah." David pointed again at the boy's pocket. "But it's Valentine's Day."

"It's Valtime's *Night*," Kevin corrected.

But finally he remembered.

His eyes widened, and his mouth made a big, delighted "o."

"That's right!" He pushed at his booster seat, trying to get a little room so that he could reach his pocket.

"Wait, wait!" Kitty made a desperate lunge with the napkin, in hopes that she could get at least some of the marinara sauce off his fingers first. But it was too late. He was so excited about his present that he couldn't be thwarted.

He scowled when he didn't immediately reach his hidden prize. But then his fingers apparently closed around the treasure. His face beamed.

"I waited," he said. He grinned up at David. "So no dog gone mad for me, right, Daddy?"

"Right." David laughed. "Now give it to Mommy."

Kevin complied delightedly. With a dramatic flair that called for a drum roll, he held out his hand.

For a minute, she honestly had no idea what on earth he had in there. It looked…

Actually, it looked disgusting.

Brown. Crumbly from being in a little boy's pocket for so long. Now stained with marinara sauce. About an inch long and hard, with rounded bumps on each end.

"Oh!" She laughed out loud as she figured it out. "Oh, my heaven. Is that a…dog biscuit?"

"It is," Kevin confirmed, followed by a whoop of triumph. "Because Daddy's present is guess what…a dog!"

She glanced at David, disbelieving. They'd been married nearly three years now, and neither of them had ever mentioned the idea of getting a pet. She hadn't wanted David to feel any pressure. And besides, with a new husband and then a new baby…she had been overflowing with warmth and love and cuddles.

And then she'd been so busy with The Three Swans.

But lately, she'd begun to wish that, at least for Kevin's sake…

Blissfully unaware of the history of this subject, Kevin babbled happily about the dog for a while, and they indulged him. It would be a small rescue puppy, nothing as elegant or as large as the Irish setter Murphy would have been. But the kind of dog who would be satisfied with the yard at home, and who needed a family bad, as Kevin put it. He and his daddy had clearly talked this over many times.

Kitty hugged him and thanked him, until he grew bored with that and began to watch the waiter at the next table, who was serving Baked Alaska.

In the momentary quiet, Kitty reached across the table and took David's hand. "Are you sure?"

"I'm sure," he said. He squeezed her fingers gently. "He's sinfully cute. We'll pick him up tomorrow."

No more *it* references, she noticed. Their new puppy would be a *he*. And, she hoped, he would heal some very, very old wounds.

She tried not to give into her emotions. She blinked hard to hold back the stinging in her eyes. She wondered if it tempted fate, being too happy and contented with your life.

But surely not… Otherwise, fate wouldn't have given her David, and Kevin…

And this new gift.

She swallowed the hot lump in her throat.

"I'm sorry I can't give you your present tonight," she

said quietly to David. "But it's going to take a while before we can pick it up."

He shook his head. "You are my present," he said.

She smiled. She'd heard a million people say phrases like that, and she'd always rolled her eyes. But she'd never realized they could be absolutely sincere.

It was the simplest, most clichéd sentence ever, but it was also the most earth-shattering truth. David was life's gift to her. He was the recompense for all the years of fear and loneliness. He was the harbor after the storm. He was her joy, her courage, her rock and her future.

And apparently she was his gift, too. Sometimes it was hard to believe, but he proved it to her every day.

And every night...

She tightened her grip on his hand. "This present... well, we won't pick it up, exactly. More like...it will be delivered."

He hesitated, as if he couldn't quite allow himself to believe. But he knew. She could tell by the sudden tension in his fingers, and the light that flared in his eyes.

"Delivered?" He cut a glance at Kevin, who thankfully was still mesmerized by the waiter. "Delivered... when?"

"Early October. At least that's what Dr. Tapia thinks." She had to smile at the shock that paralyzed his face. It was as if he'd been struck dumb with joy. "Happy Valentine's Day, David."

He made a small, choked sound. And then he brought her hand up to his lips, and kissed her knuckles.

"Are you happy?" His voice was husky, slightly ragged with emotion.

Happy? She searched for a bigger word. *Happy* was far too trivial a description for this heaven she held inside her.

Three years ago, when she'd learned she was pregnant with Kevin, fear had turned everything gray, until even the instinctive thrill of new life had been muted. But this time—this time everything in her heart was sunshine and gold. There was no ambivalence. Just these never-ending bubbles of eager, inexpressible delight.

"I'm ecstatic," she whispered.

He leaned across the table, and she leaned in, too, meeting him halfway. So what if others saw...

"Hey!" Kevin's voice broke into the moment.

They both turned, but their son wasn't talking to them. He was standing backward in the booth, trying to get the attention of the people behind them. Luckily, it was a kind-looking elderly couple who didn't seem a bit annoyed. In fact, they were smiling, and they waved at Kitty to indicate that she didn't need to worry.

Still...her cheeks flushed. She'd become one of those mothers who didn't control her children. She tried to imagine handling two little whirlwinds like Kevin, and she almost burst out laughing.

Maybe, with any kind of luck, the new baby would have David's dignity and self-control instead.

"Sit down, Kevvie," she said, settling him back into his seat.

"Mommy, no. Wait. I need to tell the lady what's our news."

Kitty's eyes shot to David's. Could he possibly have heard? Could he actually have understood what she and David had been saying?

"Kevvie," she began anxiously. "When we get home, Daddy and I will explain—"

But Kevin wasn't listening.

"Lady, guess what?" Though he didn't dare get back out of his seat, he raised his voice and hollered over his shoulder. "My mom and dad are going to get a puppy!"

* * * * *

COMING NEXT MONTH

Available November 8, 2011

REQUEST YOUR FREE BOOKS!
2 FREE NOVELS PLUS 2 FREE GIFTS!

❧ Harlequin®

Super Romance®

Exciting, emotional, unexpected!

YES! Please send me 2 FREE Harlequin® Superromance® novels and my 2 FREE gifts (gifts are worth about $10). After receiving them, if I don't wish to receive any more books, I can return the shipping statement marked "cancel." If I don't cancel, I will receive 6 brand-new novels every month and be billed just $4.69 per book in the U.S. or $5.24 per book in Canada. That's a saving of at least 15% off the cover price! It's quite a bargain! Shipping and handling is just 50¢ per book in the U.S. and 75¢ per book in Canada.* I understand that accepting the 2 free books and gifts places me under no obligation to buy anything. I can always return a shipment and cancel at any time. Even if I never buy another book, the two free books and gifts are mine to keep forever.

135/336 HDN FC6T

Name	(PLEASE PRINT)

Address		Apt. #

City	State/Prov.	Zip/Postal Code

Signature (if under 18, a parent or guardian must sign)

Mail to the Reader Service:
IN U.S.A.: P.O. Box 1867, Buffalo, NY 14240-1867
IN CANADA: P.O. Box 609, Fort Erie, Ontario L2A 5X3

Not valid for current subscribers to Harlequin Superromance books.

**Are you a current subscriber to Harlequin Superromance books
and want to receive the larger-print edition?
Call 1-800-873-8635 or visit www.ReaderService.com.**

* Terms and prices subject to change without notice. Prices do not include applicable taxes. Sales tax applicable in N.Y. Canadian residents will be charged applicable taxes. Offer not valid in Quebec. This offer is limited to one order per household. All orders subject to credit approval. Credit or debit balances in a customer's account(s) may be offset by any other outstanding balance owed by or to the customer. Please allow 4 to 6 weeks for delivery. Offer available while quantities last.

Your Privacy—The Reader Service is committed to protecting your privacy. Our Privacy Policy is available online at www.ReaderService.com or upon request from the Reader Service.

We make a portion of our mailing list available to reputable third parties that offer products we believe may interest you. If you prefer that we not exchange your name with third parties, or if you wish to clarify or modify your communication preferences, please visit us at www.ReaderService.com/consumerchoice or write to us at Reader Service Preference Service, P.O. Box 9062, Buffalo, NY 14269. Include your complete name and address.

Harlequin® Special Edition® is thrilled to present a new installment in USA TODAY bestselling author RaeAnne Thayne's reader-favorite miniseries, THE COWBOYS OF COLD CREEK.

Join the excitement as we meet the Bowmans—four siblings who lost their parents but keep family ties alive in Pine Gulch. First up is Trace. Only two things get under this rugged lawman's skin: beautiful women and secrets. And in Rebecca Parsons, he finds both!

Read on for a sneak peek of
CHRISTMAS IN COLD CREEK.
Available November 2011 from Harlequin® Special Edition®.

On impulse, he unfolded himself from the bar stool. "Need a hand?"

"Thank you! I..." She lifted her gaze from the floor to his jeans and then raised her eyes. When she identified him her hazel eyes turned from grateful to unfriendly and cold, as if he'd somehow thrown the broken glasses at her head.

He also thought he saw a glimmer of panic in those interesting depths, which instantly stirred his curiosity like cream swirling through coffee.

"I've got it, Officer. Thank you." Her voice was several degrees colder than the whirl of sleet outside the windows.

Despite her protests, he knelt down beside her and began to pick up shards of broken glass. "No problem. Those trays can be slippery."

This close, he picked up the scent of her, something fresh and flowery that made him think of a mountain meadow on a July afternoon. She had a soft, lush mouth and for one brief, insane moment, he wanted to push aside that stray lock of hair slipping from her ponytail and taste her. Apparently he needed to spend a lot less time working and a great deal *more* time recreating with the opposite sex if he could have sudden random fantasies about a woman he wasn't even inclined to like, pretty or not.

"I'm Trace Bowman. You must be new in town."

She didn't answer immediately and he could almost see the wheels turning in her head. Why the hesitancy? And why that little hint of unease he could see clouding the edge of her gaze? His presence was obviously making her uncomfortable and Trace couldn't help wondering why.

"Yes. We've been here a few weeks."

"Well, I'm just up the road about four lots, in the white house with the cedar shake roof, if you or your daughter need anything." He smiled at her as he picked up the last shard of glass and set it on her tray.

Definitely a story there, he thought as she hurried away. He just might need to dig a little into her background to find out why someone with fine clothes and nice jewelry, and who so obviously didn't have experience as a waitress, would be here slinging hash at The Gulch. Was she running away from someone? A bad marriage?

So…Rebecca Parsons. Not Becky. An intriguing woman. It had been a long time since one of those had crossed his path here in Pine Gulch.

Trace won't rest until he finds out Rebecca's secret, but will he still have that same attraction to her once he does? Find out in CHRISTMAS IN COLD CREEK. Available November 2011 from Harlequin® Special Edition®.

Harlequin
Super Romance

Discover a fresh, heartfelt new romance
from acclaimed author

Sarah Mayberry

Businessman Flynn Randall's life is
complicated. So he doesn't need the
distraction of fun, spontaneous Mel Porter.
But he can't stop thinking about her. Maybe
he can handle one more complication....

All They Need

LONGER
BOOK
Same Price!

*Available November 8, 2011,
wherever books are sold!*